A WARNING FROM INSPECTOR FINCH

Finch nodded. "There's the possibility that you may find yourself in considerable danger."

Louise shook her head. "I don't think that's likely," she said decidedly. "With the possible exception of Roger Crane, the Maules are all madly respectable."

"My dear girl, it's the respectable ones who are most to be feared because they have the most to lose. Consider, for instance," Finch begged her earnestly, "the high ratio of murders committed simply to avoid the scandal of a divorce."

Louise suppressed a giggle with difficulty. "You're not suggesting that anyone's likely to try and murder me?"

"I'm suggesting that someone at Tammerton has a very good reason for not wanting you there. And, that being so, they may try to remove you."

BANTAM BOOKS offers the finest in classic and modern English murder mysteries. Ask your bookseller for the books you have missed.

Agatha Christie

DEATH ON THE NILE
A HOLIDAY FOR MURDER
THE MYSTERIOUS AFFAIR
   AT STYLES
POIROT INVESTIGATES
POSTERN OF FATE
THE SECRET ADVERSARY
THE SEVEN DIALS MYSTERY
SLEEPING MURDER

Carter Dickson

DEATH IN FIVE BOXES
THE SKELETON IN THE
   CLOCK
THE WHITE PRIORY
   MURDERS

Catherine Aird

HENRIETTA WHO?
HIS BURIAL TOO
A LATE PHOENIX
A MOST CONTAGIOUS GAME
PASSING STRANGE
THE RELIGIOUS BODY
SLIGHT MOURNING
SOME DIE ELOQUENT
THE STATELY HOME
   MURDER

Patricia Wentworth

THE FINGERPRINT
THE IVORY DAGGER
THE LISTENING EYE
MISS SILVER COMES TO
   STAY
POISON IN THE PEN
SHE CAME BACK
THROUGH THE WALL

Elizabeth Lemarchand

BURIED IN THE PAST
DEATH ON DOOMSDAY

Margaret Erskine

THE FAMILY AT
   TAMMERTON
NO. 9 BELMONT SQUARE
THE WOMAN AT
   BELGUARDO

Margaret Yorke

CAST FOR DEATH
DEAD IN THE MORNING
GRAVE MATTERS

Ruth Rendell

A DEMON IN MY VIEW
THE FALLEN CURTAIN
A SLEEPING LIFE

June Thomson

ALIBI IN TIME
CASE CLOSED
THE LONG REVENGE

E. X. Ferrars

ALIVE AND DEAD
EXPERIMENT WITH DEATH
FROG IN THE THROAT
LAST WILL AND TESTAMENT
MURDERS ANONYMOUS

THE FAMILY AT TAMMERTON

Margaret Erskine

BANTAM BOOKS
TORONTO · NEW YORK · LONDON · SYDNEY

All of the characters in this book are fictitious, and any resemblance to actual persons, living or dead, is purely coincidental.

*This low-priced Bantam Book
has been completely reset in a type face
designed for easy reading, and was printed
from new plates. It contains the complete
text of the original hard-cover edition.*
NOT ONE WORD HAS BEEN OMITTED.

THE FAMILY AT TAMMERTON

*A Bantam Book / published by arrangement with
Doubleday & Company, Inc.*

PRINTING HISTORY
*Doubleday edition published February 1966
Bantam edition / October 1982*

ISBN 0-553-22826-9

Published simultaneously in the United States and Canada

*Bantam Books are published by Bantam Books, Inc. Its trademark,
consisting of the words "Bantam Books" and the portrayal of a rooster,
is Registered in U.S. Patent and Trademark Office and in other countries.
Marca Registrada. Bantam Books, Inc., 666 Fifth Avenue, New York,
New York 10103.*

PRINTED IN THE UNITED STATES OF AMERICA

O   0 9 8 7 6 5 4 3 2 1

THE FAMILY
AT
TAMMERTON

Chapter 1

If Miss Mathews had not known Isobel Crane for so many years she would not have agreed to send one of her nurses so far from London.

If Louise Morton had not had a sudden longing for the country she would not have agreed to go.

Now, as she sat rocking and swaying in the train which was taking her to the seaside town of Lockbridge in Somerset, her face stared back at her, reflected against the passing scenery. A pale oval face with gooseberry green eyes and dark sleek hair which lay like black silk in a fringe on her forehead. It was a lively, intelligent face, at the moment a little pensive, for the countryside reminded her of the father she had lost as a child.

Why hadn't she revisited it before now, she wondered? As she looked from the carriage window, she was aware of delight, of a sense of homecoming that was, under the circumstances, rather illogical, for the case to which she was bound had got off to a decidedly queer start.

Thinking of this, she took a telegraph form from her handbag and smoothed it out on her lap. Sent from Lockbridge two days before, it read: "MRS. CRANE IS DEAD. DO NOT SEND NURSE." Signed Maule—just Maule. And there had been three of them in the house, James, his wife Agnes, and Jason Maule, their nephew. Furthermore, the message had not been true. There had not been a word of truth in it. Mrs. Crane was not dead—and she was expecting a nurse as arranged.

When Matron had rung up to express her sorrow and make further enquiries, the nephew, Jason, had answered the telephone. He had said that the telegram must have been meant as a practical joke. "Although he agreed that it had been in very poor taste he actually sounded amused," Matron had reported indignantly. "An insolent voice." Adding intriguingly, "Just what one might have expected from a young man of his reputation."

But even a practical joke, Louise reflected, must have some

1

point. This one seemed to have none. And supposing it had not been meant as a joke but had some other purpose behind it? The wording certainly was rather gruesome, if not downright sinister.

If only I could decide which it was, she thought, joke or threat. She could find no answer. She put the telegram away and went along to the restaurant car.

It was full of men. As Louise appeared in the doorway they all looked up. Someone gave a wolf whistle. To her annoyance she felt herself blushing. It was years since anything had put her so out of countenance. A waiter hurried up. "This way, miss." Adding confidentially, "We're a bit full today owing to a congress of sorts at Lockbridge but there is one place left."

This was at a table laid for two. A man sat in one of the seats. He was large and bland. His face wore a look of almost benign disinterestedness. When the waiter had left with her order he spoke.

"You'll be quite safe here," he said in a voice that was soft and small as a woman's. "I'm a policeman."

Louise smiled rather stiffly. "I was taken by surprise. So many men. I didn't expect it."

Recovering her equanimity and over the inevitable tomato soup, she observed her companion with a lively and wholly unself-conscious interest.

There was something phoney about him, she decided. He did not look like a policeman. And, anyway, wasn't the correct term a police officer? And, if not a police officer, what was he? His face told her nothing, but instinctively she distrusted the expression on it.

In the rack above was a well-worn briefcase and a hat—

She felt triumphant. The hat was no ordinary affair. It was a curious blackberry shade, in size first cousin to a Stetson. A giveaway of a hat. Only—what did it give away?

That the owner had a flamboyant personality? That he was an extrovert? Either an actor or a confidence man, Louise decided, pleased at her own perspicuity. But how to find out?

"Why not have a look at this?" the soft voice enquired.

Louise stared. Just like the caterpillar in Alice, only it had said, *"The other side of the mushroom."*

She picked up the case he had produced. *Detective Inspector Septimus Finch, C.I.D., New Scotland Yard.*

So he was a policeman—police officer—after all.

"But you don't look like one," she said rather indignantly.

"Much better to look like a con man. Leads to more interesting results."

"Well, I wish you wouldn't sound as if you were reading my thoughts."

"Up to date, it hasn't been very difficult," he offered in a reasonable tone of voice.

She ate in an offended silence for a while.

"Are you going on a case?" Louise enquired, relenting.

"I'm going on leave. I'm breaking my journey at Lockbridge, but I don't expect to be there more than twenty-four hours."

"So am I—going to Lockbridge, I mean. I'm a trained nurse."

The big man raised one eyebrow. "An hereditary calling, no doubt."

She stared. "Why should it be?"

He gestured with a strong, well-kept hand. "Well—the glamour."

Louise dimpled. "I really wanted to be a doctor like my father but Aunt Phyllis said she couldn't afford the training. I think the real reason was that she thought it an unwomanly calling."

"In this day and age?"

"Oh, yes."

"And now you're on your way to a patient."

Louise nodded. "Yes, to a place called Tammerton Hall."

Finch looked at her enquiringly. "You don't sound too happy. What's wrong with it?"

Louise wrinkled her forehead. "I don't quite know. It's all so senseless. It simply doesn't seem to mean a thing."

"It must do—looked at in the right light."

"But what is the right light? Lots of people have suggested reasons but none of them seems to make sense."

"Suppose you tell me. It won't go any further. Policemen talk only to policemen." Finch added thoughtfully, "Except perhaps the commissioner, and he, I suspect, like the Cabots, talks only to God."

Louise smiled. "Absurd," she said indulgently. "Still, it would be a relief to get some sort of expert advice."

"Then shoot," said Finch, sitting back in his chair and preparing to listen.

"My name," said the girl obediently, "is Louise Morton. I'm a nurse at the Welbeck Street Nurses Association. As a rule we work only in London, but this was a special case. My patient, Mrs. Crane, was a Miss Maule before she married, and Matron had been brought up on the Maule estate. Mrs. Crane was an only child. She inherited a lot of money when her father died eighteen months ago, and a few months later she married this man, Roger Crane.''

Finch nodded. "Aha! Enter a sinister figure."

"Did I sound like that?" There was a faint note of dismay in the fresh young voice. "I shall have to be careful. But it's Matron's fault really. *She* looks on him with the greatest suspicion because of the way he met his future wife. And then there's his having no money. Matron doesn't believe his story either."

Finch nodded. "And a very lucid explanation, too."

"I was coming to the explanation." Louise looked dignified. For a girl who was five feet two she really did it very well. "Isobel Maule, as she was then, lived at Lockbridge in a house built by her father. She was walking home one day—Matron said she used to be a great walker—when she saw an old rattletrap of a car broken down just at her front gates. The driver asked if she could tell him where there was a telephone so that he could ring up a garage. She said he could use hers—and that's how it began. She told Matron that it was love at first sight on both sides."

Again Finch nodded. "Highly suspicious so far."

"Well, Roger Crane's story is that he became tired suddenly of living in England and decided to go out to Alaska. There was some scheme by which you got a large tract of land free provided you worked it. He put all his money into setting up as a fur trapper and then, six months later, he was involved in an air crash. He was the only survivor and was in hospital for four months. When he came out his health had gone and so had his savings, so he decided to come back to England. When he met Isobel Maule he was pretty well on his beam ends."

"And that's the yarn Matron disbelieves? I don't know that I blame her."

"She thinks he made it up to explain how a man of thirty-seven came to have no prospects, no money, and no job."

"Has she met him?"

"Only at the wedding. She got back from a visit to the States just in time. The marriage was at a registry office and Matron didn't like that either."

"How old was Mrs. Crane when she married?"

"Forty."

"Spinster or widow?"

"Spinster." When Finch offered no further comment Louise went on. "Two months after the wedding Mrs. Crane contracted polio. She's been an invalid ever since, although she's much better now and in her letter said she really only wanted a companion. Someone young, who wouldn't mind the country since she was staying with her uncle and aunt."

"Mr. and Mrs. Maule of Tammerton Hall?"

Louise nodded. "The family have been there for centuries."

"What do they consist of?"

"There's the Squire, James Maule, Agnes, his wife, and a nephew, Jason Maule."

"James and Agnes having no children of their own?"

"Matron says they had two children, a boy and a girl, but they were both killed in the last war."

"So Jason Maule is now the heir?" Finch added, "All plain sailing so far—except for the slightly sinister note struck by Roger Crane."

"He didn't strike the note. At least, not the one I was going to tell you about. It was a telegram. Matron got it in answer to her last letter." Louise took the flimsy paper form from her bag and passed it to her companion. She explained what had followed its receipt. "I can't see any sense in it but somehow it does seem rather—horrid."

"What does Matron think?"

"She thinks that Roger Crane must have sent it so that his wife wouldn't have a nurse."

"But he's had plenty of time to retard or prevent his wife's recovery. It seems a bit illogical to act now."

"I know. Matron sees that but, as I told you, she's prejudiced against him."

"Anyone else know about the telegram?"

"There were only four nurses in the home at the time. We're never there for more than a few days. They all knew and were madly excited."

Finch gave her an interested glance. "What did they think?"

"As I've already told you, Matron suspected Roger Crane. Nurse Brown thought that the uncle and aunt, having lured their rich niece into the house, had some dark plot of their own and didn't want any outside interference. Nurse Blackett"—Louise was ticking them off on her slim fingers as she spoke—"said that it was lucky my patient hadn't answered Matron's telephone call because it wouldn't have done her any good to know that someone in the house was projecting a death wish against her.

Nurse Gadsby said that a nut case must be involved, and that most old families have them.''

"But Matron never hinted at any insanity in the family?"

"No." Louise hesitated. "Nurse Gadsby said that that was nothing to go by because, even after thirty years, whenever Matron mentions the Maules, her voice simply drips with respect for the Squire and his lady."

Finch looked thoughtfully down at the telegram lying on the table before him. "Tell me, what happened when Mrs. Crane engaged you? Did she simply write asking for a nurse and Matron write back to say that you were coming?"

"Goodness, no! Everyone's been writing to Matron for the last six weeks—ever since Mrs. Crane came out of the nursing home at Lockbridge. You see, *she* didn't want a nurse and everyone else *seemed* to think she ought to have one. Matron was the obvious person to supply one so they all kept exchanging letters as hard as they could go, although Matron didn't expect anything to come of it. According to her Mrs. Crane is a very obstinate woman. So you can imagine Matron's surprise when she got a letter, last Friday, from this Mrs. Crane to say she'd changed her mind and would Matron send someone as soon as possible."

"And Matron wrote back mentioning you by name for the first time?"

"Oh, yes. Until Mrs. Crane said a young nurse there hadn't been any idea of my going."

"So now we have this sequence of events. Mrs. Crane came out of the nursing home six weeks ago. Letters have been passing between the family and Matron for roughly the same period. Then on Friday, October 30th, Matron received a letter to say Mrs. Crane would like a nurse. She wrote by return, her letter arriving at Tammerton probably by the second post on October 31st. Matron then received this telegram, which I see was handed in at Lockbridge at 2:47 P.M., and arrived in London 5.25 P.M. Matron then telephoned the Maules. And now on Monday, November 2nd, here you are on the way to Tammerton?"

Louise nodded.

Said Finch, "Then there is a distinct possibility that the telegram was sent by someone who did not want you at Tammerton. Not any nurse, but you, personally."

Louise stared in astonishment. "But that's absurd. I've never met any of the Maules. I've never even been to Somerset."

"Yet think what the telegram might have accomplished. If

Matron hadn't known Mrs. Crane so well she would have written a letter of condolence and not telephoned. In which event she wouldn't have heard the truth for three or four days. By which time, on your own showing, you would have gone out on another case and no longer have been available."

Louise was silent a moment. She stared unseeingly from the window, her small face troubled. "That sounds logical enough."

"It not only sounds logical. It is logical. Furthermore it was only the fact that the telegram was sent off in a moment of panic that prevented it from succeeding."

"How d'you mean, panic?"

"Take the wording. It's so extravagant that it defeats its own purpose. If the sender had put something like 'Plans changed. Don't send nurse.' If they'd even added 'Letter follows' or 'Writing' to the original telegram, Matron might have accepted it and waited."

"But even so, the fact remains that I don't know any of the Maules. Not one of them. Nor Roger Crane."

"How can you be sure?"

"Why—" Louise frowned. "Of course I can't be sure until I've seen them. But—oh, it'd be too much of a coincidence. Besides, why should anyone not want to meet me?"

Finch's expression was one of pure pleasure. "That is the point, isn't it? And it's one with infinite possibilities."

"Such as?"

He answered her question with another. "Where were you trained?"

"At St. Ursula's Greenwich."

"Then that's where it happened."

"Yes, but what?"

Finch shrugged. "Roger Crane may have been in St. Ursula's at a time that disproves his story of having been in Alaska. Mrs. Crane, under another name, may have given birth to an illegitimate baby—"

Louise gave a gurgle of amusement. "If Matron could only hear you. Isobel Crane is her ideal of pure English womanhood."

"Like that, is she? Then I call it jolly noble of you to have agreed to go to her."

"Oh, well! I was a bit tired of London and wanted a change."

Finch nodded. "I'd say you were going to get that, all right. There's also the possibility that you may find yourself in considerable danger."

Louise shook her head. "I don't think that's likely," she said decidedly. "With the possible exception of Roger Crane, they're all madly respectable. Mrs. Crane even now is a do-gooder on a big scale. Mrs. Maule was a Miss Sidbald from the other side of the county—whatever that may imply. And old Mr. Maule is a local J.P. and quite a well-known historian."

"My dear girl, it's the respectable ones who are most to be feared because they have most to lose. Consider, for instance," Finch begged her earnestly, "the high ratio of murders committed simply to avoid the scandal of a divorce."

Louise suppressed a giggle with difficulty. "You're not suggesting that anyone's likely to try and murder me?"

"I'm suggesting that someone at Tammerton has a very good reason for not wanting you there. And, that being so, they may try to remove you."

Louise remained unconvinced.

Chapter 2

By the time the train drew into Lockbridge, the sky was leaden and a cold wind was blowing in from the sea. As a porter came along the platform Louise let down her window and he opened her carriage door.

"Any luggage, miss?"

"Yes, two suitcases—but I'm expecting to be met."

An elderly man, very thin and respectable looking, in a chauffeur's uniform, stepped forward stiffly. "Would you be for Tammerton?" he asked doubtfully, touching his cap. Louise was not his idea of a nurse.

"Yes, I'm Miss Morton." Louise smiled delightfully at the porter. "I shall be all right now, thank you."

Out of the corner of her eye she saw her late table companion walking down the platform in front of her. At the ticket barrier she fancied that he looked back and stared a moment in her direction as if interested to see whether she had been met and, if so, by whom.

The chauffeur's thin sad voice came to her above the wind. "Mrs. Maule is waiting in the car, miss." He pointed out an ancient Rolls.

Louise gave up her ticket at the barrier and walked forward with a feeling of expectancy which quickly faded.

The little woman peering from the window of the car was a complete stranger to her. But even if she'd been disguised when I saw her last, Louise told herself, I would have recognised *her*.

Mrs. Maule was a short, excessively ugly woman. Her face was broad with a blunt square-tipped nose and a wide mouth. She wore no make-up, and her skin shone as if it had been freshly scoured with kitchen soap.

She reminded Louise of nothing as much as a stoutly built pink pig—even to the shrewd, rather small, bright eyes. A pig in a violet-coloured coat and a curious fur hat with ear flaps tied under the chin. It was like the hats worn in films of the Frozen

North, Louise reflected. Later she was to find that it had been brought back from Alaska by Roger Crane and given by him to Mrs. Maule, who, in the cold weather, was seldom to be seen without it.

"You must be Miss Morton," she said, greeting Louise in rather a hoarse voice. "Get in and sit by me. Why, you're just a girl." Only she pronounced the word "gal."

"I'm twenty-three."

"So old?" Mrs. Maule's small twinkling eyes seemed to disappear behind soft rolls of fat.

The chauffeur's lugubrious face appeared at the window. "I've put the two suitcases into the back, ma'am. Will that be all?"

"Yes, Goodlife. We'll go home now." Mrs. Maule sank back in her seat, sighing. "The great thing is that I've met you. Such a relief."

Louise looked at her quickly. "A relief? Is Mrs. Crane worse?"

"I don't know. That's the trouble." Mrs. Maule chewed her lower lip and her small eyes were worried. "You see, it was so odd. Roger bursting in on us with the news that Isobel was lying unconscious on the floor. A blackout, he said. Doing too much, was her explanation. But how could anyone in a wheelchair do too much? That's what I'd like to know."

There were several things Louise would have liked to know. Their number seemed to be growing. "What does the doctor say?"

"He said that there was nothing to worry about—but Isobel's my niece and I have a right to worry." The hoarse voice added, "Of course, Roger's wonderful with her but I never do think a beard is very hygienic in a nurse."

So Roger Crane had a beard. Hastily Louise reviewed the beards she had known at St. Ursula's. The hospital being near the river, they had been mostly of a nautical type, and some, she reflected, sinister enough to satisfy even the inspector.

There was silence for a while. Goodlife drove at a stately thirty-five miles an hour. Houses grew fewer, the landscape more rural.

Flat fields and old apple orchards appeared, a solitary farmhouse or two with their attendant buildings and cottages.

"Tammerton is one of those really isolated spots," Mrs. Maule remarked. "I hope you won't hate it."

Louise turned from looking out of the window on her side. "Oh, no," she said smiling. "I lived in the country until my father was killed in a motoring accident. Coming down in the train I was thinking how nice it would be to be back. And I don't know Somerset at all."

"Your father is dead? Are you alone then?"

"Not really. I have an aunt and several cousins."

Mrs. Maule screwed up her little eyes. "I had a father—and I was the loneliest person alive." She sighed deeply and, laying a friendly paw on Louise's arm, added, "If you want to see something of the county my husband will take you. You couldn't have a better guide. For instance there's Bristol. Such an historic town. Nelson, Edmund Burke the Parliamentarian, and Mrs. Dyer, the baby-farmer. I expect you've seen her effigy in Madame Tussaud's, so it'll be interesting to you to see where she actually lived. Then there's the Cheddar Gorge and Sedgemoor. What a pity you weren't here for the sixteenth. Then we could have shown you Monmouth's ghost."

"But I don't think I believe in ghosts," Louise protested.

"That," Mrs. Maule told her, "is because you have never seen one. But lots of people have seen Monmouth, gaunt, unshaven. Poor fellow, he was found in a ditch, his pockets stuffed full of talismans. There's a story that a soothsayer once told him to beware of the Rhine and that it wasn't until the eve of the battle that he learned that it was the local name for the Somerset dykes."

The car had turned off the main road into one that was little better than a lane. The few fine trees which had given a parklike appearance to the countryside were now merging into a great wood lying directly in their path.

"Are we getting near Tammerton?"

"Yes, these are Tammerton Woods. They extend almost to the walls of the house. Of course before the last war they were kept in much better shape. There wasn't all this undergrowth." Mrs. Maule added plaintively, "Nowadays there seems no money for anything."

The car emerged from the trees and entered the village. Louise saw a cluster of picturesque thatched cottages, a village store-cum-post office, and pub, the Maule Arms, a small Norman church and some fine yew trees round what was probably the vicarage—and that was all.

They drove between hedges again, turned in through great

double wrought-iron gates and up a winding drive. The house
came to view, enormous, rambling, with mullioned windows and
a great front entrance like that of a church.

Goodlife got down stiffly and opened the car door for the
two women to descend. He rang the front doorbell before driving
away round the side of the house. It was not quite dark yet. The
smell of late autumn, sharp and bitter with its hint of corruption,
was in the air.

"We've arrived," said Mrs. Maule.

"Yes." Louise shivered as she felt again the slight tremor
that was half excitement, half apprehension.

"You should be plump like me," said Mrs. Maule. "You
wouldn't notice the cold. But then I eat too much." She sighed,
a little gusty sigh as if there were something inevitable and
therefore tragic about her appetite.

The heavy door was opened by an elderly woman with a
pleasant expression. She wore a black frock and a small fancy
apron.

Mrs. Maule stepped over the threshold. "You see! I've
brought Miss Morton back safely." She smiled at Louise. "Come
in and get warm by the fire whilst Mrs. Dunn lets your patient
know that you're here. We'll meet again at dinner." She hurried
away on small plump feet.

Left alone, Louise looked about her with sharpened interest.

Half a tree seemed to be burning above a bed of wood ash.
The chimneypiece was of Caen stone with a coat of arms set in
an oval panel. The floor was scattered with fine old rugs. The
furniture was large and dark. The walls were panelled to a height
of about twelve feet. Above this hung a row of family portraits
and, high above again, was a great hammer beam roof. An
ornate staircase with polished treads vanished into the gloom of a
poorly lit landing. For all its dark magnificence, it was a lived-in
room and had the friendly feeling of a home. Louise liked it.

She turned her attention to the portraits. They were nearly
all of men. Many were in heroic poses and the magnificent army
uniforms of their period. She decided that if the Maules looked
like that, then she had never met any of them. They were so tall,
so thin, so elegant. So world-weary and supercilious.

She noticed something else about them.

Except for those in uniform every Maule had been portrayed
as a sportsman. Some were on horseback. Some carried guns or
fishing rods, a hare or a brace of pheasants. A stag lay at their
narrow-booted feet. They rested a slender hand on the head of a

greyhound or stood in negligent fashion amid the piled trophies of the chase. The army portraits had fiery backgrounds, littered with dead horses and expiring foes.

The murderous Maules. Then she remembered an attribute that Finch had mentioned as being more dangerous.

The respectable Maules. But suppose the inspector were wrong? Suppose she didn't recognise anyone in the household? She wondered again which of the family had sent the telegram. And at once a plaintive voice seemed to echo in her ear, *"Now-adays there seems no money for anything."*

The housekeeper returned. "Will you come this way, please, miss." She retraced her steps down a long corridor and threw open a door. "Miss Morton," she announced.

Louise was conscious of warmth and comfort. Of old-fashioned chintz and flowers, expensive knicknacks in profusion, and photographs in handsome frames. Of books in bright dust jackets and magazines. Of another great wood fire. But these were background impressions. Louise's interest was centered on the woman who sat in an armchair before the fire, a light mohair rug over her knees.

She was tall and thin—too thin. A very plain woman with irregular features, and a long humorous face. She had a look of the Maule portraits and the Maules' long elegant hands. Her dark hair was simply dressed. She wore clothes that were unobtrusive and yet had about them a look of Paris. Her voice, when she spoke, was pleasant, for all that it sounded accustomed to giving orders—and to having those orders carried out.

She looked in no way the nonentity Louise had expected. She appeared capable and level-headed, secure in her possession of wealth. It was difficult to imagine her as the prey of a fortune hunter, and the shadow of the illegitimate baby suggested by the detective vanished away.

Mrs. Crane was a stranger to Louise.

"Nurse, how delightful! I've told Mrs. Dunn to bring tea now. I'm sure you must be dying for a cup after your long journey. But perhaps you'd like to go to your room first?"

"No, I'd love some tea."

"Then take off your coat and hat. Leave them on a chair somewhere and come and sit down where I can look at you. Oh, I feel sure that we shall get along splendidly."

"Miss Mathews sent you all kinds of messages," said Louise, doing as she was told. "She said I wasn't to leave until I'd got you on your feet again."

Isobel Crane made a slight grimace. "My wretched health! Still, we'll talk about that later." Adding, smiling, "Tell me, how is the great Miss Mathews?"

They were still talking about her when Mrs. Dunn returned pushing a loaded tea trolley.

"It has to come like this," Isobel explained. "The kitchen's so far away. The Maules have always had a passion for building. Whenever they thought of it they just clapped on a few more rooms or threw out a new wing. But come and have your tea, Nurse. Meals on trains, I always think, have a way of soon becoming only a rather dreary memory."

"The food wasn't very interesting," Louise admitted, "but I shared a table with a Scotland Yard detective and that helped to pass the time." She wondered what her patient would have said if she had known the subject of their conversation.

Her eyes were caught suddenly by a photograph standing by itself on a side table. A photograph of a bearded, virile-looking man with deep-set eyes and a scar on one cheek. He reminded Louise of someone but she thought that it was a type, a stock character of the screen or television rather than anyone whom she had known.

Isobel noticed the direction of her eyes. "That's my husband," she said. "He met with a dreadful accident a couple of years ago. He was sensitive about the scars it left, so he grew a beard."

"Matron told me about the air crash. In Alaska, wasn't it?"

"He was on his way *back* to Alaska—from San Francisco," Isobel corrected. "His plane crashed into a wooded hillside in the Yukon. Owing to the snow and pine trees the wreckage wasn't sighted for six days. By then my husband was the only one still alive. There'd been a young woman who'd died two days after the accident, and a man who held out until the very morning of the rescue. It was a terrible experience for my husband, and *he* only survived because of his magnificent physique."

"He looks very strong," said Louise, seeing that they had struck on a subject of real interest to her patient. "Doesn't he find life very quiet here, after Alaska?"

"Oddly enough he doesn't. Of course he's been through a bad time. At the moment he's managing my business affairs, but I don't suppose that'll satisfy him forever. I'm quite expecting that one of these days he'll come to me and suggest we set off for some remote corner of the earth.''

"What would you do then?" Louise thought rather uneasily that Matron had been right in one thing. Isobel Crane was infatuated with the man whom she had married.

"Go, of course." Isobel looked as if the idea pleased her. "I'm not really the useless female I must seem now." She fell silent a moment, staring into the fire. Her eyes dreamy, her chin cupped in a be-ringed hand. "That's what I always feel with Roger. His strength, both moral and physical. One of these days perhaps a moment of crisis will arise. And then he will emerge in his full stature for all to see.''

Later Louise was to remember those words. At the time she was more preoccupied with the thought of Roger managing—or mismanaging—her patient's affairs. Only—could he do that and get away with it? Looking at the thin sardonic face, Louise doubted it—and felt more cheerful in consequence.

Isobel stirred, laughed. "Dear me! What a bore I'm becoming. And yet I daresay happiness is always a bit of a bore to other people—and I must admit, when Roger's away, I spend a good deal of the time dreaming about him.''

"Is he away now?"

"He went to London two days ago on business and isn't due back until Thursday." Isobel added in a tone of rueful surprise, "I'm almost ashamed of the way I miss him.''

"Today is Monday. The time will soon pass," said Louise encouragingly.

"So I tell myself." There was faint dryness in Isobel's voice as if she were discounting this professional cheerfulness. "But I was going to tell you about my health, wasn't I?"

"Please. Matron is expecting a full report."

"I'm sure she is—the bully. But then everyone has been bullying me on that score and probably with justice; for left to myself I must have overdone things. I passed right out in this very room. Gave my poor Roger the fright of his life. He found me unconscious on the bedroom floor.''

Isobel was silent a moment. Then she said reflectively, "It's always difficult to admit that one is wrong. Particularly"— and she glanced at the girl with a look of amusement—"when one is used to being right. I suppose that was why I wrote off to Miss Mathews, and told no one what I had done until I had had her reply.''

The words brought with them an odd little feeling of shock to Louise. They fitted in so well with what the inspector had said. The secrecy and then the mention of her own name.

The girl's eyes were drawn enquiringly to Roger Crane's photograph. But now it was just the face of her patient's husband, a strong, unusual face but still that of a stranger.

"Everyone must have been delighted when they heard."

"They were—but not so pleased that I'd stipulated that my nurse must be young and more of a companion than a nurse." Isobel laughed. "My last one was an old dragon. She did disapprove of Roger so thoroughly. He used to say that she had a very poor opinion of men in general. But I've sometimes suspected that she must have overheard the very rude name he insisted on calling her behind her back."

"And, apart from fainting that time, you really are better?"

"So much better—and that needs an explanation. Friday is the anniversary of our marriage. I shall have been married a year—and for most of that time I've been ill. I know that my husband has been planning a little celebration. Just for the two of us. He's been so patient, so wonderful, that I planned a little surprise for him." She added with a mock rueful air, "I suppose it's rather childish of me but the fact is, that with the doctor's connivance, I've concealed from everyone just how much progress I've made.

"I've been doing a few exercises. Walking a little. With a stick of course, but still walking. Sometimes I've wondered whether Aunt Agnes doesn't suspect but the only one who really knows is a great friend of mine whose father is a retired judge and lives near here. And of course Dr. Reed." Isobel added happily, "He says I'll soon be able to resume a normal married life."

"That's splendid." Louise wondered soberly whether it was safe to love anyone as wholeheartedly as Isobel seemed to love the enigmatic man whom she had married. She wondered too just how he would react to his wife's news. She enquired if her patient slept well. "I find a hot drink last thing at night often works wonders."

Isobel made a little grimace. "I was taking all sorts of things. Last thing at night. First thing in the morning."

"And they went out with your last nurse?"

"I suppose you could say that," Isobel admitted, with a

twinkle. "And I suppose they're going to come in again with my nurse."

"Well, you are too thin. And you must keep up your strength if you're going to surprise your husband with anything but a blackout," said Louise firmly.

"Yes, Nurse," said Isobel Crane meekly.

Chapter 3

Mrs. Dunn led Louise back through the winding corridors. "How did you find Mrs. Crane, miss?" she enquired. "Too easily tired if you ask me."

"It always takes a long time to recover from poliomyelitis," Louise answered.

"She gave us all a nice fright fainting like that." Mrs. Dunn was panting slightly as she went. "Mr. Crane was nearly off his head with worry."

"Then I shall have to see that it doesn't happen again, shan't I?" Louise answered sedately. She followed Mrs. Dunn up the stairs and threw a backward glance over her shoulder at the disappearing Maules—the impossibly elegant Maules. They crossed a wide shadowy landing, where only one electric bulb burned and the dark walls absorbed what light there was so that the two of them seemed to swim in a gloomy twilight.

Mrs. Dunn stopped, her hand on the door knob of one of the rooms. "I'm glad you've come, miss. Miss Isobel's too much alone, what with Mr. Crane having to go into Lockbridge nearly every day on her behalf," she confided. "It was Mr. Desmond who turned the place from little more than a village into a thriving seaside resort. That's how he made his fortune. His second fortune, that is. He'd already made one after the First World War, buying up government surplus stock."

"Mr. Desmond? He was Mrs. Crane's father, wasn't he?"

"That's right, miss. He was the Squire's brother and next to him in age. Mr. Jason's father was the youngest of the three. He was a very fine gentleman but it was Mr. Desmond who went into business. The first of the family ever to do such a thing." If he had been a cosmonaut Mrs. Dunn could not have sounded more proud and astonished.

She turned the door knob. "This is your room, miss. If you don't find everything you want you just let me know."

It was a comfortable room, warmed by an electric radiator.

18

There were an electric kettle and some tea things. Louise found a
shower and a wash basin fitted into a large cupboard. The room,
panelled in dark wood, was furnished with antiques. There was
a small four-poster with red brocade hangings.

She unpacked her two suitcases, washed, and changed into
her nurse's uniform. She clasped a wide white belt round her
twenty-two-inch waist and set a stiffly starched cap like a fluted
cake tin on her dark head.

She let herself out into the passage and set out to find her
way back to the West Wing. She came to the head of the great
staircase. There was no one about. As she went down the stairs
her heels made a clicking sound on each step, echoing faintly
like an unseen neighbour. She crossed the hall and went down
the long corridor. She was surprised and obscurely flattered at
the ease with which she found her way through the intricacies of
the West Wing. Almost as if she and the old house had a feeling
of affinity, she thought, then grinned derisively at her own
conceit.

Isobel Crane, who had a girl from the village as personal
maid, had changed into a green velvet housecoat lavishly trimmed
with mink. She sat in the light wheelchair which Louise had
noticed earlier, standing outside in the passage.

She regarded Louise with a faintly sardonic air. "The garb
of authority. Now I shall never dare to dispute any of your
decisions. But get yourself a drink. Then it will be time for you
to push my chair into the hall—although I do believe that I could
walk there." She smiled mischievously. "*How* surprised they
would all be."

There were three people in the hall. Louise had already met
Mrs. Maule, but they were all strangers in the sense that the
Scotland Yard inspector had meant.

Agnes Maule was wearing a rather bright shade of nastur-
tium yellow and a lot of amber beads. She seemed pleased to see
Louise and her eyes became narrow twinkling slits.

Her husband, James Maule, was a disappointment to the
girl. True, he was tall and thin, but there the resemblance to the
portraits ceased. He wore spectacles and had a scholar's stoop.

The third person was an elderly woman, small, neat, and
plainly dressed. She was wearing a serviceable grey twin set and
a very heavy grey tweed skirt. Her feet were shod in sensible
low-heeled black tie shoes. She was introduced as Miss Chumleigh.

"Not spelt in the aristocratic way, I fear," she said. She
gave a deprecating little laugh.

"James has kept Edith working so late that I insisted on her staying to dinner," said Mrs. Maule. "Afterwards Goodlife can drive her home."

"I'm sorry about that," said Mr. Maule. "I can't think how things manage to accumulate as they do."

"At least you know that Edith will sort them out," said Isobel pleasantly. "She's wonderful at figures."

"And at faces, eh?" laughed Mr. Maule.

Miss Chumleigh looked arch. "I shall remember," she declared. "I pride myself that I never forget a face."

Goodlife appeared, a bent figure with a sour expression. He announced dinner, for he doubled as chauffeur and butler.

The dining room was a handsome room. The table was lit by candlelight, which lost itself long before it reached the ornate plaster ceiling. Objects on the polished surface were repeated in pale reflection. Creamy chrysanthemum heads floated in a low black bowl.

The conversation was desultory. Agnes Maule enquired after Isobel's health and her husband asked when Roger was expected back. Isobel wondered how her uncle's family history was coming along. Her clever face was polite rather than animated. These three had taken too many meals together. Louise suspected a lack of sympathy between the two women.

Jason's empty chair remained like a question mark to the girl.

The conversation turned to Miss Mathews—Rosie Mathews to the Maules. They spoke of her two brothers, who had gone to the 1914 war with the two eldest Maules, James and Desmond, and failed to return. Of the farm itself, now worked by other hands. James Maule quoted from Houseman's *Shropshire Lad*. He spoke of other wars. Of the walls of Tammerton being new when the beacons, flaring on the hills above it, warned of the approach of the Spanish Armada.

A feeling of timelessness crept over Louise. The past seemed not so much gone as just around the corner. She felt as if she were in a dream—a sensation intensified by the pale riders in an enormous hunting scene that dominated the wall opposite her. Figures that came to brief life as a candle flared, only to re-enter the gloom of that enchanted canvas as the light died down again.

"Your husband has a wonderful mind," Miss Chumleigh assured her hostess. "It is a privilege to listen to him."

In the distance the front door banged.

"Jason!" said Agnes Maule. She sent Goodlife to tell him

not to change but to come to dinner as he was. A moment or two later the dining room door opened. A young man stood on the threshold. A young man who might, in the flickering candle-light, have stepped from any one of the family canvases, except that his expression was hard, bitter, and reckless. The long slender feet were there, the heavy drooping lids. He was tall and excessively thin. He wore an old tweed suit with an air of careless elegance and looked superbly certain of himself.

"I'm sorry I'm late, Aunt Agnes," he said, waving away the soup Goodlife offered him. "There's so much to catch up on that I forget the time. Then I ran into old Philby in the village and had to stop and have a word with him."

Mrs. Maule lifted a small, plump paw. "Goodlife, put back Mr. Jason's soup," she commanded. "You must eat more, Jason. You're too thin. Nurse, don't you think he's too thin?"

Louise didn't feel that she was expected to answer. She was aware of a quick impatient glance from under the newcomer's drooping lids as if he asked himself what business it was of hers before obediently picking up his soup spoon.

"And what did the vicar have to say?" Mr. Maule enquired.

"Some very pertinent things about my duty." Jason gave his uncle a singularly sweet smile. "Funny, I'd always thought of him as having died or retired. Yet there he was and looking as indestructible as God's uncle. He gave me a message for you, sir. He said he hoped you wouldn't do anything about the death-watch beetle in the church roof until he'd seen you."

Mr. Maule groaned. "Another of his bright ideas, I suppose." He turned to Miss Chumleigh. "And how is the feud going?" he asked, his eyes twinkling.

"I shall now write to the bishop—and so I told the vicar," said Miss Chumleigh firmly.

"Edith and Philby have never exactly hit it off," Mr. Maule explained, dividing a smile between Louise and his neph-ew. "Edith is evangelical. Philby always had leanings towards ritual and Anglo-Catholicism."

"He wouldn't find the Pope supporting him over this," said Miss Chumleigh with spirit. She turned to Jason. "The vicar actually gave out from the pulpit that, in his opinion, the inno-cent party in a divorce was entitled to be married in church."

"The text, I remember, was 'let him who is without sin cast the first stone,' " said Isobel, her face alight with amusement.

"And what happened?" Jason asked curiously.

Said James Maule, "Then up sprang brave Horatius—Miss

Chumleigh—the captain of the gate. Now who will stand on either hand and keep the bridge with me? We were all very impressed.''

Jason smiled at her, that curiously heart-catching smile. ''From what I remember of the vicar there would have been few takers. Unless, of course, he's changed? Mellowed, perhaps?''

''It was no less than my duty,'' said Miss Chumleigh, ''although the Judge tells me what I did amounted to brawling in church.''

''I wish I'd seen it,'' Jason assured her, adding, carelessly, ''You can count on me. A bit of feuding should serve to keep my hand in.''

Isobel looked at him enquiringly, lifting her fine brows. But she did not say anything and the conversation drifted to other matters. Jason finished his soup and joined the others in eating pheasants, which had been shot on the estate.

Miss Chumleigh cast several surreptitious but searching glances across the table at him, one or two of which he intercepted.

''Edith believes that she has met you somewhere,'' his uncle told him.

''I feel sure that I should have remembered,'' said Jason politely.

''Not met—seen,'' corrected Miss Chumleigh. ''I feel certain of it. And in rather extraordinary circumstances.'' She wrinkled her forehead at him. ''Abroad somewhere, was it?''

''Have you been abroad, Jason?'' his aunt asked.

''All over the place,'' answered Jason briefly.

''Edith, your passion for travelling is the one thing I have against you,'' said James Maule. ''Since you took over I seem to have lost my taste for the clerical work entailed in running this place.''

''My great regret is that I discovered the joys of going abroad so late,'' Miss Chumleigh declared. ''For over thirty years I went every summer to Bournemouth when I might have gone to Arabia, Turkey, or Peru.''

''Perhaps it's just as well,'' said James Maule. It amused him to tease her and watch her face turn pink. ''You seem to attract adventure. Chinese pirates. Corsican bandits. Even bank robbers in the City.''

''Not Chinese pirates,'' Miss Chumleigh begged. ''I have not yet penetrated to the Far East. As for the bank robbers, I fear I only managed to strike one with my umbrella as he fled with the loot.''

It was at this point that Louise noticed Jason. A curious stillness had come over him. She wondered whether, perhaps, at some time during the conversation, he had remembered where it was he and Miss Chumleigh had seen each other. If so he did not appear to derive much pleasure from the knowledge.

"I hear that the Judge is well again," James Maule remarked. "He telephoned to say that he was ready to resume our games of chess."

"Yes, K-Kathie"—Isobel stumbled over the name—"is able to go out again. She is coming in here tomorrow on her way to Lockbridge."

"We've got to get used to mentioning Kathie's name in front of Jason," said Mrs. Maule, "otherwise it will become more and more difficult."

"If I don't find it difficult," Jason remarked, "I don't see why anyone else should."

He leaned forward as he spoke, to stare mockingly at Isobel. The light fell on his face. Louise could have cried out, so bleak and hard was its expression.

"I'm sorry, Jason," said Isobel. "It was stupid of me." She smiled at him but it was easy to see that she was annoyed at her own gaucherie. "Particularly as Kathie will be coming to dinner with the Judge."

Agnes Maule looked belligerent. "We can't have Kathie. She'd be an odd number. We'd want another man." She spoke very fast. When she had finished she eyed her husband warily.

"I don't think we need trouble about that," he said equably. "It's happened often enough before and it's only a family party." The smile he gave his wife was very like that of his nephew, sweet, loving. "And to even the number perhaps Edith would give us the pleasure of her company?"

Agnes tried to look cross and failed. "Well, it sounded very grand when I said it," she admitted. She chuckled hoarsely. "And from me, who never saw any man but my father when I was a gal."

"You should have cast one of your spells," Jason said, grinning.

"Darlin'," said his aunt comfortably, "wasn't that how I met your uncle?"

James Maule chuckled. "Queerest thing I ever knew. For no apparent reason my horse bolted straight up her father's drive and threw me right at her feet." Adding gallantly, "Where I have been ever since."

When the women had left the dining room Miss Chumleigh announced her intention of 'slipping away without disturbing the gentlemen.'

She put on a hairy coat to match her hairy skirt, and tied a silk handkerchief over her hair, throwing up her chin as she did so. She paused for a moment, her eyes caught by the portrait of a Maule who had taken part in the storming of the Heights of Abraham.

"The military tradition," she murmured. "So romantic."

"They do look rather nice in uniform," Isobel admitted. "They were mostly younger sons who chose to go into the army in preference to the Church."

The conversation was cut short by the arrival of Goodlife with the ancient Rolls.

"See you tomorrow at ten," Isobel called.

"Without fail," Miss Chumleigh called back. "And for dinner," cried Agnes Maule. "Lovely!" Miss Chumleigh was wafted away emitting little cries of mingled thanks and farewell.

"For a sensible woman Edith has the silliest manner of anyone I know," Mrs. Maule commented.

"Uncle James calls her a woman of marked moral fervour," said Isobel smiling.

"Then she must find it difficult to countenance your friend Kathie," Mrs. Maule retorted, before trotting away on some domestic errand.

Isobel shrugged. "Aunt Agnes is a good hater. But wheel me back to my room, Nurse." Explaining as they went, "Miss Chumleigh worked all her life in London for a firm of solicitors. When she retired the Judge persuaded her to settle here, where, to keep from getting bored, she deals with Uncle James's affairs on Mondays and Thursdays, and with mine on Tuesday mornings."

Back in her own room she gave a sigh of relief. "How Aunt Agnes can—All those dishes and she had to do most of the cooking herself."

"I thought it was heaven," said Louise candidly.

Isobel laughed. "That should make you madly popular with Aunt Agnes. But you just watch your waistline, Nurse. Now—give me a cigarette. Take one yourself if you smoke. Then poke up the fire and we'll settle down to a nice long gossip."

Louise did as Isobel suggested, at least as far as the fire was concerned. Then she sat down in one of the low chairs and prepared to listen. She had found that nurses, like hairdressers, were liable to be the recipients of the most intimate disclosures—and on the shortest of acquaintanceships.

It was warm and quiet in the room. What light there was came from a single standard lamp and the leaping flames. Isobel Crane seemed in no hurry to begin.

At last she said slowly and picking her words, "Since Kathie may be coming to dinner tomorrow I think I had better explain why I was embarrassed mentioning her name. She and Jason were once engaged to be married."

Louise turned her head sharply to look at Isobel. "Engaged?"

"Jason jilted her within three days of the wedding. Just like that." She snapped her fingers. "Sent her a short note and cleared out. Vanished completely. That was seven years ago. Kathie was broken-hearted. We quite thought she'd have a breakdown. She kept crying and screaming. Declaring that there was a curse on her and that she was fated to be unmarried. Unfortunately it was the second love affair to go wrong. She lost her first fiancé in an accident. The Judge, although he had opposed the match, even to the point of swearing that Kathie should not touch a penny of his money if she married Jason, was furious to find the whole thing off." She gave a rather mirthless laugh. "Kathie has been away for a fortnight, and then the Judge was ill. So tomorrow, if the Kelvins come to dinner, will be the first time the three of them have met since Kathie was jilted."

So that was it, Louise was thinking. Jason had a bad reputation with women. And no wonder! She said aloud, "Hasn't Mr. Maule been back in all that time?"

"Back? My dear girl, he hardly even sent as much as a postcard. Aunt Agnes was heartbroken."

"And why has he come back now? I mean, at this particular moment."

Isobel shrugged. "He says he felt like it—always a sufficient reason for Jason."

Louise was silent a moment, considering. "Perhaps Mr. Maule didn't like to come back?"

"Ashamed, you think?" Isobel laughed shortly. "Not he. He'd die before he'd admit, even to himself, that he was in the wrong. Far less that he had done something shabby."

"And Miss Kelvin? Hasn't she married?"

"No."

"Perhaps she's still in love with Mr. Maule?"

Isobel shrugged. "Kathie never mentions Jason's name. Nor allows anyone else to mention it." She smiled to herself as she stubbed out her cigarette end. "All the same I admit I find it a little hard to believe that she is still carrying a torch for him. Or, for that matter, that there hasn't been anyone else. Kathie radiates more sex appeal and, on occasions, more sheer feminine sensuality than anyone else I've ever known. When you meet her you'll see what I mean. Even my husband scoffs at the idea of her living like a nun. Not that he approves of her. He's the only man I know who doesn't." Isobel's voice had softened again, as it did whenever she mentioned her husband. "Perhaps you've noticed it too, Nurse? How a simple man like my Roger is far more censorious than a more worldly one like Jason or Uncle James."

She yawned a little. "Still I'm glad he wakes up occasionally to what's going on," she murmured. "Uncle James, I mean. Otherwise Aunt Agnes would never have invited Kathie to the house."

"D'you mean she wouldn't have invited her because of young Mr. Maule being back?"

Isobel shook her head. "The Sidbalds are a queer lot. Aunt Agnes was a Miss Sidbald before her marriage. They've always been queer. Centuries ago one of them was actually burnt as a witch."

"Yes, but I don't see—"

"Aunt Agnes," said Isobel in a resigned tone of voice, "suffers from what Uncle James calls 'messages from outer space.' And the queer thing is that they're usually right. For instance, last week, quite suddenly, she announced that Jason was coming back. She had his bed made up and his room aired and sure enough that evening he just walked in. With Kathie it's rather different. Aunt Agnes declares she brings misfortune with her, but the plain truth is that she has never liked her. She blames her, too, for Jason's disappearance."

Louise nodded. In this isolated house, lost between the dark woods and the wild bare hills, it was not so hard to believe in second sight—which was what it amounted to—or even in witches. Indeed, a clear picture came into her mind of Mrs. Maule, stout and pink, riding a broomstick. Rather an endearing picture. She stifled a chuckle.

Looking up, she caught Isobel's amused eye. "I suppose it is funny to an onlooker. But not so funny if you have to live with it. You just wait and see. All this cooking too. So unnecessary but Aunt Agnes does love rich food, and the old-fashioned ritual of dinner. The reaction, I imagine, from a drab childhood.

"Her mother died when she was small and her father was a most peculiar man. He never allowed anything to be bought that could be made at home. Candles and soap and something called bath brick. Oh, a host of things. Their house, a great barracks of a place, had no gas and no electricity. No candles or lamps either if there were a full moon to light the room. If anyone fell ill leeches would be fetched from the ponds. And if anyone was in pain, opium could be made from the common poppy. When she was first married she used to dose the village. Dr. Reed used to get furious but he got no sympathy from Uncle James, who just roared with laughter. Of course, when the National Health Service came in she had to give it up."

"She must have missed it." Louise was thinking of her own thwarted ambition to become a doctor.

"Not for long. Aunt Agnes took to betting instead—and not always successfully. Once or twice she has been so much in the red that Uncle James has had to come to the rescue." Isobel took another cigarette from the box. "Draw the curtains, Nurse. After all this talk of witches and premonitions I shall be glad to shut out the night." Adding after a moment, "D'you know, I might even be having a premonition of my own."

Louise paused looking back over her shoulder. "What kind of one?" she asked cautiously.

Isobel laughed. "Don't look so alarmed. It's of quite a mild character. Just that we're in for a very sticky evening tomorrow. Sticky—but interesting, I hope. I can't help wondering about Kathie and Jason."

There were two windows in the room. The light shining through lit up part of a formal garden and the end of a grey stone wall. Just outside the area of light Louise noticed a shrub or small tree. Noticed it because it seemed to bear a rather curious resemblance to a person in a sou'wester and raincoat.

When she reached the other window she paused to take a second nearer look. She stood very still for a moment, then very quietly and thoughtfully drew the curtains.

The tree—or shrub—or person—was no longer there.

Chapter 4

Louise stood by the open window, taking in great breaths of morning air. The day was overcast, yet everything appeared wonderfully clean and fresh. Reluctantly she turned away. Her gaze went round the room, paused a few moments at the little four-poster with its rosy red brocade curtains, and she wondered who else had slept in it. And, if it were haunted, then by whom? Recalling her thoughts to the present, she left the room and went downstairs to her patient.

Isobel was writing out a shopping list. She looked up as Louise came into the room. "There you are, Nurse! Kathie is going to do some shopping for me in Lockbridge. When you hear her blow her horn perhaps you'd take her this list."

Louise was delighted at the thought that she was to see Jason's unfortunate ex-lady love. She had toyed with the idea of trying to bring them together again, for she was a kind-hearted girl. She had decided that too long a time had elapsed. It was highly probable, too, that a second disappointment must have had a pretty blighting effect on Kathie—

A motor horn sounded outside, blown in a gay fanfare of sound which seemed to give the lie to Louise's mournful conclusions. She picked up the list and hurried out with it.

A smart M.G. sports car, painted cream, was drawn up outside the house. A woman sat alone in the driving seat. A woman very smart and soignée. A woman with gingery hair, reddish amber eyes and a band of freckles sprayed across a slightly tiptilted nose. A woman with a wide mouth and hollow cheeks—

A great roaring sounded in Louise's ears. The plain, and yet in some indefinite way oddly captivating face of this other woman swam in a mist before her eyes. A mist shot through with the maimed and distorted shapes of memory.

The years dropped away. She was a child again, motoring

with her father along the highway—and again a powerful sports car came tearing straight at them, out of a side turning.

"So you did learn to drive after all," she heard herself saying. And the words seemed to her ears to be coming from a long way off.

Kathie looked bewildered. "What on earth are you talking about?" she asked—but not before a betraying flash of fury had flickered across her face.

"Don't tell me you've forgotten," said Louise scornfully. "After the crash that killed my father you swore not only that you'd never driven a car in your life, but that you wouldn't ever want to drive."

Kathie gave an elaborate sigh. "So you're that girl! And still suffering from the same delusion. Well, well!"

Louise's hand strayed to her cheek. "D'you think I've forgotten any single detail of what happened?"

Kathie's lips curled. "I slapped your face, didn't I? And said that as you howled every time you saw me, you might as well have something to howl about. Well, you're a big girl now and if you go round saying that I was driving the Bentley I can tell you you won't get off as lightly."

Louise met the narrowed, dangerous gaze with her own level one. "As you say, I'm a big girl now. People might be more ready to believe me than they were when I was only a child of twelve."

"So you're threatening me." Kathie threw open the car door and stepped out. "We'll see about that." She walked arrogantly away on her long lovely legs. "Believe me," she threw over her shoulders, "you may find yourself on the train back to London."

Louise remained where she was. Gradually the roaring in her head died down. Her heart ceased to thump. The Inspector was right after all, she thought. Kathie must have sent that telegram. For some reason she didn't want me here. She became aware that she was still holding Isobel Crane's shopping list. She put it on the seat of the car before turning away.

She walked slowly into the house and along to the kitchen. She had almost reached her destination when the thought struck her. Kathie was not only the woman of detestable memory. She was also the fiancée whom Jason had jilted so unceremoniously.

Agnes Maule was in the huge, old-fashioned kitchen. Plump and pink, sleeves rolled to her elbows, she was beating eggs in a brown and white bowl. The table was littered with their shells.

She became aware of Louise's presence. "I do like a recipe that says 'take a dozen eggs,' " she remarked with gusto and without looking up.

"I didn't know that any of them did."

"Some recipes did—and a few still do." Mrs. Maule continued beating vigorously. "I'm making a cake for my nephew. Don't you think he's too thin, Nurse?"

"Yes—except that all the Maules seem to have been thin."

Agnes Maule looked faintly abashed. "I'm just a doting old woman," she admitted. She looked up and saw Louise. "Heavens, child! What's the matter with you?"

"I've just seen—Miss Kelvin. She was the woman in the car the day my father was killed."

"Are you that gal?" The small brilliant eyes were round pools of surprise and sympathy. "No wonder you're upset. Here!" Mrs. Maule abandoned the eggs to pull a chair out from under the long scrubbed table. "You sit there. Put your head between your knees."

"I shall be all right, thank you. I really came to make an eggnog for my patient." She wondered fleetingly how long Isobel Crane would remain her patient.

"That can wait. You stay where you are and I'll make a cup of tea." She bustled about, muttering disjointedly, and what gradually emerged was a premonition of disaster. "Ever since I was a child I could tell . . . I know and I'm never wrong . . ." She paused to favour Louise with a strange blind stare. "It's very near now . . . A dark cloud . . . That young woman brought it . . . A dark cloud . . . Death . . . I can't see clearly . . ."

Louise felt her spine crawling. There was something so convincing in Mrs. Maule's manner—something so strange and inward-looking in her gaze. And was she, Louise, the young woman? Or was it Kathie? She would have said something. Something broken, inadequate, but before she could speak Mrs. Maule had done so. The blind look was fading fast.

"What does Kathie do to them?" she demanded, in her hoarse voice. "Harry was just the same. He'd have gone to the stake for her. They both would."

"But I thought that your nephew jilted her?"

"So he did. But why? Answer me that. What makes a man jilt a woman he loves so much that for seven long years he won't even risk being in the same neighbourhood?"

* * *

When Louise went back to the West Wing she found that Kathie had gone. Isobel was there. With her was Miss Chumleigh, who clasped a large notebook and pen. She stared at Louise and her amazement at the turn of events was plain.

Isobel sat in her usual chair, her head back, her eyes closed. To the girl's relief, when she spoke it was with a distinct note of amusement.

"Well, Louise Morton," she said. "You seem to have frightened Kathie pretty thoroughly."

"Did I? I don't see why." Louise added unguardedly, "At least, not to the extent of making her try to prevent my coming here."

Isobel said without opening her eyes, "I didn't know that she had tried to prevent your coming here. She forgot to mention it I suppose."

Louise bit her lip, annoyed at her indiscretion. "I thought from something she said—"

"Oh no, you didn't." Isobel's tone of voice made it clear that she meant to have a truthful answer. "Now tell me, just what did Kathie do?"

"She sent a telegram to Matron." Hurriedly Louise juggled with the wording. "It said that your plans had changed and that you no longer needed a nurse. When Miss Mathews rang up about it she found it wasn't true."

Miss Chumleigh looked shocked but Isobel laughed heartily. "How like Kathie! She is the most unprincipled creature. But we must keep this from Roger. He'd be so furious."

"And who could blame him?" said Miss Chumleigh. "Oh, dear! How naughty of Kathie. But whatever she may feel, the Judge will be delighted you're here, Miss Morton. He has always kept in touch with your aunt." Louise stared. "Oh, in the nicest possible manner. Just an occasional card, you know."

"Aunt Phyllis never told me."

"I expect she felt it might upset you. You were so angry with everyone."

Isobel saw the glass Louise was still holding. "Is that for me? Well, if I must—" She took it and drank a little. "H'm! It's nice. It's the nutmeg, I think."

"I still don't see why Miss Kelvin should mind my coming here," Louise persisted. "Or, for that matter, why she's called Miss Kelvin. When I knew her she was called Lynch."

"I know. But she's lived with the Judge for so long that it's become less confusing to speak of her as if she were his daughter."

"But actually," said Louise, groping after the truth, "her fiancé who was killed in the accident was Mr. Kelvin's son."

"That's it. And since the Judge is a rich man, Kathie doesn't want to do anything to upset him. Oh, I know it sounds mercenary put like that but it's just a recognition of the facts. Kathie was earning quite a good income designing textiles when she gave it up to go and live with the Judge. But she was young then. Now she's thirty-four and used to luxury. It wouldn't be exactly easy for her to make a fresh start. In fact I doubt if it would be possible."

"But why should my coming here have such a devastating effect?"

"Because the Judge has always believed that Kathie had told him the truth about the accident. Because he has a great regard for all the virtues that make life difficult. Kathie feels that he might have forgiven her for killing his son but not for having lied about it."

Louise laughed shortly. "I don't think she need worry. I've never found anyone yet who believed me when I said she was driving and not her fiancé."

"The trouble down here," said Isobel soberly, "is that anyone who knows Kathie might prefer to believe you."

"Then," said Louise decidedly, "the Judge must suspect the truth already. After all, he knows her better than either of you." Her life had not been spoilt, or even rendered unhappy by Kathie's untrue statement, but there had been times when it had been held against her—and, anyway, she resented the whole thing.

Miss Chumleigh looked at her reproachfully. "You're young," she said. And hard, her tone of voice added. "And, as far as the Judge is concerned, the question as to who was driving the Bentley has never really arisen." She spoke with a sharpness that surprised and antagonised Louise. "And, although it was wrong of Kathie to pretend she wasn't at the wheel one has to remember that fundamentally she is a very insecure person."

"And Jason's behaviour was hardly calculated to improve her morale," said Isobel.

To this Miss Chumleigh retorted, to Isobel's evident surprise, that no doubt young Mr. Maule had had his reasons.

"Edith, I believe you've been holding out on us," said Isobel. "D'you actually mean to tell me you know why Jason behaved so badly?"

"I know several things about Jason and Kathie," Miss

Chumleigh retorted with spirit, "but I should not dream of revealing anything of what I know without the consent of the parties concerned."

"And that isn't likely to be given? How mysterious—and how provoking. I shall have to try my powers of persuasion on Kathie."

"What Kathie tells you is entirely her own affair," said Miss Chumleigh stiffly, "but I think it very unlikely that you will learn anything from young Mr. Maule."

"You mean he is keeping something shady from us?"

Miss Chumleigh looked embarrassed. "Just something—rather silly and juvenile."

Isobel's eyes twinkled. "How offended Jason would be if he could hear you. But that will not prevent my trying to get it out of him."

Miss Chumleigh looked at her. "Isobel, I beg that you will do no such thing."

"Edith, you have such old-fashioned notions," Isobel was laughing openly.

"Perhaps if we were to return to the original subject under discussion—" Miss Chumleigh suggested in a goaded tone of voice.

"Of course. We have yet to hear Louise's account of the accident. It should be interesting, for whenever I've heard of it the emphasis has always been on poor Harry Kelvin's death."

"You knew him?" Louise asked.

"Edith and I both knew him. She was private secretary to the solicitor who gave Harry his first brief."

"And many subsequent ones," Miss Chumleigh agreed. "He and I often talked over his cases. He confided to me, too, details of his private life. It was during one of these talks that he made me promise to protect Kathie's interests."

"D'you mean *he* felt he might be going to die?" Louise thought this was too much. If everyone—

"Indeed, no. But he was afraid that Kathie might break off the engagement. He was very much in love with her and worried about her rather feckless outlook and the possible instability of her future." Miss Chumleigh's face was rather pink but she added firmly, "I look on it as a sacred trust to ensure that future."

"Yes, that sounds like Harry," Isobel agreed. "He was kind and thoughtful, and rather conventional. A stable future would have seemed to him to be essential to happiness." And to

Louise, "You see, I knew him all my life. The Kelvins have always owned Warley and the Judge has always spent as much time as possible there. When Harry became engaged to Kathie, it was natural that he should bring her down here to visit his father and be introduced to the neighbourhood. I was staying here at the time. Kathie, I remember, captivated us all. She was so gay, so high-spirited. There was a sort of wildness in her. She captivated Jason, too. That's when it began. His love for Kathie, I mean. He did the maddest, most extravagant things, and she egged him on. We were all horrified."

Louise had listened, fascinated. "What happened?"

"In a way, nothing. Harry was much older than either of them. He did threaten to give Jason a damned good thrashing if he made a real nuisance of himself and he might have done it if he hadn't been killed, for Jason really was outrageous. Fortunately for him Harry thought of him as a boy—but he wasn't. He was never a boy as Harry Kelvin meant it."

"How old was Jason then?" So absorbed was Louise in the story that she was unconscious of having used his Christian name.

If Isobel noticed it she gave no sign. "He was eighteen. A dazzling golden eighteen. Kathie, in spite of being five years older, would not have been the first young woman to succumb to his charms."

"And after Harry Kelvin's death Kathie and Jason got engaged?"

Isobel shook her head. "It wasn't until three years later that their engagement was announced. It was a few weeks before Christmas I remember. We were very gay. By the beginning of February the engagement was off and Jason had disappeared."

"I see," said Louise slowly. And what she saw was only confusion, mystery, and pain, and no straightforward facts at all.

Isobel smiled, sighed, and looked across at her. "You still haven't told me about the accident. But perhaps you don't like to speak of it?"

Louise shook her dark head. "No, it isn't that. After all, it was eleven years ago." She began her story. "As you may remember my father was a doctor. His practice was in Plymouth but we lived outside the town. My mother died when I was born so that we only had each other. As far as was possible we went everywhere together. We were motoring near Princetown one day and I was watching a group of convicts being taken back to the prison—"

"Convicts?" Miss Chumleigh sounded surprised. "The newspapers said nothing about convicts."

"I know one shouldn't stare," Louise spoke rather apologetically, "but somehow one does. And in summer literally dozens of people park their cars outside the prison gates for no other purpose."

"I wasn't blaming you. It was simply that in all the accounts of the affair, no mention was made of convicts."

"I don't suppose it was important enough," said Louise simply. "They were just there and I was looking at them. That's how it was I didn't see the Bentley at first. Not until I heard my father cry out. Then I looked round and saw it coming out of a side road straight for us. It struck our car, overturning it, and buckling in one side. I was thrown against the door. I can still recall the smell of hot oil and petrol—and of some oranges that had rolled out of their bag.

"I can remember one of the convicts putting his head in at the window and saying, 'The kid's all right but the bloke's had it.' Then someone else shouted that someone was dead. It was a rough sort of voice. I didn't hear what was said very distinctly, but something warm and sticky dripped on to my face. I looked up and knew that the words were true. My father was lying across the steering wheel, dead. There was blood trickling from his mouth. I think I must have fainted then because the next thing I knew I was waking up in a strange bedroom."

Louise could not have complained of her audience. Miss Chumleigh looked quite aghast, whilst Isobel said with genuine feeling, "Why you poor child! What a terrible experience!"

"Horrible!" said Miss Chumleigh, with a shudder.

"What I can't understand," said Isobel thoughtfully, "is how Kathie got away with it."

"I expect it was as Miss Chumleigh says. No one really bothered about it. And anyway the Bentley had turned over too. Its occupants were so huddled up in the wreckage that no one could have told which of them had been driving."

"Giving Kathie every opportunity to deny that she was the culprit."

"Yes—and her prospective father-in-law—the Judge as you call him—backed her up. He said that she couldn't drive. And that, although his son had promised to teach her, he had agreed with his father that a powerful sports car was neither a safe nor a suitable vehicle on which to learn."

Isobel smiled. "Which proves two things. That the question

of Kathie driving that particular car had already been discussed. And that the Judge had forgotten what it was like to be in love and, still more, the difficulty of saying no to the beloved.''

Louise sighed. "Miss Kelvin was so clever afterwards. And I didn't help matters either by screaming whenever I saw her and shouting that I hated her and wished that *she* were dead too.''

"How was Kathie clever? In your case, I mean?''

"She kept saying how terribly sorry she was for me and that she quite understood my wishing to be revenged on *someone*. And how sad it made her that she had to be the one.''

Isobel nodded. "That's Kathie all right. But what I still can't understand is how she came to lose her head so completely and have the accident. That wasn't in character.''

"I suppose it *is* odd—but it's how it happened. I can see her quite clearly, her face wearing an expression of—well, either despair or helplessness, not doing, not saying anything, just clutching the wheel and coming straight for us.''

"And Harry? D'you remember him?''

"Oh, yes. He was a big man, wasn't he? With a rather heavy face and a lot of dark hair. He was shouting something and just looked surprised and furious.'' Louise added apologetically, "I know his face must have expressed other emotions as well but those are the two I remember. Surprise and anger—but mostly anger.''

"I expect he'd warned Kathie against doing something and she'd waited until he was off his guard and then done it, regardless of the consequence, out of sheer devilry.''

Said Louise slowly, "What an odd way for someone in love to behave.''

"Love?'' Isobel smiled a rather superior smile. "I don't know how much love entered into it with Kathie. I do know that Harry was a very good match and that we knew practically nothing of Kathie's background. Nothing, except that the firm for which she worked was situated near the Old Bailey. She used to go there in her luncheon hour and listen to the cases. That was how she met Harry.''

"He told me that he couldn't help noticing her. All that ginger hair,'' said Chumleigh, who by now looked quite distraught. "In that rather dreary setting she was like a flame, he said. Then one day he saw that she was upset and he spoke to her. She was so young and vulnerable. It broke his heart to see her unhappy. And later I promised—Now I don't see how I can carry out that promise.'' She stared at Louise with tragic eyes.

Louise had no intention of making trouble for Kathie but Miss Chumleigh's championship annoyed her. She remained obstinately silent, her small face set and pale.

"I think it would be as well if we left things as they are for the moment," said Isobel decidedly. "We don't want to make any mistakes—"

"A mistake is not a crime," Miss Chumleigh cried. "I shall have to decide what to do. Harry trusted me." She blundered awkwardly to her feet, stared for a moment distractedly into Louise's face, then fled from the room.

"Dear me," said Isobel dryly. "You are in her bad books."

"I suppose I should have told her that I had no intention of doing anything to hurt her beloved Kathie," said Louise slowly, "but she annoyed me."

"Edith Chumleigh's trouble is that Kathie isn't her beloved. She doesn't even like her. But she loved Harry like a son."

Louise was filled with remorse. "Shall I run after her?"

Isobel shook her head. "She'll be better alone. But I do wish I knew what she meant about Jason. It must be connected with that time when they '*saw each other.*' Such an odd description, I mean, why remember it at all? Jason may be good-looking but . . ."

The telephone on the table at her elbow rang suddenly. Isobel picked up the receiver. The next moment she had covered it with her hand. "Kathie!" she mouthed, "from Lockbridge."

Louise nodded. She took the empty glass and slipped from the room.

She had just remembered the telegram and the need to tell Jason Maule that she had altered its wording.

Chapter 5

Louise paused uncertainly in the hall, wondering how she could find Jason. She heard the sound of hurried footsteps outside and he came in through the front door with an air of immense but controlled vitality. He was wearing riding breeches and an old tweed coat. He was walking swiftly towards the stairs when he saw her and nodded a greeting.

"I wanted to talk to you," said Louise hurriedly. "It's about that telegram and it's rather private."

Jason looked at her, impatient at having been stopped. "Better come with me to the Long Gallery. It's as good a place as any."

He took the wide shallow steps three at a time. Louise followed, soon losing sight of him but finding him again on the landing. Seeing her, he set off again in the opposite direction to the one she knew. He threw open a door, waiting for Louise to pass him. "The Long Gallery," he said.

It stretched to right and left, an immense room, rich in the glory of old Genoese velvet, dark panelling and heavy gilt frames. Enormous mirrors filled with mottled glass hung between portraits and over everything was a faint powdering of dust.

"Hardly anyone comes here now," Jason commented. He spoke in an offhand tone but the hooded probing glances conjured up as plainly as words a picture of young lovers, of Kathie and Jason meeting secretly long ago.

He paused in front of one of the wall mirrors so that his breath filmed the dim old glass. Then, absently, he drew his initials on its surface with a forefinger, J.M., and stood there looking at it as if half expecting a ghostly finger to materialise from thin air and add its own.

Watching him, Louise realised that, when she had stopped him in the hall, he had been obeying a sudden whim in visiting the Long Gallery. She saw, too, that it was her utter unimportance to his scheme of things that had made him bring her along.

He crossed to one of the long windows and forced it open. It swung out with the protesting whine of hinges stiff with disuse. Louise saw an inner courtyard, full of late straggling roses. It was as neglected-looking as the room itself and full of a deep mid-morning silence when even the birds were quiet.

She turned back to the room. "No one's likely to overhear us here. It must be about as private as the middle of the Gobi Desert," she remarked.

"It was built so that the women of the household could get some exercise when the weather prevented their going out. People didn't get about much in those days. Roads were bad. Methods of travel uncomfortable." Jason broke off to say with a kind of bitter impatience, "God! I sound just like Uncle James." He turned from the window. "What was it you wanted to say to me about the telegram?" he asked with chilling formality.

Louise saw that already he regretted bring her there. She refused to be intimidated. "I wanted to tell you that Kathie—Miss Kelvin—sent it to try and stop me coming here."

He was interested now. "Kathie? Why should she have done that?" He bent on her his intent yet haughty stare.

"It was my father who was killed in the smashup on Dartmoor years ago."

Jason's whole attitude changed. She had startled him. He looked at her, taking in every detail of her appearance in one long careful appraisal. She had the impression that he was seeing her for the first time. Before this she had been someone entirely negative. Someone sent to nurse his cousin, Isobel Crane.

"So you were the kid in the car?" Adding absurdly, "You've changed."

The words took her by surprise. "From what?"

"From a thin monkey-like child with a face about the size of a sixpence."

"Did Kathie say that?"

"No. As a matter of fact it was my own private opinion, based on your photographs in the newspapers." Again he bent on her that intent look. "You know, I used to think a lot about you. I must admit," he added meditatively, "it was mostly bloody-mindedness because everyone else was thinking of Harry Kelvin. And now, suddenly, here you are. Why, it's like meeting a distant relative. Someone one has always heard about." He smiled his fascinating smile. "May I call you cousin?"

"Miss Mathews," said Louise primly, "would be against

the idea.'' Suddenly she was conscious, frighteningly conscious, of his charm.

"How lucky then that she isn't here." He observed her rather sardonically, very much in the manner of his cousin Isobel. "But perhaps the pleasure isn't mutual? I seem to remember that when the Judge wanted to make himself responsible for your future your aunt turned on him as if *he'd* been driving the Bentley."

"Aunt Phyllis had always been devoted to my father," Louise spoke rather stiffly. "And I certainly didn't want to accept anything from Mr. Kelvin."

"The enemy?" Jason's tone was meditative. "I suppose it was natural enough."

"I can imagine that the smashup didn't seem such a tragedy to everyone."

Jason's brow darkened. "It didn't seem one to me," he said moodily. "Not at the time anyway."

"You mean—because it was Harry Kelvin who was killed?"

Jason grinned but without much humour. "So Isobel's been talking? I suppose it's natural. She and Harold practically grew up together."

"What was he like?"

"He was a bore. At least, he bored me. He was beginning to bore Kathie—and that's something I never did. He was what was known as a very sound man. Sound in law, politics, and religion. He played a sound game of golf—likewise tennis—and," Jason added mockingly, "his obituaries were far more flattering than any I could ever hope to achieve."

"I only saw him once—in the car. A big dark man, very angry-looking."

"Angry? Good Lor'! I wonder why? Kathie could be the most ghastly irritant, but that was hardly the moment to choose—even for her."

He showed a tendency to brood. Louise brought him back to the present by telling him how she had altered the wording of the telegram.

"That was pretty sharp of you. But then women are pretty sharp. They can run circles round the mere man in that respect."

His tone was so bitter that Louise fancied he must be recalling just why he had broken his engagement to Kathie.

"I couldn't allow my patient to be upset by knowing what had really been written," she said. "That was one reason why I wanted to speak to you. So that you can warn anyone else who knew about the telegram.''

Said Jason coolly, ''I didn't tell anyone else.''

Louise stared. ''You didn't tell anyone?'' she spoke incredulously.

He gave her a haughty look and, for a moment, she thought that he was about to say something crushing. But, if that had been his intention, he changed his mind.

''You've got to remember that I'd only just come home,'' he said. ''I couldn't think what was happening. Then Miss Mathews sounded so self-righteous she put my back up. So I decided to say nothing but try to track down the sender of the telegram. I did find out that it had been sent from a call box in Lockbridge, but, after that, the scent was dead.''

''Didn't you suspect Kathie?''

''No. Did you?''

Louise shook her head. ''How could I suspect anyone?'' she answered promptly—too promptly.

''But someone did.'' Jason's eyes narrowed. ''It must have been Miss Mathews.'' And, as Louise remained obstinately silent, ''She wouldn't have had any reason to think of Kathie. She wouldn't have suspected one of the Maules—not Rosie Mathews. So there remains only Roger Crane. Well, to be truthful, he was my choice too—only I couldn't see how he stood to benefit.''

''There's Mrs. Crane's money,'' cried Louise incautiously.

It was Jason's turn to stare. ''But Miss Mathews must have known that Uncle Desmond left his money tied up on Isobel and any possible children. If she dies Roger gets nothing.''

Louise looked at him blankly. ''Then who would get it?''

Jason gave her the smallest of bows. His dancing eyes surveyed her mockingly, prepared for her discomfiture and rather amused by the prospect. ''Uncle James—and myself,'' he told her. ''And you can't think how we need it.''

''Oh, dear!'' said Louise inadequately. And then in despairing tones. ''But Matron was so certain—'' She broke off, her eyes widening. ''I've just remembered. Matron must have been in the States when Mrs. Crane's father died. She only got back in time for the wedding.''

Jason nodded. ''I suppose that would explain it. Still,'' he added judicially, ''it's bad staff work. Not what I would have expected of Miss Mathews.''

Louise gave a small hiccup of amusement. ''You do all seem to have a thing about Matron.''

"It's a case of local girl makes good. She's been an example to all us lazy layabouts for the last twenty years."

"Silly," said Louise. "Well, I must go back to my patient."

"Yes, there's still the patient." Jason fell into step beside her. "Although I think you're going to find it difficult from now on to hide behind that stiff white apron of yours." Adding conversationally, and with a sidelong glance from his great height, "I suppose Kathie was afraid that you'd tell the Judge that she was driving?"

Louise came to a halt. "You knew that Kathie was driving?" They had stopped and were facing each other.

"She had to tell someone."

"D'you mean that you knew *at the time* that she was lying?"

"What did you expect me to do? Recoil from her in disgust?" Jason asked impatiently. The old bleak look was back on his face. "My dear girl, one doesn't love a person for her virtues. Nor cease to love her for her faults—more's the pity." And something in his voice told Louise that, in some way, he was still tied to the woman whom she had hated for so long.

"My guess is that Mr. Kelvin must have realised long ago that Kathie had been driving. Living with her I don't see how he could help it."

"The idea has crossed my mind," Jason admitted. "On the other hand, when I left home, Kathie had succeeded in creating a certain image of herself in the Judge's mind. It may have persisted."

"I shouldn't have thought it very wise to pretend to be something different from what one is."

"What a very matter-of-fact young woman you must be." The mocking note had come back into Jason's voice. "Now I should have thought it wholly admirable to create an image of oneself that pleases. In fact almost a social necessity."

"Kathie certainly does that." There was scorn in her clear young voice. "But we needn't argue about it. I promised that I wouldn't say anything to disillusion the Judge. And that's what you all want, isn't it?"

"You do dislike her, don't you?"

"She stands for everything I detest. She's a liar and a cheat."

"And what has it brought her that you—or anyone else—would envy?" Jason asked. And when Louise could find no answer, "The truth is that Kathie was born under an evil star.

Nothing ever goes right for her. And, from what I can see, it never will.''

''Well, I can't feel sorry for her. I can't even like her,'' said Louise in a dogged tone, ''but I'll do my best not to show it.''

At the door of the Long Gallery they shook hands solemnly. It was only later that Louise wondered rather ruefully whether they hadn't been sealing a bond drawn solely in Kathie's favour.

The Reverend Oswald Philby was returning from a visit to Warley. He felt surprised and a little hurt at the Judge's lack of enthusiasm for the project he, the vicar, had outlined.

It had been no less than an offer to deal singlehanded with the deathwatch beetle in the church roof.

It seemed to him that it had every advantage. He had read up the subject exhaustively. He knew everything that was needful to be known about the habits of the beetles and of their extermination. He was certain of the success of the enterprise. And it would save everyone concerned a great deal of money. In fact it would cost no more than the price of putting up some form of scaffolding to enable him to reach the roof.

Of course he hadn't called at a very opportune moment. He could see that. But then again the Judge had seemed relieved at the interruption—which made it all the more strange that he had not jumped at the opportunity afforded him to get the church roof repaired for nothing. Or practically nothing.

It was true that things didn't always turn out as he, Mr. Philby, had intended. There was the time when, in using a blow lamp to remove the weeds from the drive, he had burnt down one wing of the vicarage. But as he had pointed out to the church commissioners, not only was its rateable value lessened, but the house itself had become more manageable. He had thought their reaction to this most unreasonable.

He emerged from the woods and shortly afterwards turned into the lane that ran past Glebe Cottage. It reminded him that the Judge had given him a letter to leave for Miss Chumleigh. He had no intention of seeing Miss Chumleigh. He would just put the letter in the letterbox and come away. He had already made his answer to her threat to write to the Bishop.

Too broadminded, was he? And too high? Wait until she saw the latest addition to the board outside the church. It came after *Baptisms, marriages, and funerals by arrangement*. It read in letters of gold that stood out shining and bright against the older weather-worn announcements, *Confessions heard by appointment*.

Mr. Philby chuckled to himself. It was with a decidedly un-christian expression on his face that he pushed open the garden gate of Glebe Cottage and walked down the path.

Louise was off duty. She felt her spirits rise at the prospect of getting away from the house and its occupants. Particularly its occupants.

It had turned into a blustering day and, once outside the house, Louise walked briskly down the path which skirted the lake and led to the woods. She could not help being struck by the mournful character of the scene.

The woods were little better. Outside the light had been sad and grey. Here great cedars and firs, their branches locked together, conspired to keep it out almost entirely. Brambles encroached on her path, threatening to trip her, and all about her was the mournful loneliness of a great estate in decay.

She was glad to emerge on the other side, to see open country, well cultivated if still somewhat heavily timbered. There was a hill crowned with a ring of trees. She decided to walk around it. She set off, feeling her spirits rise as she did so.

Half an hour later, on her return, she found herself walking down a lane sunk deep between high grass hedges. She came on a cottage standing a little way back. She stopped to admire its neatness, its freshness and order.

Its walls were washed pink, its roof thatched. A rambler rose bush trailed over a rustic porch and Glebe Cottage was painted in black letters on a white wood gate.

So this was where Miss Chumleigh lived. It occurred to Louise that here was an excellent opportunity for her to go in and apologise for the misunderstanding of the morning. Yet she did not do so immediately. She stood there, considering the cottage, wondering whether its tenant was in.

She decided that she could admire the effect without really ap-roving of it. There was something odd, even a little unnatural, in the juxtaposition of picture-book prettiness and wild woods behind.

Louise shook her head as if to free it from these uncomfortable and indeed unwonted thoughts. She began to see what Isobel had meant when she complained of the effect of living in the same house as Mrs. Maule.

She looked up at the windows, catching sight as she did so of a face behind the frilled muslin curtains at one of the upstairs windows—a face which gazed down at her and then vanished suddenly.

Louise was conscious of an instinctive and absurd desire to move on. There had been something so strange, so—furtive about the half-seen watcher. And that, she told herself the next moment, must be Mrs. Maule affecting her once more, for Miss Chumleigh was neither odd nor furtive. And it must have been Miss Chumleigh at the window. There, to prove that she was at home, was her bicycle leaning against the garden hedge.

Louise opened the little painted gate and walked down the neat paved path. The knocker, she saw, was a pixie, the brass polished so brightly that it gave back a lopsided reflection of herself.

She knocked. The sound seemed to echo, then die abruptly. It was followed by so complete and utter a silence that Louise had a sudden impression of someone holding his breath on the other side of the door.

It was the accumulation of all these sensations so foreign to Louise's equable and indeed levelheaded nature that was responsible for her next action. In a fit of irrational and violent irritation she seized the door handle, at the same time giving the door a push. It opened for about six inches quite freely. Then she felt a pressure being exerted from the other side, a far more determined pressure than she herself had used. The door closed in her face. She heard the tongue of the lock click into place. She had been locked out.

She stood staring at the white shiny surface in disbelief. Then anger rose. She banged on the door. "Miss Chumleigh!" she called. "Open this door. It's me, Louise Morton."

There followed no movement. No sound but that of her own voice calling emptily in an empty garden.

Suddenly the door opened—opened very slowly and only a little way. Mrs. Maule's face peered out, a grey bloodless face against a dark formless background.

"So it is you," she said, slowly. "I was afraid."

"Mrs. Maule! What is it? What has happened?" Their two voices met whispering, mingling with an odd effect of stealthy panic.

"It's Miss Chumleigh."

So that was it. "Where is she? Perhaps I can help?" Some measure of common sense returned to Louise, only to be struck from her by Mrs. Maule's next words.

"She's here, in the hall. And no one can help her. She's dead. Stabbed to death with one of her own knives."

"Oh, no!" The blood drained from Louise's face. "But—but when did it happen?"

"I don't know." The small light eyes slid away from hers. "She was alive when I found her. She died just as you knocked."

Then who was it at the upstairs window? Louise wondered. She made an effort to appear calm. "Then there's nothing we can do for her, except to ring up the police."

Mrs. Maule backed away. "I'll do it," she cried. "I'll ring the police."

Louise saw now that Miss Chumleigh's body lay just in front of her, face downwards in the passage. A trail of blood extended behind it to the kitchen. The ivory handle of a knife protruded from the dead woman's back.

As Louise knelt beside the body she became aware that Mrs. Maule had closed the sitting-room door behind her. Then, to complete the mad happenings of the day, and in the face of all the mystery and horror, a jumble of verse echoed through her mind.

> *Ding, dong bell*
> *Miss Chumleigh's far from well*
> *Who heard her fall*
> *I said Agnes Maule*
> *I was in the hall*
> *I heard her fall.*

What with mingled exasperation, horror, and confusion of mind, Louise could have bowed her sleek dark head and wept.

Chapter 6

If Septimus Finch had not finished his business sooner than he expected, he would not have stood his opposite number, Detective Inspector Charles Powers, a lunch. And if he had not done this, he would not have brought up the subject of the Maules.

They were sitting over their coffee. They were old friends and had had plenty to discuss. Now, relaxed, well fed, Finch enquired about the family at Tammerton Hall.

"I know of them, of course. They've been in Somerset since the flood. Mr. Maule's a J.P. His wife's family is local too."

Finch nodded. "I know. She was a Miss Sidbald from the other side of the county. There's a niece, too, isn't there? A Mrs. Crane?"

"Yes. Her father was a pretty smart businessman. Made a couple of fortunes. Then died and left it all to his daughter." A sudden thought struck Inspector Powers. He looked at his companion suspiciously. "Here! What is all this?"

Finch raised a large, rather bony hand. "Keep calm, dear boy. I was only enquiring. You know me."

The trouble was that the local inspector did know Finch. He knew that the Scotland Yard man had a reputation for recognising the first frail shoots of a criminal growth. It was a gift that did not endear him to his superiors. It did not endear him now to Charles Powers.

"I suppose you're going to tell me some queer story about the Maules, and then, before you've even left the town, we'll be up to our necks in some beastly scandal or worse."

Said Finch smugly, "I don't find scandal beastly. Jolly interesting, most of it. Particularly in the country where people know such a lot about each other. Not that I care for country cases. Rural areas? Feudal areas more likely. Every man an individualist. The local families all connected and standing togeth-

47

er, to the bedevilment of justice.'' He laughed at the other's expression. ''Cheer up, Charles. It's only that I heard of a rather curious telegram presumably sent by one of the Maules. It said that Mrs. Crane was dead—only it wasn't true.''

''And you think it will come true?''

''In a way—yes. Only I don't expect the victim to be Mrs. Crane.'' Finch leaned forward, tapping the table top with a forefinger in emphasis. ''No, to my mind, the more likely victim is a girl. Nice girl too.'' He wagged a mournful head. ''I shouldn't like that to happen.''

''And I suppose you want to be given the opportunity to prevent it happening?''

''Me?'' Finch was shocked. ''No, I'm going on leave.'' Adding inaccurately, ''Doctor's orders. I've been working too hard. I'm to relax. Think of nothing that's likely to raise my blood pressure—and that includes girls.'' Ending with an air of conscious virtue, ''No, I'm just passing the story on so that, if anything breaks, you'll be in the picture. Now, this is what I was told—''

Finch plunged into the story of his encounter with Louise Morton. Charles Powers listened gloomily at first. Then an idea came to him and he cheered up. When Finch had come to an end he remarked that it was a jolly interesting yarn and liable to lead to jolly interesting results, and that it was jolly good of Septimus to let him in on it.

''Think nothing of it, dear boy,'' said Finch grandly.

As they were parting after mutual expressions of pleasure at their renewal of an old friendship, Powers enquired with a casual air, where his companion was spending his leave.

''At home.'' (This meant Cornwall.) ''My people are celebrating their golden wedding anniversary on Saturday. Most of the family will be there.''

''Going now, are you?''

''I'm not expected until late this evening. I shall catch the 5.15 from here. That way I'm certain to be met at the other end.''

Which was why he found Inspector Powers waiting for him at the railway station. ''One minute, Septimus. The Chief Constable wants a word with you.''

Finch halted. ''With me? What about?''

''There's been a murder at Tammerton.'' Finch's heart missed a beat. ''No, it's not the girl—an elderly woman. A Miss Chumleigh.'' Finch's heart settled down again. He listened incredulously as his friend went on, "The Chief Constable has been on to Scotland Yard and it's all arranged. They've agreed that you should take on the investigation."

"But I'm going on leave," said Finch in tones of outrage.

"Not now you aren't," Powers retorted, grinning.

"Why can't you do your own dirty work?" Finch added bitterly, "As if I didn't know."

Powers' grin broadened. "Shall we say we're short-handed?"

Finch was silent a moment. He had reduced the catching of trains to a fine art. Now he heard his train drawing out of the station without him. He sighed deeply. "The trouble with me is that I talk too much."

"Too right, dear boy," said Powers unfeelingly.

Superintendent Ennis was a large, pale, bloodless-looking man. Grown up under a stone, Finch thought unkindly. A cautious man, the superintendent lacked humour and imagination. His welcome confirmed Finch's suspicions as to why he, Finch, had been asked to take over. Indeed, the local man made no secret of the fact.

"A case like this may have repercussions," he said heavily. He and the Scotland Yard man were in a police car, on their way to Tammerton. "Indeed, the whole relationship of police and public may be—er—impaired. That is, in certain quarters." He shook his head. "It could be very awkward. Very awkward indeed. It was certainly providential that you were in the area and already familiar with a certain aspect of the case."

"You mean the telegram?"

Ennis nodded. "Exactly."

"It seems a possible motive for the murder?"

"By no means. But it does appear to explain Miss Morton's call at Glebe Cottage."

"So she discovered the body?"

"No, no. Mrs. Maule discovered it." Ennis looked uneasy. He put a pale sausage-like finger inside his collar as if it were suddenly too tight for him. "Only at that time Miss Chumleigh had not become an—er—body. At least, not quite. It was Mrs. Maule who opened the door to Miss Morton."

Finch perceived that the Burford Point superintendent was not a man who relished responsibility. He was a hedger.

"So Mrs. Maule shut herself in with a dying woman. I wonder why."

"Surely that is hardly a fair comment. One's natural instinct would be to close a front door—particularly on such a day as this."

"D'you think Mrs. Maule opened the front door, saw a dying woman lying there, and turned back to close the door? Rather an odd sequence of events if she did."

Ennis gave him a glance almost of dislike. "What reason in your opinion would she have for such an action?"

"That she wanted to look round the cottage. Make sure that none of her household had been there and left evidence of the fact behind them. She might even have been looking for some specific object." Finch gave the superintendent a bland but sidelong glance. "Or, of course, Miss Chumleigh herself might have closed the front door."

The superintendent looked aghast. "But that would have meant that Mrs. Maule killed her."

Finch looked at him. "I imagine that you've got rather a restricted choice of suspects," he said in his small voice. "Otherwise I shouldn't be here."

Ennis sighed heavily. "I hardly like to contemplate how restricted."

"Tell me about Miss Chumleigh."

Here the superintendent felt himself to be on less painful grounds.

Edith Chumleigh, he told Finch, had been a spinster, aged sixty-four. A woman with no close relatives. She had been a Londoner and before coming to Tammerton had lived alone in a small flat in Bloomsbury. She had spent her entire working life with the firm of Spooner and Silk, an old established firm of solicitors with offices in High Holborn. She had gone to them as a junior typist. She had been, for over thirty years, private secretary to the senior partner, Reginald Spooner.

He had retired three years previously on health grounds, and had gone to live in the South of France. Miss Chumleigh had retired at the same time. She had known Judge Kelvin, who was also retired ("No doubt you would have heard of him?") and living in the neighbourhood with his adopted daughter, Miss Katherine Kelvin.

It was through the Kelvins that Miss Chumleigh had come to live in Tammerton. She had been there just over two years.

Her movements that day had been unexceptional. She had spent the morning at Tammerton Hall. Here Superintendent Ennis digressed to explain the working arrangement that the dead woman had had with James Maule and his niece. After lunch

Miss Chumleigh had gone down to the village store, which was also the post office. This had been about 2.15 P.M. After that she seemed to have remained in her cottage until the time of her death.

Ennis went on to tell Finch about the telegram, the reason for its having been sent, and the events that had ensued that morning.

"So you see Miss Morton never had any intention of harming Miss Kelvin's prospects. She regretted not having made this plain to Miss Chumleigh. And when, in the course of a walk, this afternoon, she found herself outside Glebe Cottage, she decided to call in and explain matters. She knocked and the door was opened, not by Miss Chumleigh but, as I said, by Mrs. Maule."

"And what had been Mrs. Maule's reason for calling?"

"Merely to talk over the rather strange coincidence of Miss Morton's arrival at the Hall. Mrs. Maule had bicycled down to Glebe Cottage, knocked, and, getting no reply, had opened the door meaning to call Miss Chumleigh by name. She was horrified to see her lying in the passage, or hall, and with a trail of blood leading from the kitchen. She says that as she knelt down beside the injured woman she saw the ivory handle of a knife sticking out of Miss Chumleigh's back—"

"Miss Chumleigh's knife?"

"Yes, a carving knife from the kitchen—and it appears that Miss Chumleigh was attacked whilst in the kitchen and had then dragged herself along the passage. When she saw Mrs. Maule she made a great effort to speak."

"Did she succeed?"

"Yes—in a way. Mrs. Maule thinks she said 'Take care—Kathie.' She is certain about the last two words 'care' and 'Kathie.' "

"What did she make of them?"

"She says it is impossible to make anything of them. Miss Chumleigh had great difficulty in speaking at all."

"I see. But she did say 'care' and 'Kathie.' And then?"

"She died." Ennis sighed heavily. "After that Mrs. Maule admitted Miss Morton and telephoned the police. The time was then 3.43 P.M."

"Which police?" Finch asked curiously.

"As a matter of fact she 'phoned the Chief Constable. He is a distant connection."

"What does the police surgeon say about the murder?"

"He says that Miss Chumleigh had been stabbed in the back, considerable force having been used. That the blow could have been delivered by either a man or a woman. That the attacker was tall and right-handed. The blow, he says, must have penetrated the heart. And Miss Chumleigh might have lived as long as fifteen minutes. He said death isn't necessarily instantaneous—not unless the wound in the heart is very large—but I expect you know that."

"And the time of death?"

Said Ennis rather smugly, "The police surgeon said that Mrs. Maule's time was as good as any—round about 3.43 P.M."

"Any fingerprints?"

"None on the murder weapon. Several about the cottage. Miss Chumleigh had plenty of visitors calling socially."

"Including one this afternoon? How about any bloodstains on the murderer?"

"The police surgeon says there may not necessarily be any. The deceased, at the time of the attack, was wearing a heavy sheepskin coat which would have caught the first flow of blood."

"Was she going out? Or had she been?"

"Her shoes were dry and clean so I imagine that she was going out. The ones she'd worn up to the Hall and those worn earlier this afternoon in the village are in the airing cupboard, drying off. I understand she was faddy about keeping her feet dry and always changed her shoes for indoor slippers as soon as possible."

Finch nodded. "I think that's pretty conclusive. She's hardly likely to have changed her wet shoes and not taken off her coat."

"And if she *was* going out, then it wasn't far, for the handbag she usually carried was put away upstairs in her wardrobe. All she had with her was her latchkey carried in a leather purse in her coat pocket, along with a little silver and a few stamps."

"Going to post—perhaps?"

"If so, there was no sign of a letter. Nor that Miss Chumleigh had written one."

Finch nodded. "What sort of woman is Miss Kelvin?"

Ennis pursed his lips. "Oh—I suppose you'd call her the athletic type. She plays in the local golf and tennis tournaments. Rides but doesn't hunt. Drives a sports car a great deal too fast but hasn't had an accident—as yet."

"Except for the one in which her fiancé and Dr. Morton were killed."

Said Ennis stiffly, "We have no evidence to suggest that Miss Kelvin was driving at that time."

Finch stared. "Oh, Mr. Ennis, sir! What other reason had she for sending the telegram?" The question—or rather its answer—seemed to strike him as important. He fell silent, turning the matter over in his mind. He was still lost in thought when the car drew up outside Glebe Cottage.

The plan of the cottage was simple. The front door opened directly into the hall or passage. Off this passage there opened three doors. Those of the two sitting rooms which faced each other and the back door opened directly into the kitchen. It was a good-sized room and one corner of it had been taken off to make a larder.

Upstairs there were two bedrooms, a small boxroom, and a bathroom with a hot water tank and the airing cupboard.

The photographers and fingerprint men had done their work and gone. The body too had gone. It was represented now by no more than a chalk outline. The blood which Miss Chumleigh had shed showed as a long dark stain and sundry dry spots and splashes. Police Constable Sampson had mopped it up as far as possible.

This was the local man. He was very large and very red. He was popular in the village since he was in the habit of issuing a general warning when he was about to go round making enquiries as to licences or such other matters as might have been overlooked. It was years since he had made an arrest, consequently he wasn't thought much of at headquarters.

The kitchen was a very pleasant room in a colour scheme of white and yellow, so cheerful even on this dull day that the dark deed of murder seemed to have no place in it.

A table with a white formica top stood against the wall just inside the inner door. On it was an open canister of tea and a teapot with the lid off. A teaspoon lay where it had been dropped amid a scattering of tea leaves.

There was a small pile of groceries bought by the dead woman earlier that afternoon. Automatically Finch's gaze took in the items. Half a pound of tea, half a pound of butter, a bottle of rennet, potted meat . . .

The murder weapon was there too. A carving knife, thin and sharp, with a blade some seven inches long.

"The electric kettle was plugged in," said Ennis, "but not

turned on. However"—he cleared his throat importantly—"the water in it was still warm when I got here."

Finch nodded. "A good point. Did Mrs. Maule or Miss Morton turn it off?"

"They say not."

"So it was done probably by the murderer. What about the back door?"

"As you see it. Closed but not fastened. Mrs. Maule says it was usually kept bolted."

Finch opened it. Outside was a kitchen garden. A path, similar in construction to the one in front, led to a small gate opening directly into the woods.

"There's a path beyond that gate," said Ennis. "Short cut to the Hall." Adding, hurriedly, "But, of course, one could equally well get to Warley or the village through the trees."

The back door was fitted with a draught excluder. This, brushing against the floor, and the working of the rather stiff hinges, satisfied Finch that, with Miss Chumleigh in the kitchen, no one could have entered without her hearing.

"So we have Miss Chumleigh letting in an unexpected visitor," said Finch.

"Unexpected?"

"She was dressed ready to go out."

"She might have put on her coat in readiness to accompany her visitor somewhere," Ennis argued.

"In which case she would surely have had tea with her visitor first and then put on her coat. No, I think we can say with safety that her visitor was unexpected. Tea was suggested—perhaps by the visitor. They came out here—" Finch broke off to enquire whether anyone knew where the carving knife had been kept.

"In the drawer of the kitchen table, alongside the carving fork, sir." Sampson had a way of addressing his conversation to his boots, which were large, shiny, and obtrusive. He did so now.

"Which suggests that the murderer had a certain familiarity with the cottage—but then everything about the crime suggests that." Finch continued, "Miss Chumleigh switches on the kettle." There was a row of canisters on the wall opposite the one against which the table was standing. One of the canisters was missing. "That was probably when the knife was extracted. While Miss Chumleigh had turned to take down the tea. Then, as she went to spoon it into the teapot, the murderer struck.

"What happened after that we don't know. Did the murderer,

believing Miss Chumleigh to be dead, search her pockets? The cottage? We don't know. All we do know at present is that he, or she, was interrupted by a knocking on the front door—''

"Do we know that?"

"Surely—unless, of course, Mrs. Maule killed Miss Chumleigh and her whole evidence is a pack of lies.''

"I don't think that's very likely," said Ennis hurriedly.

"And it's not very likely that Miss Chumleigh would still have been alive when the murderer left the cottage if he hadn't been scared off.''

Finch himself fell silent. Standing very quiet and still and rather formidable-looking, he was thinking himself back in time. Back to such daylight as there had been. Back to when a defenceless elderly woman lay dying in her own kitchen where the kettle boiled for tea that would never be made and the murderer—?

What had he been doing when he was interrupted? Had he looked up and seen Mrs. Maule coming down the garden path? Or had he been so absorbed that the sudden knocking on the front door had been the first intimation that someone was outside and demanding admittance?

Mentally Finch shook his head. No, that couldn't be right. The unfortunate Miss Chumleigh had had time to crawl out of the kitchen and along the passage in the time left between the murderer's departure and Mrs. Maule's arrival.

He said aloud, "If Mrs. Maule didn't murder Miss Chumleigh then someone other than Mrs. Maule and the murderer called at the cottage this afternoon.''

"Mr. Philby, the vicar of Tammerton, called with a letter," said Ennis. "He'd been to see Mr. Justice Kelvin at Warley and had been asked to leave the letter on his way back to the vicarage.''

Sampson made a slight movement as if he had something to contribute if encouraged.

"Yes?" Finch looked at him.

"I was only going to say, sir, that Mr. Philby's an unpredictable gentleman. Anyone knowing both Mr. Philby and Mrs. Maule would have been more alarmed to see him coming down the path than her.''

"But I understood you to say that Mr. Philby and Miss Chumleigh were on bad terms," interposed the superintendent rather testily. "In which case the murderer would have expected him to do no more than he did do—namely, to drop the letter into the letterbox and go away.''

"But if he had wanted to see Miss Chumleigh," Sampson persisted with sturdy independence, "he'd have thought nothing of trying both doors and looking in all the windows.''

"And might he have wanted to see her?" Finch asked amused.

"Well, sir, they have been saying in the village as how Miss Chumleigh would be getting herself cursed if she didn't give over. Vicar warns 'em first. Then he does it on the next Sunday from the pulpit. Ah! It's a rare show is that.''

"Fills the church too, I expect." Finch's solitary chuckle had a faintly sinister sound.

"I suppose the vicar suits his service to his congregation." From the superintendent's tone of voice Finch gathered that Mr. Philby too was related to everyone else. Possibly even to the Chief Constable himself.

He said aloud, "To go back to the letter. What was in it?"

"I don't know. I left it for you to open. You'll find it on the desk in the sitting room.''

"Then let's have a look." As Finch followed Ennis from the kitchen he paused to ask, "What was the trouble between the dead woman and Mr. Philby?"

"Mostly a difference of opinion over church matters," Sampson answered. "Miss Chumleigh was low and the vicar high. Not as high as he'd like to be but as high as the Squire will allow.''

The sitting room was a charming room, if a little too determinedly old world. There was order, a chilling, rather unnatural order. Not a chair was out of place. Not a book nor a newspaper lay about. There were no signs that Miss Chumleigh had occupied herself in any way before the coming of her attacker. On the desk two fountain pens lay neatly in the pen tray. Even the red leather blotter contained only unused blotting paper.

"It's like a showroom in the window of a furniture store," said Ennis uncomfortably. "To my mind it doesn't seem natural.''

"No, someone's been at pains to leave it like this. I wonder why?"

Finch, prowling about, could see no possible reason. Unless the murderer, coming in from the kitchen, had tried to wipe out the image of his late hostess; the woman whom he believed to be lying dead in the kitchen. And that would make him a nervous neurotic type—but no less dangerous for that.

And what had spelled out that image? Two armchairs drawn up cosily to the fire? A knitting bag spilling out its contents instead of lying as now, pushed into the back of an otherwise tidy drawer of the bureau bookcase? A cigarette box, half full, thrust behind a cushion on the couch? A library book pushed down the crack behind?

A small leather purse lay on the desk. It was the one taken from the dead woman's coat pocket. Next to it lay an unopened letter, addressed in a small neat writing to "Miss Chumleigh, Glebe Cottage." "By hand" was written in the lower left hand corner.

Finch opened the envelope and took out the letter. He read it aloud.

> *My dear old friend, Kathie has followed your, as ever, excellent advice and has admitted that she was driving the Bentley on the day Harry was killed. This was something I have long suspected and indeed, my pride is a little hurt that you should not have realised this. However, that is merely an old man's vanity. The great thing is that Kathie's mind is now at rest—on all points.*
>
> *She has also admitted to the many foolish fears entertained over the years. They must have been very real to her. I cannot recall ever having seen her so distraught. But then she always does go to extremes, does she not?*
>
> *I hear that we are to have the pleasure of seeing you at the Hall tonight. Shall we pick you up in the car? I hope about 7.45 P.M. but you know what Kathie is. Time and she are the merest of acquaintances. It is alas, Expediency, with whom she is firm friends.*
>
> *Yours sincerely, Horace Kelvin.*

"So Miss Kelvin *was* driving that day," cried Ennis chagrined. "She admits it—and incidentally to perjury."

"It was eleven years ago," said Finch thoughtfully. "Why should she get so worked up about it now?"

"She must have been under oath when she swore that she wasn't driving," Ennis persisted.

"You have to remember that the alternative was to face a charge of manslaughter."

"But she did kill someone—two people." Ennis seemed to find this very sinister. "And *that* time she got away with it."

"Yes—but since the Judge knew that she was driving, the fact can hardly be a motive for Miss Chumleigh's murder." Finch had perched himself on one corner of the desk. He sat there, one long leg dangling. "You know," he added thoughtfully, "it's like having a game with a professional card sharper. We keep having one particular card palmed on us—the fact that Miss Kelvin was driving the car when Harry Kelvin and Dr. Morton were killed. The telegram was sent to keep Louise Morton away. Why? Because she knew that Miss Kelvin was driving the car, etc. Miss Chumleigh was upset this morning. Why? Because she knew that Miss Morton knew etc. Miss Kelvin becomes distraught. Why? Because she had confessed that she was driving the car that etc. But the fact that the Judge had known all the time—that everyone concerned had known—makes nonsense of that particular card."

"Then you believe that Miss Kelvin came back here and killed Miss Chumleigh?"

Finch had been taking out the contents of the drawer nearest to him, diary, book of telephone numbers, household account book. Now he murmured, "I'd say that if the murder and the disturbance over Miss Morton's arrival have no connection, then it's a pretty rummy coincidence." He picked up the diary, ruffling through its pages.

"You won't find much there," said Ennis. "Miss Chumleigh used her diary mostly to record appointments. Visit to hairdresser, Women's Institute, and so on."

Finch nodded. "V. expensive against the first and V. interesting against the second aren't going to get us far," he agreed.

He turned to the household accounts book. The last entry read "Half pound of tea, half pound of butter, bottle of rennet"— he turned the page—"Potted meat . . ."

He laid the book open on the desk. "Look at this," he said. "A list of groceries bought this afternoon and entered after 2:15 P.M. It was written in ink and both pages were blotted."

"So what?"

"So where is the blotting paper that was used? There are several scraps of paper thrown into the wastepaper basket." Finch had slid off the desk and was taking them out as he spoke, after first removing a copy of the day's newspaper. There were a circular, two business envelopes, a broken rubber band—but no blotting paper.

"You're thinking the murderer took it?"

"Someone took it. And that suggests that Miss Chumleigh *did* write a letter—and blotted it. A letter that was of particular interest to the murderer." Finch had sunk back on his heels, his forehead puckered. "Now, who would she have been writing to?"

"I don't see that we can possibly answer that."

"Miss Chumleigh had no near relations. She had lived alone in London. But if she had wanted advice, had anything important to impart, there was one person to whom she would write—her late employer, the man to whom she had been private secretary for thirty years, Mr. Reginald Spooner."

Finch's gently drawling voice died away. A sudden thought struck him. He sprang to his feet. He picked up the purse that had been found in the pocket of the dead woman's coat. He shook out its contents on to the desk top. The latchkey tinkled down. It was followed by the stamps. *Four sixpenny stamps.*

Finch regarded them with the innocent pleasure of the amateur conjuror whose trick has come off successfully.

"Is that the postage to France?"

"Sixpence, yes. Now we know just why Miss Chumleigh had to go out."

"She wanted some groceries."

"Not really. She had tea and butter in her store cupboard. She even had potted meat. No, what she really wanted was a sixpenny stamp so that she could send a letter to Mr. Spooner."

"D'you think that letter was—well, her death warrant, as you might say?"

"I don't know." Finch spoke slowly and very quietly. "I don't know anything yet. I'm just feeling my way around. That's all."

And something in the Scotland Yard man's manner made Ennis decide that if he were the murderer he'd be frightened. Very frightened indeed. Rather hurriedly he told Finch that he must be getting back to Burford Point, assured him that he would telephone next day, and took himself off.

Left alone, Finch called in Sampson and asked him what sort of woman Miss Chumleigh had been.

Sampson consulted his boots. "Well, sir, she was a great joiner."

Finch had no difficulty in following this: "Oh? What did she join?"

"There was the Women's Institute, the Church Council—voted on to that she was—Tammerton and Triston Magna Amateur Dramatics, the Church Working Party . . ."

Finch regarded Sampson with amusement. "I see what you mean. What else?"

"She was a great one for putting folk right."

One of Finch's eyebrows climbed. "That couldn't have made her popular."

"At first, sir, folk were fair wild. Then it became a sort of joke. Quite a catch phrase as you might say. 'Miss Chumleigh says so' settled many an argument. Real knowledgeable too she was. The only one who took it amiss was the vicar. There was a proper feud there. Going to write to the bishop, Miss Chumleigh was—or so I've heard."

"You don't think—?" Finch paused delicately.

"Bless you, no, sir. Vicar looked on it as—as a sort of game. Mock warfare you might call it. But as for bodily harm—why, he'd never think of it!"

Finch accepted this. He changed to another aspect of the case. "How long would it take to get from Warley to here?"

"About ten minutes walking fast. Miss Kathie could have done it in less on her bicycle. It wouldn't have been difficult either to have ridden it through the woods."

"And from the Hall?"

"That'd take a bit longer. Fifteen minutes walking. Mrs. Maule and Mr. Jason both have bicycles but he doesn't use his much. He walks or rides on horseback."

Chapter 7

Finch was still talking to Sampson when he became aware of a car stopping outside. "Just see who that is, Sampson."

The constable was soon back. "It's the Judge, sir. Wants a few words with you."

Finch glanced at his wrist watch. Three minutes to eight. "I'll talk to him. You go back to the kitchen."

Mr. Justice Kelvin was a tall thin man. He had an austere face, long, thin-lipped. He looked much older than when Finch had seen him last but this, the detective decided, was the result of shock. His skin was pallid and he was suffering from an anxiety he could not quite hide.

"Good evening, Inspector." The Judge extended a veined hand. "I got my daughter to drop me off on our way to the Hall, thinking I might be of some help to you." He remarked as he followed Finch down the passage, "I never imagined that we two were destined to meet again. And certainly not under such strange and indeed tragic circumstances. Poor Edith Chumleigh! The very last person I should have expected to fall victim to a crime of violence."

"You knew her well?"

"Yes, and for a great number of years. My daughter and I were devoted to her and she, I believe, to us." As he spoke the Judge's eyes flickered about the room, to come to rest with a peculiar intentness on the letter he had written to the dead woman. "I wonder how many times I have dropped in here, congratulating myself on my cleverness in getting Miss Chumleigh to settle here."

"Tell me how that came about."

"I'll tell you how I first met her." The Judge had sunk wearily into a chair. "It was typical of her and so may be of use to you. Miss Chumleigh came into my life when my son, Harry, was still a schoolboy. At the time she was secretary to Mr.

Reginald Spooner, of the firm of Spooner & Silk, Solicitors. You probably know them." Finch nodded. "We, my entire household, including the servants, were down with influenza. Mr. Spooner came round to see us—we were friends of many years' standing—and I can remember my dear wife throwing the front door key down to him from the bedroom window. He was horrified at our predicament, and insisted on lending us his Miss Chumleigh, whom, up to then, we had not met. She took charge in a most wonderful manner. Conjured up some sort of staff. Even a nurse and that in the middle of an influenza epidemic. Organised the work in shifts, did the housekeeping, ordered the food—everything. It was our little joke that she could quite well have deputised for me on the bench. It was during this time that she and my boy became friends."

"And she came here at your invitation?"

"Yes. My friend, the Squire, had recently lost his bailiff. His nephew was away and he was hard put to it to keep up with things. As you can imagine the management of a big estate entails a great deal of bookkeeping and paperwork. It was then that I thought of Edith Chumleigh and her gift for organisation. My daughter needed no persuasion to ask her down on a visit. And, somewhat to my surprise, Edith took to country life as a duck takes to water. This cottage happened to be empty and Mr. Maule did it up for her." The Judge sighed deeply. "Up to now I had thought it a perfect arrangement."

"Can you think of any possible motive for her murder?"

"None at all. She was deeply respected and well liked."

"You sent her a letter earlier this afternoon?"

The Judge nodded. "That was one of the matters about which I wished to speak." His glance, like his voice, had sharpened. He was more like the man whom Finch had known. "No doubt you have been given enough information to understand to what I referred in the first page of my letter. It is about the second part that I wish to speak."

He hesitated, as if he had difficulty in choosing his words. When he did speak he had lost his judicial calm and it was in a low, rather broken voice. "I had no idea until today that my daughter worried about her future. Still less that she had infected a sensible woman like Miss Chumleigh with those fears."

"What fears were these?"

"She actually believed—" Mr. Justice Kelvin broke off, then began again. "My daughter, who, as you probably know, is

adopted, seems to have believed that I might tire of her company. Or, alternately, that she herself might do something that I
would find unforgivable.'' He added, with a jocose air that Finch
found positively ghastly, ''She felt that in either case she would
find herself thrown penniless on the world.''

''Extraordinary,'' said Finch.

''So I thought. I fear it sprang from the fundamental differences in our outlook—in our ages.'' The Judge spoke rather
drearily, ''My standards were not hers. Indeed, how could they
be? We belong to different eras. Then she appears to have
believed that sitting in judgement on others had made it inevitable that I should always be weighing her up—and finding her
wanting.'' He fell silent, to remark with considerable vehemence,
''But, taking everything into account, I still find it hard to credit
that two people could so misjudge the position.''

''I myself would have difficulty in believing that you had
made no provision for Miss Kelvin's future.''

''Exactly. When my son died, I made a new will naming
my adopted daughter as chief beneficiary. This afternoon realising that a will, being revokable, would not entirely rid her mind
of misgivings, I promised to settle a sum of money on her. Not a
fortune but enough to render her financially independent.''

''That must have pleased her.''

''Pleased her! She was transported with delight.'' Mr. Kelvin passed his hand wearily over his face. Then he essayed a
smile. ''I shall have to see that the money is tied up or it will just
slip away. Borrowed by her friends. Bestowed on any charitable
cause that cares to make an appeal. Half of which, you may be
sure, will be undeserving and the other half downright fraudulent.''

''How about Miss Morton? Do you feel any responsibility
for her?''

''Not now. When she was a child it was different.''

''Perhaps Miss Kelvin may have been afraid that you would
make provision for Miss Morton at her expense?''

''No, no. We have often spoken together of Louise Morton.
Kathie knew my views.''

Finch nodded. ''I see from your letter that your daughter
had been in touch with Miss Chumleigh this afternoon?''

''Yes, indeed. She called in here on her way back from
Burford Point.''

''What time was this?''

''I think you'll have to ask her, Inspector. I know it was

about half past two when she got home but I have no idea how long she was here with Miss Chumleigh.''

"I understand that they were friends?"

"They were more than that. Miss Chumleigh was Kathie's conscience, her sheet anchor, her adviser. Indeed I find it difficult to imagine how Kathie will get on without her. Miss Chumleigh not only had a great deal of influence over her but she helped her a great deal in a practical manner. Reminded her of anniversaries, of letters that must be answered, bills that must be paid. She even, I suspect, acted as banker on those occasions when my daughter ran short of money. In fact, in every way she carried out the promise she made to my son to look after her.''

"A promise? Forgive me for bringing up a matter that may still be painful but I understood that your son was killed instantaneously?"

"You're quite right, Inspector, he was. The promise he extracted was in no sense a deathbed promise. Indeed it originated in no more than a request on his part that Miss Chumleigh would be Kathie's friend. It was only after his death that this request assumed the seriousness of a vow. Edith Chumleigh was devoted to my son and I believe did not find it very difficult to transfer some of that devotion to his fiancée.''

Mr. Justice Kelvin having, in Finch's estimation, said what he had come to say, now rose to his feet, "Well, I must be getting along. It won't do to keep my hosts waiting for dinner.''

"It was very good of you to come." Finch enquired how the Judge proposed to get to the Hall. When he heard that His Lordship intended to walk he insisted on putting him into the police car.

"Although I'm afraid it's not the last you'll see of me tonight," Finch said in parting. "I shall be coming round to the Hall myself later on.''

"Then make it after dinner," Mr. Justice Kelvin advised. As he was driven away he smiled faintly, raised his hand in farewell.

Finch fancied that, whether he realised it or not, he was saying goodbye to peace of mind.

To Louise as she stood at her bedroom window on that dull evening, twilight did not seem so much to fall as to swoop out from under the trees.

She was still pale from the shock of Miss Chumleigh's death, nagged at by the suspicion, implanted in her mind by her late dining companion, the Scotland Yard inspector, that somehow she was responsible.

Someone has a strong reason for not wanting you at Tammerton.

He had said that and now Miss Chumleigh had been murdered. Miss Chumleigh and not herself. But was there any connection?

Someone at Tammerton—

And the list of suspects was so small. Not a tramp. Not a gipsy. Miss Chumleigh had disapproved of both, as being feckless and antisocial. She would never have invited either into her kitchen. Or so the local policeman had said, although not quite in those words. Then who had it been? Figures passed through her mind, in ghastly procession. The lithe, tall figure of Jason Maule with his bitter reckless face. Kathie slipping from the back door of Glebe Cottage as Mrs. Maule knocked on the front. Mrs. Maule herself. Mrs. Maule who had looked down from an upstairs window and then had tried to bar the door to her—

There were other less likely contenders for the fearful post of killer. James Maule, Goodlife, Mr. Philby the vicar. Last of all there was the murderer from outside this circle. Faceless, formless, and, she feared, the most unlikely contender of all.

She turned rather wearily from the window and went downstairs to her patient. The sitting room in the West Wing was empty, the two long windows black and steely. The murderer could be standing outside these now, she thought. She recalled the figure—if figure it had been—that she had seen on the previous evening. It seemed, looking back, to have been infinitely threatening, sinister.

She stared out, pressing her face to the windowpane. As she did so the first rain fell, whispering across the glass. She drew the curtains and turned away, shivering a little. Now, she thought, we are quite isolated from the sane safe world that still exists beyond the woods and hills.

The door opened. Isobel came in propelling herself in her wheeled chair. She was wearing a black frock, mourning for the dead woman. She wore it with extreme elegance but it did not suit her. It took the last of the colour from her face, making her appear even more sallow than usual.

She, too, glanced at the windows. "I'm glad you've drawn the curtains." She propelled herself right up to the fire, bending towards it as if feeling that she would never be warm again. "I wish now that we'd called the dinner off. We shall all be conscious of the empty chair. Kathie will behave badly and pick a quarrel with Aunt Agnes. We shall talk about poor Edith. Or if we don't, her death will be at the back of our minds all the time.''

"Why don't you cry off and go to bed," Louise suggested. Her patient's face was pale, and there was a faint bluish look about her lips.

"No, I think I must go through with it now." Isobel consulted the small diamond studded watch on her wrist. "A quarter to eight. The Kelvins should be here at any moment. The Judge is the most punctual of men but with Kathie one never knows.''

It was past eight o'clock when the door opened. Kathie came in. "Late again," she cried, enveloping Isobel in a soft scented embrace. "Mrs. Maule, I feel, will never forgive me and I shall find henbane in my soup.''

She was wearing a graceful ankle-length frock in thick grey corded silk. It had long tight sleeves and was cut low to show off the smooth creamy flesh and long graceful neck. She wore satin slippers dyed to match the frock. There were emeralds in her ears and a couple of emerald clips in the front of her dress.

Kathie, Louise reflected rather scornfully, had changed in only one respect. She was used now to what the girl thought of as a mink-coat life.

"You look lovely." Isobel held her friend at arm's length to admire her. Their eyes met and all their pleasure was quenched.

"Isobel, isn't it awful? Poor Edith!" Kathie's voice broke.

"I know. It seems incredible.''

"God, yes! I don't know what I shall do without her." Kathie drew away from her friend's embrace. She saw Louise. "Oh—hullo!" She studied the girl, her amber eyes narrowed. It gave to her face a curiously sly, feline look. "Still in uniform? I'm surprised.''

A faint shadow of annoyance passed over Isobel's face. "Louise can dress as she pleases. And, if she seems like an old friend to us, that is entirely your own fault.''

Kathie grimaced. "I admit it. In a life made up of regrettable incidents, I admit it.''

She appeared to dismiss Louise from her thoughts. She wandered about the room, picking up things at random, holding them to her eyes without really seeing them, then putting them down again in the same heedless manner.

"Of course it's easy for you," she burst out at last. "You're one of the few people who couldn't be suspected of killing Edith."

A spot of colour tinged Isobel's cheeks. "Kathie, what an awful thing to say. Even if I hadn't been—incapacitated I should still not have looked on myself as a possible suspect."

"Wouldn't you?" Kathie was holding an open book. She stared over the top of it. "You're lucky. But then I haven't had the advantage of being a Miss Maule of Tammerton." She replaced the book, flouncing away down the room. "Why Mr. Maule ever agreed to calling in a detective from Scotland Yard I don't know. Left to himself Superintendent Ennis would just have shelved the whole thing, and we could have forgotten all about it."

"My deat Kathie, one can't shelve a murder." Isobel spoke rather wearily. She had closed her eyes and so missed the darting look of fury her friend directed at her. "As for blaming Uncle James, you know as well as I do that Colonel Snow"—this was the Chief Constable—"makes his own decisions." She changed the subject. "Where is the Judge?"

"I left him at Glebe Cottage." Kathie answered sulkily. "He wanted to have a word with this Detective Finch. He seems to know him quite well."

"Louise knows him, too. At least, she had lunch with him in the train coming down yesterday."

"Oh, did she?" Kathie stared at Louise. Her eyes were cold, watchful. "Then I suppose you'll be running to him with all sorts of tales?"

Louise stared back. "I suppose I would—if I knew any."

Isobel made a determined effort to restore some degree of normality. "Stop bickering, you two, and let's have a drink. Louise, be a dear and pour out. Sherry for us. You have what you like."

Kathie grimaced to herself, but accepted the glass Louise offered her. Then she went with it to the far end of the room, walking about in front of the long looking glass hanging on the wall.

Isobel turned her head to watch her. "Backwards and forwards and sideways did she pass, making up her mind to face the cruel looking glass."

Kathie took up the quotation. "The Queen was in her chamber, her sins were on her head—" She halted. Her eyes sought those of her friend in the glass. "Isobel, how can you stay so calm when I feel so—so churned up?"

"It's simply a matter of temperament. You're easily moved. I'm not. It's as simple as that," answered Isobel. Adding coaxingly, "Come and sit down by the fire and tell me just what you're planning. To bewitch poor Jason all over again?"

Kathie came trailing back. "I must admit I wouldn't want him to think me an old hag."

The talk turned to clothes. Louise fancied that Isobel kept it there deliberately, calming her more volatile friend.

Presently the door opened. Mr. Justice Kelvin came in. It seemed strange to Louise to be actually about to meet him. She had hated him for so long. Now she felt no animosity. He was far older than she had expected. Older, more tired, and more frail.

"I'm afraid I've held up dinner," he said to Isobel, their greetings over. "But I'm glad to say that I've managed to make my peace with my hostess."

"You know that Aunt Agnes would forgive you a far more serious fault than being a few minutes late for dinner," Isobel assured him. "And here is someone you've always wanted to meet—Louise Morton. Isn't it the strangest thing?"

"The working of Fate, perhaps." The girl became aware of the appraising gaze of a kindly but very penetrating pair of eyes. "Little Louise Morton." His smile broadened. "And, if I may be forgiven the comment, still little Louise Morton."

"I know. It's mortifying."

"It appears to me a very delightful height. As high as some young man's heart you'll find, if you have not done so already." Mr. Justice Kelvin's face sobered. "I only wish we could have met under happier circumstances."

Isobel caught her breath in a quick sigh. "Poor Edith! It doesn't seem real."

"I'm afraid that you'll become more and more conscious of its reality as the police investigation goes on. Questions—and more questions. All sorts of things that one has left hidden brought out into the light of day."

"Why, Judge, you sound as if everyone had some disreputable secret," Isobel protested.

"Not necessarily disreputable. But a secret? Yes, I fancy most of us have one. Unless"—he smiled at Louise—"we are very young."

"I'm not as young as all that," Louise protested.

"Then I shall await with interest the unearthing of some quite appalling aspect of your past," the Judge declared solemnly. "And now I must go and have a word with my host. Look at the chessboard too. I don't doubt that James has worked out some surprise for my undoing."

Chapter 8

Jason was alone in the hall when the three women appeared. Lounging against the tall chimneypiece, he looked wonderfully handsome and romantic in his dinner jacket.

Kathie went to meet him, smiling, fluttering her eyelashes in an absurd parody of pleasure. The murder of Edith Chumleigh seemed to have slipped from her mind. "Jason, my dear! Long time no see."

Jason grinned rather derisively. There was, Louise thought, nothing of the lover about him, only a certain wariness. "Come off it, Kathie. Didn't we run into each other in Piccadilly a fortnight ago and have dinner together?"

Kathie dropped the hand she had been holding out to him. "I thought we were keeping that secret?"

"And have you use it to bludgeon me with at some inconvenient moment of your own choosing? No, thank you."

"Jason! You ———!"

"Kathie!" Isobel was shocked.

Kathie turned a face of innocence. "What's wrong with that? I've heard Roger say it."

"I've never heard him," said Isobel stiffly.

Kathie slipped her hand through Jason's arm. "Then perhaps I learnt it from someone else," she said airily.

Agnes Maule came into the hall, followed by the Judge and her husband. Her hair was done in a row of tight little curls; her frock was of a rather startling shade of purple. Long jet drops hung from her ears. A cherub mourned under a weeping willow on a brooch cushioned on her plump bosom and a cascade of what looked to Louise like jet tiddlywinks encircled her neck. She had gone into half mourning in a big way.

The Judge greeted Jason kindly enough. "I see you two have broken the ice."

"Not broken—melted," Kathie answered.

They all laughed except Mrs. Maule. She said nothing, but regarded her guest rather balefully.

Goodlife announced dinner. They all went into the dining room, Jason pushing the wheelchair regardless of Louise's protests.

"Don't let's talk about Edith," Kathie begged. "Let's just pretend nothing has happened to her."

Mr. Justice Kelvin looked gravely across the table at her. "I doubt whether that will be possible."

"Or even desirable," said Mrs. Maule.

"We could try," Kathie urged. She began to speak about a play she'd seen on her last visit to London. Jason had seen it too. Louise saw Isobel's eyebrows go up at this but all she said was to regret her own present inability to go to the theatre.

Surprisingly enough the conversation flowed easily. Kathie seemed in high spirits, and if there seemed an extravagance, even a wildness, in her words, it did not distract from the enchantment she wielded.

The talk turned to motor racing. An argument developed between Jason and Kathie as to the winner of a recent event. Louise, who had been present, which was the case with neither of the other two, found herself drawn into the argument and, indeed, settling it.

"So you can drive a car, Louise," Isobel remarked, breaking into the conversation. "That's splendid. I have a job for you—that is, if you can manage a Jaguar and have your driving licence with you. It's to go into Lockbridge on Thursday, and bring back some things from my house there."

"Better let me do it," Kathie urged. "That Jag of yours is not to be trifled with."

Louise had been conscious of Jason's eyes resting on her in a thoughtful stare. Now he said, "No need for that. I'll give Louise a driving lesson."

"You'll find her an apt pupil," Mrs. Maule declared. "Louise is a very capable gal. She'll do you credit."

"But I've driven a Jaguar before," cried Louise. "A friend of mine has one. And I always have my driving licence with me."

"There! I told you she was a capable gal."

"Dear Mrs. Maule, if you call her that once more I shall scream," Kathie declared with an angry laugh. "Or perhaps Louise will. After all, it's not a madly glamorous description."

"I suppose," said James Maule suddenly, "that we can

expect that Scotland Yard fella to turn up either tonight or tomorrow morning."

"Tonight," said the Judge.

"Alibis, I suppose," said Jason. "God, doesn't it sound incredible?"

"An alibi is a nice thing to have," said Kathie. Her giggle held a faint note of hysteria. "I don't know if mine counts. I was in my bath."

James Maule peered at her over the tops of his spectacles. "I doubt if that will hold water," he said blandly.

"I don't suppose one of us *has* an alibi," said Agnes in a gloomy way. "I know mine is nonexistent. I might have stabbed Edith and then reported it to the police."

"I understand from the colonel that the murderer is thought to have been tall," said Mr. Maule.

"I might have stood on a stool just to mislead the police." Agnes Maule was obstinately gloomy.

"So you might," said the Judge. "And I might have slipped out as soon as Philby had left me. He always walks very slowly. I could easily have beaten him to the cottage."

"I was in the library working at my book," said Mr. Maule. "Alone for most of the time. And Jason, I imagine, was on his way to Grigg's Farm, and so would have had to pass Glebe Cottage."

Jason smiled rather sourly. "A highly suspicious lot. Not an alibi among us."

"Don't let us talk as if one of us stabbed poor Edith," Isobel begged. "After all, we all knew her. She was our friend."

With the words a silence fell. The room itself seemed to become alive and full of the past echoes of that other happier meal.

"I wish Roger were here," Isobel said suddenly. The blue look about her lips seemed to have become more accentuated.

"Damn Roger!" cried Kathie violently. "What use would he be?"

"He'd be a great comfort to me," Isobel declared.

"And he'd have an alibi, lucky fellow," said Jason.

Kathie planted her elbows on the table. "I can't help feeling glad that I don't live here," she said with a provocative sidelong glance at her hostess. "I mean now that there's a murderer about. Warley is such a compact, friendly sort of place. But here at Tammerton it's all so old and echoing. So full of vast pieces of furniture and enormous billowing curtains. Rooms that are never visited, let alone used. Who can tell who may be hiding there, waiting a chance to spring upon another victim?" She shivered, half persuaded by her own words. "And it could be hours, even days, before the body was found."

Agnes Maule's small bright eyes were angry. Now she burst out laughing.

"You are droll, Kathie. A real comic. And such absurd ideas about Tammerton. Here we have Jason and Goodlife—even James if he could wake up to what was happening in time. Three excellent shots. But at Warley." She pulled down the corners of her mouth. "There are no cottages within hearing. At five your gardener goes home. At this time of year he probably goes earlier." Her eyes caught and held those of her guest rather after the manner of the Ancient Mariner. "Yes, I don't suppose he stays after dark. That leaves only the Templetons. She's as nervous as a mouse and he's deaf as a post. You could scream and no one would hear you. Cry out and no one would come. We're your nearest neighbours, and we certainly wouldn't hear you. No, I don't suppose anyone could be more cut off from help than you."

James Maule lowered his head, peering over his spectacles from one speaker to the other. "Far be it from me to spoil your entertainment, peculiar as it may seem, but just what are you two ladies trying to do? Make our flesh creep?"

"Agnes is right about Mrs. Templeton," said the Judge pacifically. "Ever since she heard about poor Edith's death she has been on the verge of hysterics. Swears we'll all be murdered in our beds. Demands that we close the house and go back to London. What the poor husband must be suffering at this moment alone in the house with her I shudder to think."

"It's a strange thing that one can get a really satisfactory married couple," said Isobel. "Either the wife is wonderful and the husband no good. Or one puts up with the wife for the sake of the husband's work."

The conversation had been turned into safe channels, but a residue of uneasiness remained. There was a strangeness in the room as if the talk had brought home to them the fact of their own mortality.

Leaving the men to their wine, the women retired to the yellow drawing room, a room so called from its walls of faded apricot silk. Soon Agnes Maule made the excuse of domestic duties, and trotted away. Kathie went upstairs to put on a new face.

"I hope you don't intend to stay up late," said Louise.

"No, I shall make an excuse soon and go to bed," Isobel answered. "From the look of things we can safely leave Jason to entertain Kathie." Adding with an amused air, "I can't help wondering if that meeting in Piccadilly was the only one. Or, indeed, the accident they were at such pains to make it appear."

She was interrupted by the door being flung open violently. Kathie burst in, white-faced and shaken. "Oh—there you are!"

"Kathie! How you startled us."

"I'm sorry but really I had such a fright on the upstairs landing. The light was poor and everything so quiet. I was just by the big window. And then suddenly I saw something moving." There was a quality of stark horror in Kathie's voice.

Isobel's face paled. "What was it?" she asked, whispering.

But Kathie had been making a great effort to regain composure. "I'm sorry. It was silly of me to get so worked up. But that's what I'm like—silly."

Isobel stared. "So—there was nothing there?"

Kathie hesitated. "You're wrong. Quite wrong." She made round eyes at her friend. "There was a suit of armour—positively breathing down my neck." She laughed, the ghost of a high-pitched giggle, the sound of which set her hearer's nerves on edge.

Isobel's face was troubled. "Kathie, don't let Edith's death get you down. It's horrible, tragic, inexplicable, but it's happened. We've just got to accept the fact with as much equanimity as we can manage."

"Equanimity!" Kathie helped herself to another cup of coffee. The spoon rattled in the saucer. She made a grimace. "Serves me right. I set out to scare you all at dinner and only succeeded in scaring myself."

She walked over to stand before the fire, her back to the room. She put her cup on the high mantelshelf and, clasping the cool stone in her hand, rested her forehead in the crook of her arm.

Isobel looked at the slim drooping figure with concern. "Kathie, what is the matter? Is there anything I can do to help?"

The gingery head was shaken. "I told you—no." The earlier note of hysteria had been replaced by a flat, factual voice. "I think someone must be walking over my grave."

"Tramping backwards and forwards I should have said." Jason had entered the room in time to hear Kathie's last words.

Kathie lifted her head, staring towards the windows with dilated eyes. "Listen! What's that?"

Very faintly from somewhere in the depth of the house a bell shrilled.

"The front door," said Kathie incredulously. "Someone rang the bell."

"Oh, come off it, Kathie. What's so extraordinary about that?" Jason gave her a good-humoured thump on the behind.

Kathie rounded on him. "I've told you before not to do that," she flared.

Louise remarked, thoughtfully, "Didn't Mr. Kelvin say that the inspector would be up tonight? I expect that's who it is—" She was aware of having spoken into a vacuum of silence.

I've told you before—

So Isobel had been right. Jason and Kathie were not the strangers they had pretended to be.

Back in Glebe Cottage Septimus Finch, with Sampson's help, made a parcel of the books which the dead Miss Chumleigh had kept so methodically. To these he added four diaries he had found locked up in a trunk upstairs and a book of press cuttings dealing with the inquest on Dr. Morton and Harry Kelvin.

He left these for the Burford Point constable to give to the driver of the police car when it returned from taking the Judge to the Hall. They were to be delivered to the house in the village where Finch was to stay.

He set out for the vicarage with Sampson to show him the way.

It was a large gloomy looking house, in darkness except for a narrow strip of light between the drawn curtains at a downstairs window.

Finch rang the old-fashioned jangling bell and was mildly surprised that it didn't come away in his hand. He heard it ring somewhere in the house. Nearer he could hear a continuous, if slightly irregular, bang, bang, bang.

No one answered the bell.

Sampson walked away to stand by the lighted window in an attentive, listening attitude. Then he came back to where Finch stood on the doorstep. "Four hundred and thirty nine, four hundred and forty," he said, grinning all over his large red face. "We're in luck, sir. The reverend won't be long now."

"How d'you know?"

"Mr. Philby's taking his exercise. He hits a tennis ball against the wall morning and evening five hundred times. He won't let nothing distract him."

The front door opened. A small dark man stood in the

entrance. His eyes were black, his complexion dark. He had a lot of black hair above a wrinkled old face. His arms and legs were match-stick-thin. Finch thought him as near a black beetle in appearance as it was possible for a human being to be.

"If that's the pink paraffin, you're late," he said in a harsh voice, peering out. "And if it's the butcher—"

"It's the Scotland Yard inspector, sir," said Sampson in an agony of embarrassment. "He'd like a word with you."

"Indeed?" Mr. Philby put a lean brown hand up to shield his eyes in an endeavour to see better. "Come in then, Inspector." He added in a tone of distaste, "D'you need Sampson with you?"

"I'd be glad if he would come in and wait," Finch answered. "I need him to show me the way to my lodgings."

Mr. Philby switched on the lights in the hall. "Sampson can sit out here in the hall," he said at last, grudgingly.

It was an enormous room and full of enormous pieces of furniture. Enormous and gloomy oil paintings hung on the walls. Sampson politely selected the hardest of the straight-backed chairs. He took off his helmet and sat down to wait, a great red hand spread on each knee.

The vicar led the way into a sitting room even larger than the one they had left. It resembled the hall in that it was full of enormous pieces of furniture. It was very warm for a large round stove was burning fiercely in front of the hearth.

"Sit down, Inspector," the vicar invited.

Mr. Philby took out a pipe and a tobacco pouch. "Are you a pipe smoker, Inspector?" he enquired, holding out the latter.

"I'll have one of my cigarettes, if I may."

"By all means." The vicar filled his pipe, then returned his tobacco pouch to some obscure pocket under his cassock and all with an air of almost furtive haste as if afraid that his visitor might change his mind. "Now, what can I do for you?"

"I'm enquiring into the murder of Miss Edith Chumleigh," Finch answered. "I understand that the letter from Mr. Justice Kelvin found at Glebe Cottage was delivered by you?"

"That is so." Mr. Philby leaned back crossing one skinny leg over the other, exposing a sagging sock and an expanse of hairy flesh. "Unfortunately for your enquiry, Inspector, I did no more than drop the letter into the letterbox. For all I know to the contrary Miss Chumleigh might already have been dead."

"What time was this?"

"I really don't know. Round about half past three perhaps."

"Did you see anyone in the vicinity of the cottage?"

"I did not. It looked just as much an offence to the eye as usual. Women's frippery at the windows. A Cornish pixie for a knocker and a couple of fancy nesting boxes in the garden which no respectable birds would ever dream of using."

"I understand that you and the dead woman were not on good terms."

Mr. Philby drew on his pipe with obvious enjoyment. "We detested each other. And that was all to the good. Village life is very restricting, Inspector. Apart from the Christian exercise of wrestling with the devil one gets little upon which to sharpen one's wits. Miss Chumleigh, misjudged as she was, poor woman, was a positive boon. I cannot tell you how much I regret her unfortunate and untimely demise." He added, "A demise which, I rather fear, has preceded Miss Chumleigh's letter to the bishop."

"You wished her to write this letter?"

"I was looking forward to putting my case before the bishop. We have engaged in argument before and he has proved a most worthy opponent. Not like the last bishop or even the one before that. A positive craven the first, and the other so full of Christian forbearance that to argue with him was like belabouring a down pillow."

"As vicar, have you any suggestion as to which of your parishioners might be capable of a crime of violence?"

Mr. Philby's smile was positively ghoulish. "Any of us, Inspector," he said with relish. "Any one of us. We are a backward, even a primitive community. Had Miss Chumleigh been deprived of her life in any subtle or devious manner I should have said look outside the parish. But a simple case of stabbing? No, there we are all suspects."

Finch looked at him sadly. He was beginning to see that the vicar looked on him too in the light of an opponent to be outmanoeuvred if possible. "When you visited Warley how did you find the Kelvins?"

Mr. Philby gave him a quick sidelong glance. "I found Miss Kelvin in some distress and the Judge engaged in writing the letter I afterwards delivered. Miss Kelvin departed shortly after my arrival saying that she must take a bath."

"A bath? In the middle of the afternoon?"

"A purificatory bath perhaps. After all, Pilate washed his hands—although I don't, of course, know exactly to what sin Miss Kelvin had confessed. Perhaps to something very minor. Women, I find, cry very easily."

"What makes you think that Miss Kelvin had confessed to anything?"

"The Judge remarked that he had been usurping my function and that he found the confessional somewhat wearying. And I must admit he looked quite broken up." Mr. Philby added in a voice of happy appreciation of this possibility, "So much so that I shouldn't be surprised if I didn't outlive him."

There seemed nothing further to be gained from the interview. Finch rose to his feet, and Mr. Philby showed him out.

Chapter 9

Superintendent Ennis had reserved rooms for Finch and his sergeant at a house where visitors were taken in the summer. It was called Hill View for obvious reasons. It belonged to a widow, a depressed-looking woman but a good cook and glad of the extra money.

Detective Sergeant Archie Slater reached Lockbridge shortly before nine o'clock that evening. From there he was motored out to Tammerton in a police car. He was a tall young man with a long lantern-jawed face. His hair was very fair, his expression candid and solemn. In this it belied his character, for he was a very lively young man, with a taste for practical jokes of the more elaborate nature.

He had taken the precaution of having a good meal on the train. This was as well, since, on his arrival at Hill View, Finch insisted that they leave at once for Tammerton Hall.

"If you look out of the window, Archie, you'll see for yourself that it's a particularly difficult terrain," said Finch, complaining in his small soft voice. "The area in which we are interested lies in this valley. In a relatively small space there stands Tammerton Hall; Warley, where the Kelvins live; the village of Tammerton, with the church and vicarage; and Glebe Cottage, where the dead woman lived. It's hemmed in on one side by a range of hills. On the other there're these shocking great woods, an arm of which runs out parallel to the hills. And it's this arm that's the real villain of the piece—apart, of course, from the murderer. The trees there are massed behind and to one side of the Hall. They grow practically up to the back gate of Glebe Cottage. Warley stands in a clearing of the woods. In fact only the vicarage escapes them, being on the opposite side of the valley. And that stands amidst a fine display of yew trees. Fine, that is, if you like yew trees. So there you have it. An unknown murderer operating in as isolated a bit of country as one could find anywhere."

79

Finch's gently complaining voice died away. "Awkward," said Slater, who had lapsed into a pleasant state of somnolence. His superior, he knew, was fond of talking. Indeed, failing any other audience, he had even been known to talk to himself.

"You can say that again." Finch wagged his head sorrowfully. "We don't really know the motive for the murder. Nor even whether it was premeditated. And the murderer? You can take your pick. Miss Kelvin, the Judge, Mrs. Maule, her husband, Jason—"

"What a name!"

"I know. The Golden Fleece and all that." Finch ruminated a moment. "My own choice is Kathie Kelvin."

"But why should she murder Miss Chumleigh? According to what I've been told the old girl was devoted to her."

"I wonder how she managed it? To my mind Miss Kelvin ain't a lovable type."

"Have you met her?"

"No, but Superintendent Ennis described her. Said she's the athletic sort. Drives a fast car, plays tennis and golf. Rides but doesn't hunt."

"At least she doesn't seem to approve of blood sports." To Archie Slater, the townsman, this was a virtue.

Finch wagged a lugubrious head. "It wouldn't surprise me to learn that blood sports were right up her street," he commented darkly.

By now the police car had turned in at the Hall drive. It drew up before the front door. The moon had come out from behind a passing cloud and they could see grass lawns and clipped yews. The two men were aware of the velvet blackness of the woods and of the vast loneliness that lay over the scene.

"What do they want us for, anyway?" Slater muttered, suppressing a slight shiver. "Living in a place like this they must be dead anyway."

Finch shook his head. "Not yet, Archie," he said in his soft drawl. "Not yet." He put his finger on the bell-push and rang.

The door was opened almost at once by James Maule. Finch introduced himself and his sergeant.

James Maule smiled, peering at them over the top of his spectacles. "Two tall men and after ten o'clock. Who else would they be but police? But the truth is I was expecting you. So come in. It's wet and cold on the doorstep."

He led the way over to the fire, which he kicked into a blaze. "This is a shocking business. Can't make head or tail of it. Miss

Chumleigh of all people." He shook his head in bewilderment. "It doesn't seem possible."

"What kind of woman was she?"

"Miss Chumleigh had a misleading manner. Perfectly genuine, you understand, but misleading. In her appearance, too, she was a typical old maid. Arch; even coy. Apt to overpraise. Loved a compliment or a mild joke. But beneath the surface she had a very definite Character. She was a woman of integrity, of courage, both moral and physical—"

Mr. Maule broke off to offer the two detectives a drink, which Finch refused for them both. He went on, "She was essentially a kind woman. She was also a fine businesswoman." He smiled ruefully. "Since the war I have never come nearer to being solvent than since Miss Chumleigh took over the books. In the house, too, she had, with my wife's approval, put in hand all sorts of economies. Some small, some not so small."

"You saw her yesterday, I understand? How did she seem?"

"Perfectly normal. Cheerful, helpful as ever. She worked late and stayed to dinner. Goodlife ran her home afterwards in the car."

"Your chauffeur?"

"He began life as footman. Then he was butler. Now he's more of a handyman." Mr. Maule smiled slightly. "His loss of status makes him a bit querulous. Otherwise he takes it well enough."

"I'd like to speak to him. Your wife, too."

"I think Goodlife will have gone to bed but we can see. He'll probably be more approachable in his own quarters, if that'll suit you."

As they crossed the hall Finch enquired after Mr. Maule's alibi, "just for the record," and learned of the earlier discussion of that point at the dinner table.

"It's true I was in the library at four o'clock but then I knew that Goodlife would be bringing me a cup of tea at that time. So naturally, if I'd been engaged in anything nefarious," said James Maule, "I'd still have made a point of being back at my desk at four o'clock."

The passage leading to the kitchen was poorly lit. One of the economies instigated by the late Miss Chumleigh, James Maule explained. Voices came to them.

"If the Mummer's jockey is putting up two pounds overweight then King's Jester should beat it by three lengths," a hoarse feminine voice declared.

"Not in this weather, Ma'am," was the firm, if respectful, reply. "None of King Cole's stock like heavy going."

Finch observed a slight look of amusement flicker across the Squire's face. "You're in luck, Inspector," he said. "It seems that my wife has delayed Goodlife's departure for bed."

The kitchen was very warm. For this reason as many as possible of the staff's activities were carried out there. Pantries, lamp rooms, still rooms—all remained closed and unused during the winter months. Goodlife, in a baize apron, had been cleaning silver.

Mrs. Maule was standing in front of the great coal-burning range. Her appearance was bizarre. To the imperial purple and the jet she had added the fur trapper's hat. A decorative pair of horn-rimmed spectacles with wide gold sidepieces was on her nose. She held a glass of hot milk in one hand and a sporting paper in the other.

"This is the Scotland Yard detective, my dear," Mr. Maule told his wife. "Detective Inspector Finch and Detective Sergeant Slater."

Mrs. Maule tucked the newspaper under her arm. "You must be Miss Morton's inspector," she said, smiling, so that her eyes disappeared behind creases of fat.

"I had the pleasure of having lunch with her on the train," Finch admitted. He was fascinated no less by Mrs. Maule's appearance than by her complete lack of self-consciousness.

Mrs. Maule beamed. "A really nice gal, that."

Her husband had turned to Goodlife. "I believe the inspector would like to ask you some questions."

"Very good, sir." The old man looked rather angrily at Finch.

"I understand that you took Miss Chumleigh back to her cottage last night. Did she seem just as usual?"

"Yes, sir. Very cheerful she was. Told me she was looking forward to Christmas, and that this year she was going to make her own Christmas cake from a recipe the mistress had given her."

"Eight eggs, two pounds of fresh butter, two pounds loaf sugar," said Mrs. Maule rapidly and with great relish. "Mace, nutmeg, dried fruit, and blanched almonds." Her face fell. "It was a good recipe," she added, saddened by the thought that now it would not be used.

"Did you see Miss Chumleigh at any time today?" Finch asked Goodlife.

"No, sir. She was in the habit of letting herself into the house when she came to work."

"Thank you. One other thing. Where were you between three and half past this afternoon?"

"I was in the garage cleaning the car."

"Did anyone see you there?"

"Seeing that we're short-handed, no, sir. Time was when there were three men working in the stables alone, not to mention the gardeners. But in those days," Goodlife added bitterly, "I shouldn't have been in the garage, chauffeuring not being my work."

"Quite so," said Finch in his mild voice. Adding, "These are difficult times for most of us. Thank you for your co-operation."

"Thank you, sir." Goodlife, although polite, was not to be appeased. "Goodnight, sir—ma'am." He drew himself up to his full skinny height. "Had I known beforehand that I should require an alibi no doubt I could have arranged one more satisfactory to all parties." He picked up the baize-lined wicker basket containing the table silver and stalked gloomily away.

"Don't take any notice of him," Mrs. Maule advised. "He always looks as if he and ten children were all about to be evicted but it doesn't mean anything, except perhaps that he's failed to find the winner of the three-thirty."

Mr. Maule was smiling broadly. "I fancy, Agnes, that your alibi isn't likely to satisfy the inspector either."

"I don't think it even satisfied Louise," Mrs. Maule admitted. A thought seemed to strike her. "Inspector, can I offer you and your sergeant anything? Angel cake and tea? Or there's cold pheasant and orange salad. Or—"

"I expect the inspector would rather you just answered his questions," said Mr. Maule.

"Oh, very well. I don't know why it is that no one takes any interest in food. I cook and cook and my husband remains as thin as a beanpole and Jason is just as bad. It's discouraging."

"We're the lean kind, Agnes, and you'll never change us. But now it's getting late and there're still the inspector's questions about poor Edith's death."

Mrs. Maule's face saddened. "The dear, *good, useful* creature."

Said James Maule, "It's difficult to imagine anyone wanting to murder her."

His wife returned to the present in a flash. "Oh, no, it's

not," she declared decidedly. "Edith was quite inflexible. To her, right was right and wrong wrong. Why, when she took me to task about my betting losses and pointed out how much more difficult I made things for you, I could willingly have killed her."

"But fair's fair, Agnes. After I told Edith that I considered you entitled to have some enjoyment she never mentioned it again, did she?"

Mrs. Maule shook her head. "Trouble was I knew that she was right," she said in her gravelly voice.

James Maule smiled but traces of anxiety lingered in his eyes. "In any case stabbing someone would hardly be my wife's kind of retaliation."

The words raised a sudden mental picture in Finch's mind. A picture of Agnes Maule, plump and pink, sticking thorns into a clay figure. Or inscribing cabalistic signs on the floor in some disused wing of the house in an attempt to raise the devil to do her bidding.

An involuntary flicker of amusement passed across his face. "I see what you mean," he murmured.

James Maule stared. "Why, I believe you do," he said, taken aback. "I really believe you do."

Mrs. Maule remarked rather crossly, "I wish you two would stop talking in riddles. I didn't kill Edith. I didn't kill anyone. It's true I went down to Glebe Cottage but that was because I had a feeling about her."

"What sort of feeling?"

"Just a feeling. How can one define it more closely? I can only say that I'd had it for some time—only not in any specific direction. I knew that trouble was coming. Until I met her I thought that perhaps Louise Morton was bringing it." She added, still more crossly, "And now I suppose you think I'm quite mad."

"Not at all," Finch assured her. "My mother is a Cornish-woman. She is a great hand at making predictions."

James Maule laughed. "Then I can safely leave you two together and get back to my chess."

When he had gone Finch said, "So you found Miss Chumleigh dying? Tell me about it."

Mrs. Maule stared at him for a moment in silence. Then abruptly she began to speak, "I knocked, you know," she said gravely, "and no one answered. But for this feeling of anxiety I would have gone away. It was a grey day and it seemed to me that the cottage, for all its gay colours, was greyer still. None of the lights was on but that meant nothing. Edith was careful of electricity. I opened the door and the grey light from outside seemed to slip past me and mingle with the shadows inside.''

Again she fell silent. Her eyes no longer saw Finch. Only some inner vision of their own. ''I called her by name. 'Edith!' I called, and then I saw her—crawling slowly along the passage—like a brown caterpillar. I switched on the light and then I could see the knife—and the blood and that she was dying. I knelt beside her and said her name again. At first it didn't seem to register. I don't think she knew even that the light was on. Then suddenly she saw me, recognised me. She squeezed my hand faintly. So very faintly. She said 'Take care' and then a little later she said 'Kathie.' I'm not certain about the first word but the other two were quite distinct. Then the blood rushed out of her mouth. She let go my hand and she was dead.''

''And then what did you do?''

Mrs. Maule looked at him. ''I thought that murderer might still be about so I went to look,'' she said. ''But he wasn't. The cottage was empty.''

It was a good explanation, Finch thought, but unlikely. ''You told Superintendent Ennis that you were with Miss Chumleigh until Miss Morton knocked.''

''That,'' said Mrs. Maule blandly, ''was just kindness of heart on my part. I could see the superintendent was in an agony of apprehension in case I said anything to incriminate myself.''

''You went into the sitting room?''

A stillness fell on Mrs. Maule. ''It was like a different room. As if no one had ever lived there,'' she said and her eyes were fearful.

''What did you make of it?''

''I thought that perhaps the murderer had felt triumphant and that it was his way of saying, 'You're dead. Now you stay that way.' Or perhaps he was only frightened and saying 'You're dead, Edith. *Please* stay that way.' ''

Finch wondered what two characters she had conjured up. Jason and Kathie Kelvin perhaps. ''What would the room have looked like normally?''

''Very comfortable. Always in the winter there'd be a big wood fire and two armchairs drawn up before it. Then Edith would have collected everything she might need and put them within reach. Her knitting, library book, newspaper, cigarettes.

Sometimes there'd be fruit. More often there was a box of chocolates or sweets, for she adored rich things.''

"When she said 'Take care—Kathie' what did you think she meant? Was it 'Take care of Kathie' or 'Beware of Kathie'?''

Agnes Maule was silent a moment, chewing her lower lip. "I was afraid you'd ask that. At the time I was certain that she meant 'Take care of Kathie.' It was only later that I told myself that it might equally well have been 'Beware of Kathie.' ''

"You don't like her?"

"No, I don't. She's a sly secretive gal and she brings trouble with her. Always has. Besides she must have someone to run after her and that's maddening. Harry Kelvin, my nephew Jason, the Judge, Edith Chumleigh, even James. She bewitched them all.'' Mrs. Maule extinguished herself under the hat, muttering crossly from beneath its shelter, "And who is she anyway? Answer me that.''

"It's a question of some interest to me," said Finch, dryly. "D'you know anything about her?''

"Nothing." Agnes Maule sniffed. She added with a satirical note in her voice, "The Judge says it's enough that his son loved her.''

"Miss Kelvin never spoke of her parents? Nor had any relation to visit her?''

"No. Of course we tried to find out about her when she first came down here but we got nowhere with her." It was plain this still rankled.

"Where did she come from?"

"London, I imagine. I have never heard her mention any other place with affection. But London! Oh, she's always dashing up to London—to theatres or to buy clothes. The Judge spoils her and that's the truth."

Chapter 10

Mrs. Maule put one of the rooms opening off the hall at Finch's disposal. It was a small rather dismal room, obviously the repository of odd pieces of furniture not wanted elsewhere. To compensate for this Mrs. Maule produced a large efficient electric fire, which Slater plugged in. She also insisted on bringing them coffee. Then she went away promising to send Louise Morton to be interviewed.

"Bonkers," said Finch thoughtfully. "Bonkers—but in the nicest possible way. From now on she's going to be my favourite screwball."

"Mine, too," Slater agreed grinning.

Louise entered the room. She looked very efficient and smart in her crisp uniform. On closer inspection it could be seen that she was pale and her face had a rather pinched look.

"Isn't this awful?" she said at once. "I feel the most awful Jonah. If only I could be certain that Miss Chumleigh's death had nothing to do with my arrival."

"Yes, it's a queer business." For her own safety Finch was not going to attempt to reassure her. "Sit down and let's see if we can puzzle it out."

Slater was holding a chair for her. He thought himself a connoisseur of women and was already busy planning future meetings with her in London.

Finch went on. "I've a book of cuttings about the smashup on Dartmoor, so we can leave that for the present. As for the row this morning—if it amounted to that—with Miss Chumleigh, I'd like you to write as full an account of it as possible, remembering particularly what she said. And now tell me everything else that has been happening to you and talk fast. It won't make you popular with the family if they think you were too long with the police."

Louise nodded, recalling Kathie's remark earlier that evening. She began to tell Finch of the broken engagement, embarrassed at first by the realisation that the lantern-jawed sergeant was taking it all down in shorthand but it was a subject that fascinated her. It seemed to fascinate Finch too and soon she found herself ignoring Slater's flying pen.

She did not tell him about Miss Chumleigh's belief that she had seen Jason somewhere in the past, because she forgot it. She did not tell him that Jason and Kathie were still lovers because, she told herself firmly, it was none of his business.

She told him of her patient's deception about the state of her health. Of Isobel's infatuation for her husband. Of their coming anniversary. Encouraged by Finch's interest she even recalled to mind the shrub—or tree—or person—which had disappeared so mysteriously, from outside Isobel Crane's window.

Finch made no comment. His private thought was that it had been Kathie Kelvin, hoping to see whether the Louise Morton who had come to nurse Mrs. Crane was the same Louise Morton whose father had been killed in the motor accident for which she had been responsible. He thought, too, that a rather different picture of Kathie was beginning to emerge from that drawn by Superintendent Ennis.

By now they had come to Edith Chumleigh's murder. Here Finch was quick to spot some reservation in the girl's manner.

"What are you keeping back?" he asked. "If it concerns Mrs. Maule, she has already admitted that Miss Chumleigh died earlier than she had said. And that she had explored the cottage before letting you in."

The faint shadow lifted from Louise's face. "That's all right then. But it was seeing someone at the upstairs window that decided me that Miss Chumleigh was at home. It was only a sort of shadow but it was definitely *someone*. I thought afterwards that perhaps the murderer was still upstairs but I could see the stairs from where I was sitting in the dining room and no one came down so I knew that it must have been Mrs. Maule up there."

Finch nodded. And Mrs. Maule, deciding that Louise had seen her, had decided to admit to the truth—or part of it. "Tell me exactly what happened from the time you stopped outside Glebe Cottage."

Louise did so. She was an excellent witness.

"The worst part," she ended, "was waiting for the police. We sat and sat, with Miss Chumleigh lying dead in the passage, just out of sight. And Mrs. Maule didn't say anything—except to remark that she hoped the church bell would soon stop tolling. Only it wasn't tolling, so that didn't help much."

"When Mrs. Maule shut herself in the sitting room, could you hear anything of what went on?"

"Not distinctly. I could hear her voice but not what she was saying. I heard the click when she put back the receiver. After that there was silence for a bit. When she came out she looked quite blue and frozen. She said that we had to wait for the police to arrive from Burford Point, and that we'd better go into the dining room. It was terribly cold in there. Cold—and sort of shivery, although Mrs. Maule had turned on the electric fire. She was wearing the fur hat—"

"*The* fur hat?"

"Roger Crane gave it to her. She wears it at the oddest times."

"She's wearing it now."

"No?" Louise's eyes were wide. "Perhaps she sleeps in it."

"Perhaps! But she was wearing it at Glebe Cottage?"

Louise nodded. "She had the ear flaps tied on top. But she undid them and tied them again under her chin. Then she thrust her hands up her sleeves and—and sort of withdrew."

"With not a word?"

"Not one. Oh, I remember! Just before the police arrived she did say that she wanted her tea but that she supposed, under the circumstances, even a biscuit might be thought to be evidence."

"Have you any idea what her feelings were towards Miss Chumleigh?"

"She was terribly upset that she was dead, but apart from that I don't know." Louise spoke slowly, picking her words. "I'm sure she liked her, only—she was inclined to place her." She added reflectively, "It's funny to find it still going on in the country. Who was she? Where did she come from? All that sort of thing. Miss Chumleigh was a dear useful creature but the operative word, I think, was useful. It's the same with me—only in a nicer way. I was 'Nurse' until Kathie recognised me. Then, all of a sudden, I was placed. I was the daughter of the doctor who had been killed at the same time as Harry Kelvin. Someone they'd always known about and been interested in. Everyone seemed delighted to see me—except Kathie. And she, obviously, loathes my guts."

"D'you know who she was before Mr. Justice Kelvin adopted her?"

"She was a Miss Lynch. No one seems to have known much else." Louise added, "Mrs. Crane did say that she used to design textiles for a firm somewhere near the Old Bailey." At this Finch's movements were arrested. He sat quite still. Louise fancied that, in some curious way, his face seemed to have sharpened.

"The Old Bailey?" he said slowly. "What a curious expression. Why should a firm be mentioned as being near the Old Bailey?"

"Well, you see, Kathie used to slip in there during her luncheon hour. That's how she met Harold Kelvin. He'd see her there. Then one day he noticed that she was looking upset and he spoke to her. And that began it."

"Mrs. Crane told you this?"

"Yes. At least, Mrs. Crane said that Kathie used to go in and listen to the various cases and Miss Chumleigh said the rest."

But Finch seemed to have lost interest. He glanced at his wrist watch. "Time we returned you to circulation." He stood up. "About the question as to who was driving the Bentley. Surely it all happened too long ago to count now?"

"It counts with Kathie. You should have seen her expression when she recognised me. She looked as if she could have killed me."

Finch went with her to the door. "You be careful she doesn't do just that."

"Oh, I shall be all right. Kathie's cleared that all up with the Judge, so my being here doesn't matter one way or the other."

"You're sure of that?"

Something in his voice caught her attention. "I don't see how it could matter. My only connection with Kathie was because of that accident. Once the inquest was over she just vanished out of my life."

"In that case I need not worry." But Finch continued to stare after her as she crossed the hall. Almost, she thought, uneasily, as if he did not really believe what he had just said.

Kathie was the next to be interviewed. Although Finch had been ready to readjust his idea of her, her actual appearance took him by surprise. He had, too, a passing feeling of surprise for Superintendent Ennis.

Whatever else Kathie might be, athletic was not the word to describe her. True she had a strong, beautifully built body and long firm legs but it was her sheer femininity that struck Finch. It would have struck any normal male.

She was a man's woman, passionate, uninhibited, wanton perhaps. He found himself wondering about her sex life. It was difficult to think of her having none. Mentally he contradicted himself. Not difficult—impossible. Sex was the first thing he had thought of in connection with her.

Just as unhappiness was the second.

Not a sudden transitory unhappiness caused by the death of Miss Chumleigh but a deep-seated melancholy that permeated her whole being. It seemed, in some curious way, to add to her attractiveness.

As the interview progressed, Finch came to a further conclusion. She was, he thought, a person who needed security—but of affection, not money. She needed cherishing—but by a husband or lover; not by an old man. He wondered fleetingly about the men in her life. Whoever they were they had given her neither of these two things.

"I'm sorry to have to question you at such a time," he said, "but apart from the murderer, you were probably the last person to see Miss Chumleigh well and about."

"I suppose I was." Kathie sank with unstudied grace into the chair Slater had hurried to pull out for her. Her marmalade-coloured hair flared against pallour. She looked exhausted and there were dark smudges of fatigue beneath her eyes. She closed them for a moment. "I'm sorry," she muttered, "but I've had it all day. Talk, talk, talk and no one really saying anything."

"A thing like this must always be a great shock," said Finch sententiously. "Particularly when the victim happens to be a friend."

Kathie made a grimace. "A friend! That's putting it mildly. She was always a—a sort of fixed point in a changing world. She was friend, adviser—banker." She smiled with difficulty. "This very afternoon she lent me five pounds until the end of the month." Again that wry smile twisted her long mouth. "I don't really see how I'm going to get on without her."

Finch looked sympathetic. "Tell me about that telegram you sent to Nurse Morton."

"Must I? I've heard nothing but that all day. And most people seem to think that I was out of my tiny mind to have thought that the Judge hadn't guessed that I was driving that day." She broke off to glance directly at Finch's quiet attentive face. "Oh well! I suppose it was silly. But however I appeared outwardly at the time of that beastly car crash, inside I was desperately upset and feeling as guilty as hell. Shocked, too, I imagine. So that, when the Judge said that I couldn't possibly have been driving because his son had promised him that I shouldn't, it sort of stuck in my mind as—as immutable. The Judge believed his son to be incapable of telling a lie and that left me saddled with mine for evermore.

"I suppose I reasoned, if I reasoned at all, that I had caused him enough sorrow without adding to it the shock of knowing that his son was not a second George Washington after all." Kathie broke off to look appealingly at Finch. "I expect it's difficult for you to understand, but the easy way out has always been the right way for me. I found the Judge's standards as incomprehensible and as terrifying as some voodoo cult. So when Mrs. Crane told me that the only other person in the world who knew the truth was coming down here—well, I just panicked."

"You recognised the name?"

"Yes. But, of course, I couldn't be certain that it was the same Louise Morton—not until I had seen her."

Through the window of Isobel Crane's sitting-room window? Finch wondered. "And then?"

"Then I discovered that what I'd been afraid of for so long was only a turnip ghost after all. That everyone believed that I had been driving the Bentley that day."

"Including Miss Chumleigh?"

Kathie nodded. "But she thought the Judge didn't know. Not because he was—silly but because he had never considered the possibility. She thought that the only thing about the accident that had registered with him was the fact that his son was dead."

"When did you learn that Miss Chumleigh had suspected you of driving the Bentley?"

"When I called at the cottage this afternoon. I'd gone to tell her what Mrs. Crane had told me over the telephone. You know! That Louise Morton didn't intend to be tiresome. Edith said that the best thing I could do would be to tell the Judge the truth, because it was quite likely that if Louise didn't tell him someone else would." Kathie added thoughtfully, "But the oddest part of it all was that I had the feeling that she wasn't really attending."

"You think she had something else on her mind?"

"I'm sure of it. But, to be truthful, I was too full of my own woes to be interested in hers."

"Woes? You think she was worried?"

"If I hadn't been so wrapped up in my own affairs and so very much against doing anything as unpleasant as telling the Judge the truth I suppose I would have asked her what was the matter."

"But you did tell him? And found that he had guessed long ago?"

Kathie nodded, resting her head in her hand so that Finch saw no more than the flaming lovely hair and the curve of the graceful neck. "I suppose he'd seen so many shifty, irresponsible people in the dock—" Her voice trailed dispiritedly away.

"What time was it, when you called at Glebe Cottage?"

"About—oh, I suppose it must have been well before two o'clock, for when I got home the clock in the hall was striking half past two and I suppose I must have been at the cottage about an hour. I went straight into the study and was still there when Mr. Philby called. I left him with the Judge and went upstairs. It was then ten past three. I know that because I looked at my watch to see how long I could stay in my bath and still be downstairs changed and more or less in my right mind, to give the Judge his tea at four o'clock."

"A bath?" Finch sounded mildly incredulous.

The marmalade head nodded. "Yes, a bath. A long, hot, scented bath. There's nothing like it for restoring morale—and mine needed restoring, I can tell you. Just floating. Occasionally turning on the hot water tap with my toes. M'h'm. Heavenly!"

The words, no less than the sensuous way in which they were spoken, were enough to conjure up for both men a picture, disquietingly vivid, of the long pale body, floating in the scented water. The elegant toes, no doubt beautifully manicured, the whole lovely line of her—

Kathie looked amused. Amused and a little complacent. The effect of a male audience was having a reviving effect on her.

"One other point. That telegram. I understood that you're supposed to be Mrs. Crane's greatest friend?"

Kathie stared. "My God, you're sharp," she said. (And that goes for you too, Finch thought.) "Yes, it's quite true. We used to be the greatest friends. But I've never felt the same since she married."

She was silent a moment, frowning to herself. "It wasn't that I minded her marrying. It was her marrying Roger. Oh, I tried at first not to show my dislike but I never could keep things to myself.'' She shrugged. ''It ended in our having a row. At least, I rowed and Isobel froze. I told her he was a fortune hunter and not worthy of her. I said the marriage would be a failure.'' She smiled a slight bitter smile. ''But it wasn't. That's what I couldn't forgive. It wasn't a failure.''

''You felt that she had no right to be happy when you'd warned her that she wouldn't be happy?''

''Something like that.'' Kathie rubbed her forehead wearily. ''And then when I heard that Isobel's nurse was to be Louise Morton I felt that Isobel was to blame for that too.'' She hesitated. ''I suppose she was pretty sick about that telegram?''

''I understand that when Miss Morton told Mrs. Crane about it she altered the wording.''

Kathie's eyes flashed. ''Don't expect me to be grateful to her. I'm already too much in her debt—if you can understand that.''

''There's a Chinese proverb that runs 'Why do you hate me? I never did you a favour.' ''

Kathie laughed abruptly. ''Put like that my reactions sound more than a little bitchy.''

Watching the haggard yet attractive face Finch reflected that she might, or might not, have been telling the truth about her visit to Glebe Cottage. But when she had spoken of Isobel Crane's marriage—as when she had expressed her feelings towards Louise Morton—then she had been speaking the truth. He was certain of it.

He glanced at his watch. ''Past eleven. You'll be wanting to go home.''

Kathie, taking this as an intimation that the interview was over, rose to her feet with the eye-catching grace that characterised all her movements.

''The party breaks up only when the game of chess finishes. The Judge and Mr. Maule sometimes go on playing so late that I'm forced to go home alone. They're mad enthusiasts. Particularly the Judge. He even plays chess at the vicarage on Wednesdays but I don't go there.''

''Can't take Mr. Philby?''

Kathie's sauntering walk ceased. ''You've been there? To the vicarage?'' Her voice had sharpened.

''Yes, I called to ask Mr. Philby if he'd seen or heard anything suspicious when he left the Judge's letter.''

''And had he?''

"Not a thing."

"Too bad." She was moving gracefully again towards the door.

"Wow!" said Slater to himself when she had gone. And again, "Wow!"

Chapter 11

No one asked Louise what had transpired during her interview with the men from Scotland Yard. True Kathie had given her an ugly glance in return for Finch's message that he wanted to see her, but this was no more than the girl had expected. Isobel had pressed her hand comfortingly, and Mrs. Maule had welcomed her return with one of her slit-eyed smiles. Jason, lounging against the high chimneypiece, favoured her with a long intent stare.

"You were going to bed," Louise reminded her patient.

"From the number of times Isobel has glanced towards the windows, I imagine that she is waiting for Roger," said Mrs. Maule rather tartly.

"I did think he might come down tonight instead of waiting until tomorrow," Isobel admitted. "You see"—she smiled faintly—"I find Roger reassuring."

As if her words had worked some kind of spell from outside, there came the sound of an approaching car.

"That's Cartwright's taxi," said Jason. "Looks as if you're going to be right, Isobel."

The car stopped, then moved off again. There followed the sound of a key being fitted into the front door. The next moment a square-shouldered, powerfully built man walked into the drawing room.

"Roger." The colour returned to Isobel's pale cheeks. Her eyes shone. She looked rejuvenated, gay, almost a girl again. Agnes and Jason Maule, too, seemed pleased to see him. He was introduced to Louise.

He bent and kissed his wife, looking at her with a deep, intent and questioning glance. "As soon as you 'phoned about poor old Miss Chumleigh I decided to finish up my business in London as far as possible, and come back." He grinned down at her. "I had a sort of feeling you might be needing me."

Louise could see what his wife had meant. Here was someone on whom one could depend. Strong, masculine, and giving an effect of latent power. She found him rather overwhelming, which was why, she decided, she found herself staring at him.

Roger turned, his hand still clasping his wife's. "I saw a car outside. Looked like the police."

"Yes. Scotland Yard no less." Jason's grin was mirthless, rather savage. "An Inspector Finch, who happened to be in Lockbridge."

"Scotland Yard, eh?" Roger raised the thick bar of his eyebrows. "He ought to be an improvement on that fellow Ennis."

"I like him," Mrs. Maule declared. "There's something very reassuring about him."

Louise suppressed a shiver. There *was* something reassuring about the Scotland Yard detective. He was like a visitor from another, saner, world. Only, she thought drearily, he had come too late. Fear and suspicion, like a contagious illness, seemed to have infected the very air they breathed.

James Maule and the Judge appeared. They greeted Roger with impeccable politeness, if not with enthusiasm.

"Where's Kathie?" asked the Judge sharply.

"With the inspector—in the garbage room," Mrs. Maule said.

"I hope he'll remember that she's already had a cruel shock," said the Judge, "and is not fit for much in the way of interrogation."

"I expect by now she's twisted him round her little finger," Jason said with a peculiarly bleak smile.

"Young man," said the Judge sternly, "let me tell you that the inspector is not a man who can be twisted round anyone's finger."

Jason looked at him from his superior height and from under his heavy lids. "A warning, sir?"

"If it is pertinent," agreed Mr. Justice Kelvin sternly.

"I have a box of fondants somewhere," said Mrs. Maule hurriedly. "In my bedroom perhaps."

"I'll get it, Aunt," Jason promised.

It was while Jason was out of the room that Kathie returned, Finch at her side.

"My husband." Isobel introduced Roger to Finch.

"Evening!" Roger nodded. "I thought as things were down here I'd better come back."

"Yes, it's a bad business." Finch looked at Roger Crane

with interest. A strong, muscular-looking man; it was not surprising that he had survived the plane crash.

Kathie's face had hardened at the sight of Roger Crane, but all she said was, "As the last but one to see poor Edith I've been put through the mangle. So give me a drink, someone."

"But the murderer was the last but one to see Edith," said Mrs. Maule's muffled voice.

"I forgot the operative words which were 'about and well,' " said Kathie. "When you saw Edith she was already dying—or wasn't she?"

Jason had returned with the box of sweets in time to hear the exchange between the two women. Before they could carry their argument further he said, "I called at Glebe Cottage about a quarter past three. Miss Chumleigh was certainly about and well when I saw her."

Finch glanced at him curiously. A young man so elegant, so quick to come to Kathie's aid—and in such a suppressed but towering temper. "You didn't mention this before?"

Jason looked at him, a cool, hard look. "To the superintendent? And then again to you? No, thank you. Once is enough—for what it's worth."

"Why did you visit the cottage?"

"I visited Miss Chumleigh—not the cottage." Jason's voice, like his look, was insolent. "I wanted to ask her if she'd go through the books with me one afternoon. I only stopped a few minutes on my way to keep an appointment at Grigg's Farm. Certainly not more than five."

"And Miss Chumleigh?"

"I thought she seemed upset."

"What made you think that?"

"I'd heard so much about her business abilities and yet she answered me almost at random."

"Any idea what she was doing when you called?"

"She had been writing a letter. Anyway, there it was—on the desk."

Was it Finch's imagination? Or was there something odd about the little silence that followed? A coolness in the air? A sharpening of perception? He fancied that Jason's remark must have spelled near disaster to someone in the room. And it had been so easy—after all his, Finch's speculations and deductions.

"You didn't happen to notice who the letter was addressed to?"

"No. I just saw it lying there and since it was a beastly day, I offered to post it."

"Did you notice whether it was stamped?" Finch and Jason seemed to have the conversation to themselves.

"No, it wasn't. I offered to stamp the letter at the same time as I offered to post it."

Mr. Justice Kelvin joined in. "Where is all this leading, Inspector? Are we to assume that the letter was important?" and his voice was cold and judicial as if he were, once more, presiding at court.

Finch turned to answer him. "Its importance lies in the fact that the letter seems to have disappeared."

"Posted, perhaps," suggested James Maule.

"No, it was not posted."

"Then delivered by hand," Mr. Maule persisted. "After all, no stamp, eh?" And he looked at Finch over the top of his spectacles.

"And not delivered by hand," said Finch in his small voice that yet had the power to carry to every corner of the room.

The silence that followed was very odd indeed. A silence in which a tiger-presence seemed to stir and come alive among them.

Agnes Maule peered at Finch from under the fur hat. "The blotting paper," she croaked to herself darkly. "So that's why he asked."

"What you are suggesting," said James Maule, in a voice in which incredulity and horror battled for a place, "is that the murderer removed the letter after killing Edith Chumleigh?"

"Or even," said his friend, the Judge, "that the murder was committed to obtain possession of the letter."

"I must admit I'd feel happier if I knew its contents," Finch admitted.

"Even to know to whom it was written," said Isobel faintly. "That would be a help."

Roger Crane clasped her thin hand in his strong one. "This talk could go on for hours," he said roughly. "My wife should be in bed."

"We should all be in bed," Jason corrected him and Kathie's look was hard and disdainful.

"Since all speculation about the letter's probable destination must be futile, perhaps we might call it a day," James Maule agreed.

"Not futile at all," said Finch. "On the contrary, I have a very good idea to whom the letter was addressed."

Again the words were followed by a silence.

Mr. Justice Kelvin spoke. "Don't let anyone underestimate the police," he said harshly. "And, most of all, don't let anyone underestimate the inspector here."

"By Jove, no!" James Maule exclaimed. "You've known him for years, Horace. We'll take your word for it."

Mr. Justice Kelvin looked about him and his gaze was bleak. "Yes, I've known the inspector for a great number of years and I've seldom known him to fail." It was a plain warning that the speaker considered the murderer to be in the room. Finch hoped it was no more than that. For the old man's sake he hoped it was no more than that.

"The quicker he succeeds the better I'll be pleased," Roger declared. "And now, if you'll excuse us, I'm taking my wife and her nurse away."

"You do that, Roger," said Agnes Maule. "And if you want a meal there's plenty of food in the larder."

Roger's face cleared. He grinned, showing strong teeth, very white against his beard. "I don't know anything more rewarding than to raid your larder, Aunt Agnes." He took the wheel of the chair and headed it briskly for the door.

Isobel raised her voice. "Kathie, shall I see you later?"

"I expect so," was the ungracious reply.

Roger's face hardened but he said no more than an abrupt and gruff 'Good night all,' closing the door firmly behind him and his charge. "Hey, that was some do in there. All the same I could well have done without it," he remarked.

"I thought it was horrible," Isobel declared with a shudder.

When they had all three reached the sitting room he lifted Isobel into her chair before the fire, picking her up easily. Then he helped himself to a whisky and soda.

"Anyone else want a drink? No?" He returned to draw up a chair for himself close to his wife and took her hand in his. "Listen, love. It wasn't you who killed the old lady, for you couldn't have got as far as Glebe Cottage. It wasn't me, because I was in London. It wasn't Nurse because she had no motive. So let's be thankful for that and just sit tight while the police get on with it."

"Oh, Roger! What a council of perfection." Isobel was half laughing, half crying.

Louise, who had caught herself staring again, turned away to pour out a dose of her patient's heart medicine.

Roger grinned cheerfully, "It's good sense—for all those fine words of yours." He pulled a packet of cigarettes from his pocket.

"Roger! That horrible packet."

Her husband looked as guilty as a schoolboy. "And I'd made up my mind only to help myself out of the box on the table here so you wouldn't notice the carton."

"I suppose you left your case in London?"

"Must have done. They'll have to send it on." Roger's tone was rueful. "Tell you what, I'll buy half a dozen cheap cases. That way I should have one by me for quite some time." Adding teasingly, "Then I shan't offend you with my low ways."

Isobel looked at him fondly. "Darling, you haven't any low ways, as you call them. It's just that I loathe cartons of any sort. They affect me in the same way as dirty bank notes." She took her medicine from Louise. "There's a gold cigarette case in the top long drawer of the tallboy," she told her. "Please get it and give it to my husband."

"That sissy one?" Roger gave a groan. "Isobel, have a heart."

"No, you're to take it. You know it's the only one you never mislay."

"It's too damned valuable, that's why. I feel as if I'm walking around with the crown jewels."

By now Louise had found the case. It was long and slim. The initials I.M. (Isobel Maule) were entwined in diamonds and enclosed in a wreath, the leaves of which were composed of small emeralds. It was beautiful, expensive—and feminine. Roger had Louise's sympathy.

"You take that, Roger." Isobel commanded, laughing at his expression. "And, Louise, will you see if there's a tray put ready for my husband in the kitchen? Aunt Agnes is almost sure to have remembered."

As Louise moved towards the door she paused to look back, aware that husband and wife had returned to their own world. The world in which Isobel found her happiness and security.

"And how is my lady wife?"

"I wish you wouldn't call me that."

"But it's what you are. I never cease to marvel that you married a rough fellow like myself."

"Oh, Roger!"

Louise closed the door thankfully behind her. She made her way down the corridor to the hall. The police had gone. The yellow drawing room was empty except for Jason and Kathie. They were quarrelling. They kept their voices low so that no actual words came to Louise's ears but their attitudes were unmistakable. Plainly Kathie was provoking him, her expression one of mocking amusement. Jason responded with a tense, still body and a black, stony look that Louise would have found frightening.

The long scrubbed table in the kitchen was bare except for a colourful-looking tray. Louise saw that it was laid with a thermos jug of coffee and a large plate of sandwiches of the open variety, all very appetising-looking.

She carried the tray back. Jason and Kathie were still in the yellow drawing room, sitting quietly on each side of the fire. They had made up their differences—or exhausted themselves.

Isobel and Roger were still in the sitting room. Their conversation was low and confidential. Looking at her critically, Louise thought that her patient was better. The blue look had gone from her lips. Louise fancied that her husband's presence had had more to do with this than the doctor's medicine.

Roger was standing with his back to the fire. His expression was serious, even grim. He smiled though when he saw Louise and hurried forward to take the tray.

"Good old Aunt Agnes," he remarked. "And me still in this state. Not even my hands washed." He put the tray down on a table.

"Now don't be long, Roger," said Isobel.

"Trust me," was his rejoinder. He grinned at the girl, said "Thanks for the tray," and disappeared through a door communicating with the rest of the suite.

Isobel looked at Louise with dreamy eyes. "Trust me," she murmured. "And that's just what I do. When Roger's here it's as if I sink into another world. A world where I need never worry—not about murder, illness, growing old. Or even about having been born so plain." She laughed softly. "You see how egotistical I am."

"No one could call you plain now," said Louise truthfully. She was busy for a few minutes getting her patient out of her evening dress and into a housecoat, settling her comfortably before the fire.

"I've warmed you some milk. It's in the small thermos," she pointed out. "I hope you won't add any coffee to it."

Isobel laughed. "You run along to bed, Louise. Then you won't see what I do." She caught the girl's hand. "And thank you—for everything."

Louise said good night and left her.

The hall was empty, the yellow drawing room in darkness, the door slightly ajar. Louise paused, listening, looking about her, not from curiosity but to assuage the strange sense of being alone, cut off.

A voice echoed suddenly in her ear. A voice whispered from just inside the darkened room beside her. A whisper so close that Louise recoiled involuntarily.

"There's no hurry," it said, sighing voluptuously. And then, "Don't think I'll ever give you up, for I won't. Not ever."

And then, gently, silently, like a stage curtain, the door of the yellow drawing room, closed shut.

Jason and Kathie!

Louise fled across the hall and up the stairs. Her bedroom brought her no comfort. For some reason the episode had frightened her. Perhaps it had been the naked passion in Kathie's voice. The something untamed and dangerous that had seemed to seep out from behind the half-closed door.

Chapter 12

The police car dropped the two Scotland Yard men off at Hill View. Finch fitted the key into the door. "We'll have a glass of beer and make a few notes before we turn in."

"Right. I suppose Mrs. What's-her-name has gone to bed?"

"Thomas. Her name's Thomas." Finch hung up his coat. "What did you think of the battered nymph?"

"Kathie? I didn't think of her. Only of beds. Large soft beds in small discreet hotels. She must have been fab, simply fab, when she was engaged to Jason. I can't think how he could have thrown her over."

"I've had an idea about that." Finch opened the sitting room door to be pleasantly surprised. The fire, behind a heavy wire screen, was burning brightly. A crusty loaf, butter, and a large slab of some local cheese were on the table.

"Gosh! I could use some of that," said Slater appreciatively. He set about getting glasses and two bottles of beer out of a cupboard.

"So could I, but we'll have to work while we eat." Finch was taking some blank sheets of lined paper from his despatch case as he spoke.

"Pleasure. What do I do?"

"Write down a list of the callers at Glebe Cottage this afternoon and the times at which they called."

The list when it was finished, looked like this:

Miss Kelvin called at Glebe Cottage approx.		1.30 P.M.
Left Glebe Cottage	approx.	2.25 P.M.
Arrived at Warley		2.30 P.M.
Jason Maule at cottage	approx.	3.15 P.M.
Mr. Philby	very approx.	3.30 P.M.
Murder reported		3.43 P.M.

"Now take another sheet and write motives."
Another list was begun.

Mrs. Maule—Time right. Betting losses or other extravagances. Lied to Superintendent Ennis. General behaviour at cottage suspicious.

Mr. Philby—Time right. Temperamentally suited. May not be so indifferent to Miss Chumleigh's activities as he made out. Folds of cassock excellent for concealing knife. Against—inclined to trust P.C. Sampson's judgement.

Jason Maule—motive unknown. Might still be involved with Miss Kelvin. Time might be right. Temperamentally suited. Has been living hard—

"Might have been in prison," Slater suggested cheerfully.

"More likely in the army—a paratrooper perhaps." Finch had noticed the number of army uniforms among the Maule portraits.

"But would he have stabbed anyone in the back?"

"With Jason Maule's temper he'd have found back and front all the same. In fact, under certain circumstances, I don't doubt but that he'd have been capable of strangling Miss Chumleigh with the old school tie itself."

"But he did tell you that Miss Chumleigh had written a letter."

"Everyone has his own idea of what looks innocent. Besides, Jason might well have told us for the devil of it and the kick he'd get out of skating on thin ice."

Slater, recalling the hard reckless face, had to admit that his superior might well be right.

"Now we come to the less likely candidates. Mr. Justice Kelvin—motive, devotion to adopted daughter. But if had intended to kill Miss Chumleigh why get Mr. Philby to deliver a letter? Why write at all? Miss Morton, unlikely. James Maule, unlikely, but no alibi. Goodlife, the same. Roger Crane, no known motive. Alibi but unsubstantiated."

At this point both men were startled by a sudden sharp rat-tat on the front door.

Finch raised an eyebrow. "Visitors? Must be for us. Let them in, Archie."

Slater opened the front door. A dark red sports car stood

outside in the road. On the doorstep was its owner. A small neatly made man with dark eyes and a swarthy complexion. He was very well dressed in tweeds. He carried a pair of string gloves and was hatless. He looked alert and energetic. He introduced himself as Colonel Snow, Chief Constable.

Finch, as he hurried to meet him, thought that he would have made a good gipsy. He thought, too, that Mr. Philby was related to the Chief Constable after all.

"A bit late, I'm afraid." Colonel Snow spoke, as he moved, energetically. "But Mr. Maule rang me up to say that you'd just left the Hall so I thought I might find you still up. I was dining with the vicar."

"We were going over the case," said Finch. "We hadn't had a chance before, since my sergeant only got down here late this evening."

"So I heard. Well, I'll join you if I may." Finch helped him off with his coat and the colonel preceded him into the sitting room. "You comfortable here? Mrs. Thomas is a melancholy woman, I always think. Sort of perpetual widow. Makes me think suttee isn't such a bad idea after all."

"She has her points," said Finch in his mild voice. "Can I offer you a glass of beer, sir?"

"Thanks. And I'll have some of that excellent-looking loaf. Cheese too, if I may. No butter." He sat down in the chair Slater set for him. "Dining with my cousin—always a bit of an ordeal." The three men settled down at the table. Colonel Snow cut himself a crusty corner from the loaf and helped himself to cheese whilst Slater poured him out a glass of beer. "Now you two carry on—with your supper I mean." He was a companionable man.

"Awkward really, being related to everyone," he remarked. "Suppose I shouldn't have become Chief Constable but I'd too much energy simply to remain retired." His smile was pleasant, lively. "Still, it must have occurred to you that that was why you were here, eh?"

"I understood that it was to preserve good relations between the police and—certain quarters." Finch was quoting the superintendent.

"Certain quarters, my foot," said the colonel energetically. His eyes strayed to the papers lying by Slater's plate. "Mind if I look?"

"We were just getting that lot out of the way—as far as possible."

"Oh?"

"For instance, Mrs. Maule was some time in the sitting room of Glebe Cottage. What was she doing?"

"Not talking to me. That's certain. She rang me up and said 'Ron'—my name's Rodney—'Ron, Miss Chumleigh's been murdered and even Ennis will think I did it.' I said that, in that case, it was a jolly good thing that capital punishment has been abolished. She gave me a few details, which I passed on to Ennis. I told her to wait where she was for the police—and that's all there was to it." The colonel was silent a moment. Then he said with an air of caution, "So you think she was poking about, eh?"

"Would she do that?"

The colonel grinned. "She would. Agnes is a law unto herself." He went back to the list. "You think my cousin, Philby, temperamentally suited to murder? Or, to this murder anyway?" He thought it over. "He's like me. Bad-tempered. Quick-tempered. Would I stick a knife into someone?" He shook his head. "I don't know. Make an awful scandal if I did."

"I doubt if Superintendent Ennis would care for it," Finch agreed.

Colonel Snow was convulsed with laughter at the idea. "He's not going to like what's going on whichever way the chips fall. I see you're inclined to trust Sampson's judgement. Why?"

"He's one of those ruminating types. He knows his village and the results of his thoughts, I imagine, are pretty sound."

"Ennis doesn't think so."

"I fancy Sampson is a bit too independent."

"Ah! Yes—like that, is it?" The colonel put down the sheets of paper. "This is as far as you've got with the case?"

"No. I was just getting to the person I suspect of having committed the murder—Miss Kelvin. Or, if she didn't do the actual killing, then I believe the crime was committed to protect her interests."

"Miss Kelvin, eh?" The black eyes had grown intent. "How d'you make that out? The telegram and all that, eh?"

"Yes—if we looked at it apart from Miss Kelvin's explanations." Finch rose from the table and went to stand, tall, broad-shouldered and solemn, on the hearth rug, his back to the fire. "Miss Kelvin does not want Louise Morton at Tammerton. She sends a telegram in an endeavour to put her off. When this fails she tries to get Mrs. Crane to send the girl back to London. Then

follows the discussion between Isobel Crane, Louise Morton and
Edith Chumleigh, during which Miss Chumleigh appears to have
become surprisingly upset. Shortly after she has left the room
Miss Kelvin rings up and Mrs. Crane tells her what has transpired.

"Miss Kelvin then calls at Glebe Cottage. Stays there about
an hour. Goes back to Warley and sees the Judge, who later, in a
letter to Miss Chumleigh, describes her as being in a distraught
state. He says that she has told him of her fears that he may one
day throw her penniless on the world. Either because he has
grown tired of her or because she may do something that he will
find unforgivable. She told him that Miss Chumleigh shared her
fears. The Judge, much shaken to learn of this, agrees to settle a
sum of money on her, enough to guarantee her independence.
Whereupon, in his own words, she was transported with delight."

It was very quiet for a moment after Finch had ceased
speaking. So quiet that the three men could hear the whisper of
rain against the windowpane and the hiss and fizz as it fell down
the chimney on to the fire.

"It doesn't make sense," the Chief Constable burst out.
"Fears for some hypothetical action in the future? If Miss Kelvin
entertained such silly thoughts, Miss Chumleigh wouldn't. She
was too sensible. Nobody's fool."

"So we're left with the conclusion that what Miss Kelvin
really meant was that she had already done this unforgivable
something and that Miss Chumleigh was willing to keep it from
the Judge for Harry Kelvin's sake. Willing that is, until today.

"Today something happened—was said, perhaps—that made
it impossible for Edith Chumleigh to keep Kathie Kelvin's secret
any longer. She insisted that Kathie should confess, which would
account for that young woman's distraught state of mind. Miss
Chumleigh may even have threatened that if Miss Kelvin didn't
tell the Judge the truth she would do so herself. Oh yes, it hangs
together. It hangs together very well and Miss Kelvin would
have had reason to be desperate. To adopt desperate measures,
for there were only two alternatives before her. The death of
Miss Chumleigh or utter ruin."

"H'm, not a pretty choice."

"It's possible, probable even, that Miss Kelvin would have
asked for a little time in which to screw up her courage to
confess—from what I've heard of her character it would have
been quite in keeping. Miss Kelvin may even have hoped that in
this time of grace she might think of some way out—a way, that
is, short of murder. But time ran out for both of them when the

Judge sat down to write that letter to Miss Chumleigh. The letter that would tell her that Miss Kelvin had not kept her promise—and Miss Chumleigh was no farther from the Judge than the telephone.''

"Hence the alibi of the bath?"

"Yes, she'd make the motions of preparing to take a bath, in some way call attention to herself no doubt. Then she'd lock the bathroom door on the outside and slip out of the house unseen. Would that have been possible?"

"Perfectly easy. Back stairs, side door, plenty of trees."

"And Miss Chumleigh wouldn't have been surprised to see her. Kathie, the irresolute. Kathie, the vacillating. But this time she was Kathie, the determined. As inflexible as Miss Chumleigh herself. It was only afterwards that her heart failed and she was filled with superstitious terror and, by clearing the sitting room of all personal touches, tried to blot Miss Chumleigh from her memory."

Colonel Snow lighted a cigarette. "So it seems that it was beware of Kathie after all."

"I think so—yes."

"And the hypothetical person who might have murdered Miss Chumleigh?"

"Is the man in Miss Kelvin's life."

"As far as I know there isn't one."

Finch shook his head. "I don't believe it. I simply don't believe it."

Colonel Snow shrugged the subject away. "Tell me! In all this where does Miss Morton come in?"

Finch made a rueful face. "It's not her coming in I worry about. It's the possibility of her going out."

The dark-eyed regard sharpened. "You think she's in danger?"

"I think Miss Kelvin has some pretty strong reason for not wanting her about. When I mentioned Miss Morton's name Miss Kelvin practically emitted sparks."

"What does the girl say?"

"Says she can't understand it. That she'd never seen Miss Kelvin before that smashup in Devon. Nor heard of her since the inquest. Yet obviously their lives must have crossed somewhere."

The Chief Constable blew the smoke obliquely from the corner of his lips. "You have set yourself a problem. And with a pretty open field, too."

"Not so open as you might think," Finch answered. Then

he asked, "Did you know Miss Kelvin when she came down here first?"

"No—but from all accounts she was pretty lively. Dancing, riding, tennis. Fascinating too, of course. Why, she even fascinated Cousin Oswald—Philby to you. I know for a fact he offered her marriage after each of her engagements had come to grief." Colonel Snow gave his barking laugh. "He's just about old enough to be her grandfather, and has been married twice before, but that didn't deter him. The Philbys are a pretty virile lot."

"I'm told that when she worked in London she used to occupy her leisure listening to cases in the Old Bailey."

The Chief Constable stared. He burst out laughing. "That's a likely story. Who ever . . . ?" He fell silent, the smile wiped from his face. He sat quite still, regarding Finch from under knitted brows.

"The Old Bailey, eh?" He spoke in quite a changed voice.

Finch nodded. "And Harry Kelvin was a barrister."

An odd little silence fell on the room—a silence in which the three men pursued their own lines of thought, each haunted in some degree by the pale shade of the woman whom Finch had called the battered nymph.

Said Colonel Snow slowly, "If it was a *cause célèbre*, Harry would have been briefed as a junior. He was in the chambers of Mr. Charles Baron, then senior counsel to the Treasury at the Central Criminal Court."

"Miss Kelvin wouldn't have been the chief figure," said Finch, "otherwise people down here would have recognised her and the Judge would certainly have heard of her. No, she must have been a minor character." He shrugged. "Witness, hanger-on, relative of the accused? She must have been implicated in some way. Some mud must have stuck to her skirts—and of a kind that would have made her unacceptable to the Judge as a wife for his son."

"How far back does that take us? Must be ten—no, eleven years since Harry was killed. I imagine we'd be pretty safe in saying that the case must have been heard within a couple of years of that date."

Again a silence fell. Again the fascinating Kathie Kelvin haunted their thoughts, brightening, if in rather a macabre way, the prim little sitting room. Bringing a touch of the exotic to the meal of bread and cheese and beer.

Said Colonel Snow slowly, "Eleven—twelve years ago she

must have been"—he sought for the word—"bewitching. Yes, that's the word." When he spoke again the spell was still on him. "That broken engagement. Jason must have found out. He must know her secret."

Said Finch, "He'll not tell it. I fancy there's still some tie between them."

"I doubt if he'd tell anyway. Jason, like the devil, is a proud spirit. He's also a romantic. I'd have said there was no vice in him but infatuation makes people do strange things. And Kathie Kelvin's still a fascinating woman. After all, what age is she? Only thirty-three—thirty-four?"

"Had Jason Maule any money on him of his own when he disappeared?"

"I shouldn't think so. His father left him some but he must have pretty well got through that by then and I know for a fact he never wrote to ask his uncle for any."

Finch nodded. "An interesting picture, that. An extravagant, pampered young man suddenly thrown on the world to sink or swim. One wonders how he made out."

"Had a hard time by the look of him," the Chief Constable conceded. He rose to his feet. "I'd better be getting off to bed. And I imagine you'll be doing the same. You look like having a busy day in front of you."

"Mostly at the telephone, I'm afraid. I wish I could get up to London and make the enquiries myself."

"Yes, hard to wait when the scent is fresh," the colonel agreed.

When Finch was helping him into his coat he remarked, "Just struck me. You spotted the unlikelihood of Miss Kelvin worrying herself sick about some possible sin in the future. Don't you think the Judge's mind will work in the same way as yours? After all, he's an astute old gentleman. He's only got to think it over."

"I know." Finch's face was troubled. "That's what frightens me. If he begins thinking on those lines—if he tackles his adopted daughter on the subject—well, she'll stall him off as she did Miss Chumleigh. And we know what happened to her."

The Chief Constable looked uneasy. "But, hang it all, man, she owes everything to the Judge." And then, explosively, "Damn it, he loves her."

"So perhaps, did Miss Chumleigh—but it didn't save her."

"No, that is so." The Chief Constable stood still a moment, thinking. "Tell you what, I mean to speak to James Maule about having a plain-clothes man in the house. I'll speak to the Judge as well. Persuade him that he must have police protection"—he grinned briefly—"for Miss Kelvin's sake, of course. Good night, Inspector. Good night, Sergeant."

He tore open the front door before Finch had time to do it for him. He sprang into his car and roared away into the night.

Chapter 13

Septimus Finch awoke to find another stormy day. As he dressed he was conscious of a sense of foreboding that would have done credit to Agnes Maule herself. This worried him. He knew that it could not all be attributed to his Cornish blood. Nine tenths was the result of experience; of long and varied years spent in the police force.

He went downstairs to put through a call to Scotland Yard. The bulk of the enquiries must be made there. Records to be searched to find out just what had been the attraction exercised on Kathie by the Old Bailey. A study to be made of all cases in which Harry Kelvin had acted.

The firm of Spooner & Silk were to be approached to find out which of their clients had appeared at the Old Bailey in the two years preceeding Harry Kelvin's death. The textile firm was to be identified in an endeavour to discover where Kathie had lived when she had been working for them. Their staff was to be questioned to find out who remembered her and what they recalled.

Criminal Records Office was to be asked if her fingerprints were among its files. Somerset House was to be visited to look at her birth certificate. That, at least, must have an address. Then Finch wanted to be certain that she was Kathie Lynch and not Mrs. Someone-or-Other. There was still the odd fact—odd to Finch—that Kathie appeared to be still single. Interpol was to be asked to get in touch with the retired Mr. Reginald Spooner, his address to be got from his old firm. Then for good measure Finch asked that the War Office should be asked whether Jason Maule had enlisted in the army.

"And the only thing we can do," Finch complained, "is to find a photograph of Miss Kelvin in the local paper and have it blown up to a reasonable size—just in case we should need it."

"And even that," Slater pointed out, "will be done by the Lockbridge police."

Finch sighed heavily. "Better have breakfast."

And there the Chief Constable found them. "Don't let me interrupt you," he said, faintly sarcastic. "You two carry on." Plainly his opinion of the Scotland Yard men had fallen. Ostentatiously he consulted his wrist watch. "Ten minutes past ten."

"What's the news, sir?" Finch asked, ignoring his manner, about which, to be truthful, he cared little.

A shadow fell on the swarthy face. "I've just come from Warley. The Judge refuses any sort of police protection."

"On what grounds?" Finch recalled the sense of foreboding with which he had awakened. Here we go, he thought dolefully.

"He said he'd make his own arrangements if necessary— and he looked pretty ghastly when he said it. I tell you he's got me worried."

"Me too," Finch agreed. "He's supposed to be playing chess with the vicar tonight. I think I'll go round and see if the game's off."

"Of course it's off," was the short answer, "Why else d'you think the Judge refused any form of protection for Miss Kelvin?"

Finch remained unconvinced. "I still think I'd better ask the vicar. You'll have to stay by the telephone, Archie. I shan't be long."

"I'll run you round," said Colonel Snow. "My car is outside."

The church dated back to the twelfth century. Outside it was very plain. Inside it was full of colour, of old stained glass, of handsome monuments. A side chapel was dedicated to the Maules, and they had spread themselves throughout the church, in plaques, inscribed flagstones, and monuments.

The vicar was there, in the aisle of the chapel, lying flat on his back.

For one dreadful moment Finch thought that he was dead— murdered. But he had heard the detective's approaching footsteps. He rose to his feet with no sign of embarrassment and with remarkable agility, for a man of his venerable appearance.

"I was considering ways of getting to the roof," he explained, resting an elbow familiarly on the chest of a recumbent Maule and gazing upwards.

"In the body or the spirit?" Finch asked, interested.

"The body. The deathwatch beetle is destroying the fabric of the building and I have a plan for dealing with it if only I can get up there."

"You have a fine church," Finch commented politely.

"A fine number of monuments," Mr. Philby corrected. "Originally the Maule family were merchants in Bristol. This one," he took a large white handkerchief from a pocket under his cassock and dusted the effigy's face. "This one was the first member to settle in Tammerton. He built the Hall and this chapel. The family, like many another, rose to affluence under the Tudors. It was a time of expansion. When Elizabeth came to the throne the family was well established."

Mr. Philby blew his nose, secreted his handkerchief under his cassock, and said in quite a different tone, "And now what can I do for you? You didn't come to hear me talking about Tammerton Church, I feel sure."

"Not exactly." Finch put his question, thanked Mr. Philby, and hurried away with the answer.

An old man was obliterating something from the board in the churchyard. Finch guessed what it was. He was right. The information that confessions could be heard by appointment was being painted over.

"And I only painted it yesterday afternoon," the old man complained. Adding with a slightly furtive glance in the direction of the church, "Some folk don't seem to know their own minds."

"Well, man, what is the answer?" The Chief Constable was impatient.

"The game's on," said Finch shortly. He added, climbing into the car, "The Judge telephoned Mr. Philby to that effect half an hour ago."

'And Miss Kelvin?"

"He didn't say—but she's not expected at the vicarage."

"Damn and blast!" said the Chief Constable violently. He turned the car and shot back in the direction of Hill View. "I don't like it."

"Nor do I. Why is he going? To show his trust in his adopted daughter? To set a trap?"

"Tell you what. I'll have someone watching the house. Get the fella sent out from Lockbridge without telling the Judge. Give him a walkie-talkie apparatus so he can keep in touch."

"Have two men," Finch amended. "One back and one in front." To which Colonel Snow agreed, adding that James Maule had had no objection to having a plain-clothes man at the Hall, so why the hell did the Judge want to be so b——— awkward?

At Hill View the first information had come through. Kathie

Kelvin's fingerprints were not with C.R.O. There was no record
at Somerset House of any marriage. Her parents still lived at the
address in Islington shown on her birth certificate. A plain-
clothes man was on his way to interview them.

Colonel Snow was interested in this. He was interested as
well in the enquiries put in hand by the inspector. His opinion of
him rose again. He said that, if he wouldn't be in the way, he'd
wait for a bit. He put through his own call to Lockbridge Police
Station.

Finch sent Slater off to interview the Templetons. There
followed a period of silence. Finch resumed his study of the
books and papers taken from Glebe Cottage. He found it hard to
concentrate. The haggard, beautifully boned face of the woman
in whose past so much interest was being taken seemed to come
between him and the pages. A single sentence persisted in the
detective's mind.

How say you, Katherine Kelvin, are you guilty or not guilty?

None of Miss Chumleigh's papers yielded any surprises.
Her affairs were in perfect order. Her bank statements showed no
sudden change of fortune, no extremes of wealth or poverty. A
copy of her will showed her modest fortune to have been left to a
cousin living in Scotland.

Finch turned to the diaries. The first two yielded nothing of
interest. There were various small loans made to Miss Kelvin.
They had all been repaid. Sometimes Miss Chumleigh had had to
remind the borrower. Sometimes not.

In the diary for April 1962, Finch came across a more
interesting entry.

> *Kathie's quarterly allowance only just paid into
> the bank yet she wants to borrow £50. She says she
> needs the money for back bills but seems unable to
> produce any. She looks ghastly. Quite feverish. Have
> made her a present of the money but remain v. worried.*

There was no further mention of this sum, or of any other of
commensurate size.

Finch looked across to where the Chief Constable sat, neat,
alert, and smoking a pipe. "Have you any idea what the Judge
allows Miss Kelvin for her dress allowance?"

Colonel Snow raised surprised eyebrows. "None at all. But
she runs a car, dresses well, goes away. It must be pretty
generous."

Finch nodded. He passed the diary across to the colonel. "Two and a half years ago Miss Kelvin was in need of money. The entry is for April 3rd, 1962."

The sloe-dark eyes narrowed. "Blackmail?"

"As far as Miss Chumleigh was concerned, Kathie Kelvin seems to have wanted money at that particular time and no other. But, of course, we don't know who else she may have borrowed from."

"Anyone at the Hall might have obliged. Mrs. Crane, James Maule—he's a very kind man. Jason, if he were anywhere about at the time. Agnes?" Colonel Snow shook his head. "I don't think Kathie would have tried her."

At this point Scotland Yard came through with the results of the interview with Kathie's parents. The information was largely negative. The Lynches were a respectable but unsuccessful family. The father worked for a local greengrocer. His wife went out cleaning. Kathie had been the third child of seven. The bright one of the family. She had left home at sixteen and they had gradually lost touch with her.

The firm for which she had worked had been quickly identified. It had been a small business, specialising in fine handprinted materials, and owned by two brothers. Unfortunately eight years previously it had been bought up by a much larger concern who had closed it down. The staff had been scattered. One brother had since died. The other lived in Wembley. Enquiries were proceeding.

No connection had been traced, so far, between Kathie Kelvin and any case tried at the Old Bailey.

Interpol had not had much luck with Mr. Spooner. He was out sailing in a small yacht. The French police were awaiting his return. Mr. Silk had been contacted. An elderly man, he had not gone to his office that day but was now on his way to the Yard to see what help he could give.

Reluctantly the Chief Constable took his leave. Shortly afterwards Slater came back from his visit to Warley.

He had been fortunate in finding Mrs. Templeton alone in the kitchen. The woman had overwhelmed him with the tale of her fears. Prompted by Slater, she had agreed that it would be easy enough for Miss Kathie to be murdered, since she had a suite of rooms cut off from the rest of the household.

Slater had mentioned the case of Smith, the man who had drowned a succession of "brides" in their baths. This had brought fresh fears to the timorous woman. It had also brought the information that Kathie had baths at all times of the day. That she had had one about three o'clock on the previous afternoon. Mrs. Templeton knew this because Kathie had called her up to the bathroom to complain about some nail polish spilled on the floor, "though how it got there unless Miss Kathie spilt it I don't know." Yes, Mrs. Templeton had agreed, the bath had been drawn. Full of very hot water and the bathroom full of steam. Miss Kathie liked it like that. Yes, she had been all ready to get into the bath. Bathwrap and cap on, no shoes or stockings. The woman had not seen her again until she had taken tea into the study at four o'clock.

The afternoon looked like being as disappointing as the morning had been. Such reports as had come in were inconclusive. Finch suffered from an illogical and unjustifiable belief that, if only he were in London, he would have unearthed Kathie Kelvin's reason for haunting the Old Bailey.

It was in vain that Slater pointed out that less than six hours had elapsed since the enquiries were first instigated. Finch remained unconvinced.

Time dragged on. Finch visited the Hall, only to find that no one there seemed to have known of any possible need for money on Kathie's part. James Maule seemed distressed at the idea that she might have been in financial difficulties. Plainly he would have been an easy touch. Isobel Crane, like many another wealthy woman, made it a rule not to lend money. Almost, Finch could see, trembling on her firm lips the old saw about "neither a borrower nor a lender be." She was a good woman, but she had had to protect herself. Jason Maule, arrogant and indolent, had suggested briefly that Finch mind his own business. Agnes Maule would have helped him if she could but she had known nothing of any financial crisis in Kathie's life.

Finch had been driven back to Hill View, making a detour to pass Warley.

It was a charming house built in the Georgian period. It was approached by a long straight path bordered by herbaceous beds. Behind it was an orchard. Behind this again the woods rose steeply. To one side a ragged copse tossed its thinning head in the November wind.

No one was about. A thin trail of smoke rose from one of the chimney stacks and a curtain flapped from an open upstairs window.

"A pretty place," Slater commented. "Easy enough to keep a watch here."

Finch agreed. Yet even as he did so he became aware of the crystallisation of his own sense of foreboding. It was as if he had by chance come upon its source. Here in this charming house with its gleaming white paint, its graceful urns and rosy bricks— here was to be told a story of disaster.

At 3.44 P.M. the Lockbridge police telephoned. Roger Crane was at the station wishing to make a statement. They had told him that the Scotland Yard Inspector could be seen at Hill View but he had said that he wanted his visit to be kept private, and that he would either say what he had to say there and then or he would return later and tell it to the inspector.

Finch agreed to see him at Lockbridge at five o'clock.

"Obviously he's got some information to give us about the Maule family," Finch remarked to Slater with satisfaction. "Equally obviously he doesn't want his wife to know."

He gave orders for any telephone calls to be put through to Lockbridge. Then he sent once more for the police car.

He did not like being driven but at least it gave him the chance to look about him. It was because of this that he caught a fleeting glimpse of a white sports car drawn up in one of the overgrown rides of Tammerton Woods.

He stopped the car. "You hop out too, Archie. Whilst I have a word with Miss Kelvin you make your way round to where you can watch her car without being seen. If she's expecting someone I want to know who it is. When I get to Lockbridge I'll send the car back for you. If you're not waiting it'll return to Lockbridge and I'll meet you later at Hill View."

The white M.G. had been driven over briars and between overgrown bushes into a small clearing. Kathie was sitting at the wheel. She was wearing a short ocelot fur coat over a tweed suit. She was hatless and her ginger hair flared wildly. A cigarette hung on her lower lip giving her a faintly raffish air.

She was not doing anything in particular. There was no particular expression on her face. She was just sitting there, her hands resting on the steering wheel, her eyes staring straight in front of her.

She heard Finch's approaching footsteps only when he was close to her. Even so she did not turn as if she were expecting anyone. "Were you looking for me?" she asked. "Or just passing this way?"

"I happened to see your car from the road."

For a moment she looked disconcerted. Plainly she had thought herself hidden from view. She recovered quickly. "I wanted to be alone," she said. "Oh, I don't mean that I mind your coming but that was why I drove up here."

"It's certainly quiet," Finch agreed, resting his arms comfortably on the door of the car.

"It used to be such a nice walk. Harry and I often came this way. There's a pool farther on—but, of course, it was sunny then." In spite of the fur coat she shivered, as if the comparison between the blustering November day and the sun of long ago had chilled her.

When Finch did not speak she said, "I suppose you think I schemed for all this." Her gesture took in the car and her own immaculate appearance. "But I didn't. I didn't even want it. But you get used to luxury. Then you find yourself clinging to it because it's all you've got." Her voice was light, mocking. For all that Finch recognised that it came from some deep well of discontent. "You look down the years and they're empty. Meanwhile you're fed and clothed, scented and pampered. A dull perseverance keeps you going. And the times when you look back and say 'God! How did I come to this?' get fewer and fewer.

"Oh, I admit I had no intention of allowing myself to be charged with manslaughter. And I didn't care a hoot what happened to Louise Morton. But above and beyond everything else was my determination to get away from the Judge. I'd killed his son, the honourable, the truthful, the to-be-trusted Harry. And he was, too. All those things and more. Only it so happened that that day I'd nagged him into letting me drive the Bentley. Well, not exactly nagged, but the Judge wouldn't have understood."

She was silent a moment. Her amber eyes had narrowed and held a strange inward-looking brightness. A slight sly smile twisted her lips and gradually expanded. It was as if with the words she was recalling with ever-increasing clarity some slightly disreputable but amusing experience.

The memory went. She was still in the past but now it was a different, difficult, and confusing time. "After the inquest I went back to my job. I tried to forget and to avoid the Judge. But it was no good. He kept inviting me to go and see him. And when I went—always against my will and feeling like hell—I'd realise his loneliness. His dependence on me as a link with his dead son. And that was a laugh because, even before the accident, I'd known that it was no good. That I couldn't go through with it."

"Why not?"

She shrugged, tossed away her cigarette, and said with brief finality, "We were too dissimilar. It wouldn't have worked." She turned her head and looked at him. "I have to get back to Warley. Can I give you a lift?"

"Thanks, no. I have a car." Still Finch made no attempt to move. He said, "You were in the habit of borrowing money from Miss Chumleigh?"

"Yes, small sums. I was never much good at managing and she didn't mind." Kathie's voice was light but Finch noticed the sudden tightening of her grip on the wheel.

"In April, 1962, you borrowed fifty pounds."

There was a silence for a moment. Then, without looking at Finch, she asked a breathless question, "How d'you know?"

"Miss Chumleigh entered it in her diary."

"What did she say?" Still Kathie didn't look at him but her face had stiffened in a curious way.

"That she wished she knew what you wanted it for."

"But she did know. I told her. It was for bills. Back bills."

"She said you couldn't produce any."

"How absurd. Of course I could have produced them." She laughed in a brittle way. "I can always produce unpaid bills—but usually the shops will wait."

"Can you prove that that was how the money went?"

"Why should I?"

"You may have to. And there's another point raised by Miss Chumleigh in her diary. Your quarterly dress allowance. She wondered what had happened to that—and so do I. I ask myself was the fifty pounds the only money you raised? And where did it all go? Why did you need money so desperately two and a half years ago?"

"I didn't need money *desperately*. Why should I? I can always get extra money from the Judge . . ." Her voice, which had begun with such assurance, trailed away as if, in the end, she could no longer convince even herself.

"April, 1962." Finch shifted into a more comfortable position, leaning against the car. His voice was very soft and yet deliberate. "When it comes to making enquiries that's not so long ago. Come to that, it's not so long ago you were haunting the Old Bailey. And that, too, is a date that interests me."

If Finch had had any doubt of the importance of this period in Kathie's past, it had gone now. Kathie's face had turned a ghastly white. Against its pallor the powdering of freckles stood out like blisters. She seemed to have difficulty in speaking, even in breathing. It was as if she were crumbling inwardly. Dying before his eyes.

"You beast!" she whispered. "You spying lousy bastard!" And then, "Get away from my car." She leaned forward suddenly and turned the ignition key. The engine sprang to life. She swung the car round and for a moment he thought that she was going to run him down. If this had been in her mind she must have decided against it. The car swung away from his direction. Then it was gone, bumping and swaying over the rough ground until it regained the road.

Archie Slater came out from among the trees. "You seem to have touched the right spot there, sir," he remarked cheerfully.

Finch nodded. "The right spot but perhaps not the right moment." His voice was troubled. "Perhaps not even the right person with whom to have broached that subject."

Slater looked at him sharply. "How d'you mean, sir?"

Finch said slowly, "Ever since I've been here—and I admit that it hasn't been long—I've had a vague disquieting impression of a shadowy someone standing behind Kathie. Someone clever and ruthless. Someone in whose hands that woman is no more than a puppet. If now she goes to him. Tells him . . ."

Finch's voice, like that of Kathie earlier on, trailed into silence. He seemed to see again the lonely house, the rosy bricks and white paint. The thin trail of smoke and a curtain flapping in the wind.

Roger Crane was already at the police station when Finch and Slater arrived. He sat squarely in his chair, an embarrassed but stubborn look on his bearded face.

Finch apologised for being late. "Something cropped up to delay us," he explained vaguely. He sat down behind the desk occupied as a rule by Superintendent Ennis. "Now, what was it you wanted to make a statement about?"

The deep-set eyes met his. "It's about something my wife told me—but I don't want her to know I've repeated it."

"I can't promise to keep the information you give me secret if it comes to an arrest."

"Fair enough." The dark head nodded. "That's what I want. An arrest—and a conviction. My wife doesn't realise what it's going to be like if no one is charged with that old lady's murder. The suspicion, the gossip that will never entirely die down. There are a lot of jokes about knowing the facts of life but these are the sort of facts people like my wife don't know about. And I aim to keep it that way."

His brow darkened. "I remember a couple coming to live near us. A decent respectable middle-aged couple. Their son had got into trouble, bad trouble, with the police, and they'd moved to get away from the scandal. But it wasn't any good. People soon got to know. The talk and the curiosity started up again. They were back where they'd started." Roger was scowling into the distance. His voice was hard. "The woman couldn't take it any more. She was found hanging one day from a hook in a shed in the garden. I've never forgotten it."

Finch looked at him curiously. He would not have given him credit for so much feeling. "Where was this?"

"Bideford, in Devon, where I was brought up. Both my parents were killed in an air raid and I lived there with my granddad. I'd always wanted to emigrate but, of course, I couldn't go as long as the old boy was alive." Roger caught his breath in a sigh. "Alaska—the Yukon—a man's life. It was just as I'd hoped. And then, within less than eighteen months, there I was, penniless, weak as a kitten. I came back to England thinking myself the unluckiest fellow alive." He smiled briefly. "But I wasn't. I reckon that plane crash was the best thing that ever happened to me."

Finch nodded. "What was it you were going to tell me?"

Roger smiled again, a wider grin this time. "Sorry, I guess I got carried away." His smile was replaced by a rather grim look. "I've got two things to tell you. You'll have to decide their importance for yourself. Now, I've nothing against Jason Maule," he explained. "I'd never even seen him until about ten days ago. Of course, I'd heard of him—and I hadn't much cared for what I'd heard—but when I met him he seemed a nice enough bloke. I'd imagined a sort of sissy, soft and spoilt. But he's not like that." The deep-set eyes sought Finch's. "Believe you me he's not like that at all."

Roger went on to repeat part of the conversation that had taken place over the dining table on the evening of Louise Morton's arrival. That part that dealt with Miss Chumleigh's belief that she had seen Jason Maule before somewhere.

"My wife didn't mean any harm but she—well, she's always been a bit jealous of Jason." Roger smiled indulgently. "All that charm and women falling over themselves to please him. So when, next day, Miss Chumleigh described his behaviour as silly and juvenile, Isobel couldn't resist pulling his leg about it. Well, he didn't take it in good part. White with anger, Isobel said. And after he'd owned up to having called at Glebe Cottage, and her knowing what a temper he'd always had she was terrified he might have done in the old lady.''

"And he didn't give any indication to your wife as to where the mysterious meeting might have taken place?"

"None at all. Miss Chumleigh, as I said, thought it was abroad somewhere. But before that there was a queer bit of conversation." Roger's tone was dogged. He repeated what Isobel had remembered about James Maule's teasing words. "Miss Chumleigh wouldn't have the Chinese pirates. Said she'd never been to the Far East—so that's somewhere those two couldn't have met."

"Leaving us with the Corsican bandits and the London bank robbers," said Finch slowly.

"Maybe there's nothing in it. But I thought I'd tell you."

"And the second thing?"

"I don't know where this comes in either." Roger hesitated, then added in a rush of words, "The truth is that both Jason and Kathie Kelvin made a queer impression on my wife—almost as if there was still some tie between them. She had the feeling that they were very much aware of each other." He laughed, a little embarrassed. "Those are my wife's words, not mine, Inspector. Posh words—but she was right. They weren't supposed to have met for seven years but later that evening Kathie let out that they'd been seeing each other. Isobel got the idea that Jason was still in love with her. Or, at least, still her lover."

"I can see that there might be a difference," said Finch dryly. "But tell me, what's to prevent their getting married?"

Roger's eyes dropped. He looked undecided. Then he said awkwardly, "It seems the Judge didn't approve of the idea. He thought that Jason was unreliable."

"How strongly did he hold that opinion?"

Roger shrugged. "I don't know. But seven years ago it was strong enough for him to say Kathie would get none of his money if she married Jason." He rose to his feet. "Now I must be off. Got to attend to a business matter. The Lockbridge Council want to drain the small swimming pool and turn it into a tenpin bowling alley. My wife is opposed to the idea. Wants to know where are the kids going to learn to swim. There's a lot of money in these bowling alleys but I expect Isobel will get her way.''

He agreed to return the following day to sign the statement

he had made. He wrung Finch's hand, grinned at his sergeant, and took himself off with an air of relief as if a disagreeable business had been successfully accomplished.

"So it looks as if we've found the man in Miss Kelvin's life," Slater commented, closing his notebook.

Finch nodded. "That's another thing the Yard can do. Find out where Jason Maule was two and a half years ago. Meanwhile we'll try and discover just how much money Miss Kelvin raised at that time."

"I thought we did know," Slater commented, following his superior from the room. "The fifty pounds Miss Chumleigh gave her. No one else seems to have lent her any."

But Finch was not attending. He was in the charge room asking about money-lenders, adding, "I don't suppose that Miss Kelvin would have dared pawn her jewellery but I'd be glad if you'd make enquiries locally. It would have been round about April, 1962."

Superintendent Ennis came in at this point. When he saw Finch he looked as if he wished he had not done so. He asked how the case was getting on. He did not sound as if he wanted to know. Finch told him of the enquiries he had just set in motion.

A sergeant, who had been writing busily at a desk in the corner and had stopped to listen to the Scotland Yard man, got up and came forward. He was a dark, sharp-looking young man.

"Miss Kelvin may not have pawned her jewellery round about then, sir—but she did lose it."

Finch's eyes narrowed. "How was that?"

"She was on her way to London—I can't remember the exact date, off hand, but it was a bit earlier than April. Sometime in late February I think. She had her jewel case with her when she left home. When she reached her hotel in London it had gone."

"The jewellery was insured, of course?"

"Yes, sir. The insurance company paid up all right—seven hundred pounds."

Finch gave a soundless whistle. "Now, what could she have wanted a sum like that for?"

"Obviously they had no reason to think the loss anything but genuine," Ennis protested stiffly.

"And no proof that it was," the sergeant rejoined cheerfully.

"Jewellery about which a false claim has been made has a distressing way of turning up again," Finch commented.

"This didn't, sir. Not a single piece was ever found."

"Which suggests to me that the loss was genuine after all."
Ennis had the appearance of a man clinging to an untenable
position.

"It suggests to me that the jewellery was either broken up
or smuggled abroad," Finch declared roundly. "That in turn
suggests that it must have been passed to a fence. And how
would a respectable young woman know where to find such a
person?"

"Looks as if she wasn't as respectable as all that," said
Slater, grinning. "Or perhaps she just had a pretty dubious set of
friends."

"But Miss Kelvin wouldn't have had the insurance money,"
Ennis protested. "Not just to do as she liked with. Mr. Justice
Kelvin would have expected her to replace the lost pieces."

Finch nodded. "Miss Kelvin will have replaced them all
right—but with what? That's the question."

Chapter 14

The early evening darkness of November had fallen with the completeness peculiar to the empty countryside. A little group of men were gathered together at Tammerton Police Station as represented by P.C. Sampson's cottage—Septimus Finch and his sergeant, the Chief Constable, and Superintendent Ennis.

The room was warm; a bright fire burned in the old fashioned grate. Mrs. Sampson, as stout and homely a figure as her husband, dispensed tea from a large brown enamel teapot. It was all very cosy. Archie Slater had to suppress a tendency to giggle.

In spite of its air of informality the room was a centre of activity. The plain-clothes man at Tammerton Hall kept in touch by telephone. The two men watching at Warley reported regularly. Scotland Yard telephoned such information as they had been able to gather, out of which there began to emerge a picture of the young Kathie Lynch.

Kathie, the good-time girl. Fond of parties, of luxurious entertainment and expensive presents. She had made no secret of the fact that women bored her. She had had many enemies and few friends. Several men had loved her. She had encouraged them, used them, and left them the poorer for the experience.

"Not a girl you could take into a Lyons," one man had said. "I don't know what her clothes cost," said a woman, "nor how she got the money to pay for them—but I could guess."

The sales manager of the firm would have married her. A good match, surely, for a girl brought up in the slums, but she had turned him down. She'd allowed him to spend his money on her. But marry him? Not she. Led him on and then left him flat.

With a good job in another firm—married for the last six years to a pleasant handsome young woman—he still remembered Kathie with a sense of bitter injury and equally bitter loss.

"Odd thing," Finch murmured. "It's always the same story. The lady's not for marrying."

"La Belle Dame Sans Merci," Colonel Snow suggested.

"Whenever I've seen her it's been her unhappiness that has struck me." As Finch spoke he became aware of what it had been about the woman waiting in the woods that had so disturbed him. It had been her profound and utter loneliness. The sense that now she hoped for nothing, expected nothing. She was past grief, past despair. But why? The hard reckless face of Jason Maule rose in his mind's eye as if it were some sort of answer.

Superintendent Ennis stirred restlessly. His sense of the fitness of things was outraged. P.C. Sampson, in the superintendent's opinion an example of the lowest form of life in the constabulary, and his wife, seemed to look on themselves as hosts. More extraordinary still, Colonel Snow seemed to accept them as such.

"What exactly are we waiting for?" he asked impatiently.

Finch's small voice emerged from the depths of an armchair. "I don't know about you. I'm waiting for bad news."

Ennis stared. "What kind of bad news?"

A look of sadness spread over Finch's bland face. "I wish I knew," he said softly. And then, "I wish I knew."

"The rain has stopped," the Chief Constable commented as if it were a matter of congratulation.

"If only the wind would go down," said Finch.

"The wind doesn't make things happen," snapped Ennis.

"No," said Finch sadly, "but it can drown the sound of its happening."

At a quarter to seven Scotland Yard came through with more information. It had come from the late owner of the textile business, an old gentleman living in a flat in Chelsea. He remembered Kathie Lynch quite well. Remembered seeing her one evening dining at the Dorchester and not looking a bit out of place. She had had some man with her. A young man. Well dressed too. No, after all this time he couldn't remember what he looked like. He had concluded that Miss Lynch must have a rich protector. She had been an extremely clever designer, original, energetic, and dependable. Her private life had been none of his business.

He knew of nothing to connect her with the Old Bailey. He felt certain that she must have had more entertaining things to do than pass her time in such a dreary place—unless, of course, she had been compelled to do so.

"But she wasn't compelled," said Finch. "We know that

now. It begins to look as if she were there only because she was this man's mistress. That's why there's no official record linking her with the trial."

"But the man?" the Chief Constable demanded. "What was he tried for?"

Finch shrugged. "Something unsavoury, no doubt. A drug ring—living on immoral earnings."

"No wonder Kathie wanted to keep it from the Judge."

Finch looked at his watch. "If only he'd leave home we could get on with things. Miss Kelvin won't talk in front of him."

"Will she talk at all?" Colonel Snow asked dubiously.

"I think so"—Finch laughed shortly—"and then we may find that the Old Bailey has nothing whatever to do with the events of the past few days."

"You'll just have been wasting your time," said Ennis nastily.

"Not altogether. Haven't you ever noticed how people are drawn to the same types over and over? A woman will marry a waster. Get rid of him—and marry another. Kathie Kelvin, it seems, has a yen for bad men. She may have found one right here in the seemingly respectable circle of the Judge's friends." Finch added slowly, "It's that thought that makes me a bit anxious for her safety."

"My men have drawn in close enough to cover both the front and the back," said Colonel Snow sharply. "No one can get in whilst those two are on guard."

Finch nodded. This was true enough—so what could go wrong? Yet he could not help recalling the impression of power, of hidden violence, that had emanated from someone in the yellow drawing room on the previous evening. He could almost feel the strength of that mind's repudiation of any warning or caution.

Finch tried to take comfort from those two watchers whose calm unemotional voices broke in at irregular intervals.

At twenty minutes past seven the watcher stationed at the front of the house reported that the manservant had brought round the car— Mr. Justice Kelvin had come out of the house— He had stepped into the back of the car— Was being driven away in the direction of the village, or Lockbridge.

"So the chess game *is* on," said Colonel Snow under his breath.

"We must give him ten minutes," Finch muttered consulting his wrist watch.

Before the time was up the same man was reporting back. The car had returned— Miss Kelvin, wrapped in a dark cloak, had come out to speak to the driver— They had both gone into the house— Nothing more was happening— Yes, Templeton had come out with his wife— She was carrying a suitcase and appeared to be in tears— She was climbing into the back of the car— Miss Kelvin was standing at the open front door— Templeton had climbed into the driver's seat— He had slammed the door— The car was moving off in the same direction as before— Miss Kelvin had gone into the house— She had shut the front door.

"So Miss Kelvin is alone now in the house," Ennis commented.

The words brought a fresh tension into the room. A picture that, all at once, seemed disquieting, even frightening.

Said Finch abruptly, "Those two men—they must keep on the alert. Report back every five minutes."

The man on watch at the front reported that all was quiet. The one at the back made the same report. Then: "Hold on, sir. Someone is coming. It's the Judge coming through the trees." Then followed a pause. "Sorry, sir. Couldn't speak before. He passed quite close to me— Now he's letting himself in by the side gate— Can't see him now— Yes, he's at the side door. He's got a torch and is using it to see the keyhole— I think he must have gone into the house. It's so damned dark."

"What's Horace Kelvin playing at?" the Chief Constable muttered. "I thought at first that he was going to have it out with Miss Kelvin. Now it begins to look as if she isn't to know he's in the house."

Finch said slowly, "Is it because he's expecting a visitor? Better find out if any of the men of the family are at the Hall."

"They should be," said Colonel Snow. "The Maules dine at eight-fifteen."

But they were not in the house. Roger Crane had not yet returned from Lockbridge. Jason Maule was not to be found, although no one seemed to know when he had gone out. James Maule—and here a faint note of amusement had sounded in the plain-clothes man's voice—had gone to call on the Chief Constable at his private residence.

"And a fat lot of good that would have done him, even if I had been in," Colonel Snow grunted.

Finch looked at his wrist watch. "Eleven minutes gone."

Ennis stared uncomprehendingly. "Gone where?"

"Gone since we last heard from Warley. Eleven—no—twelve minutes."

Said the Chief Constable, "Damn it! Why don't they call?"

"Why not indeed?" Finch was on his feet, making for the door.

"But there were two of them," the Chief Constable protested.

"There *were* two," said Finch, on whom had fallen a sense of urgency, almost of terror. For it seemed to him that it was this towards which the whole day had been moving. This moment when Warley was empty except for a frail old man and a woman whose past seemed about to catch up with her.

How say you, Kathie Kelvin, are you guilty or not guilty?

He flung himself into the red sports car. The Chief Constable sprang in at the other side. The car shot away like a bullet, leaving the others to follow in the police saloon. Only a plain-clothes constable was left at the police station to deal with any further incoming telephone calls.

The red sports car came to the house without headlights. The two men sprang out, and stood waiting, staring about them.

There was a moon now and for the moment it was clear of cloud. They could see across the garden, remote and mysterious in its wan light. See the filigree pattern of shadow cast by trees which, farther back, formed a single band of darkness. Against this darkness Finch fancied that, for an instant, he saw a moving figure. If so it had gone now.

Apart from this there was no sign of human life. There was nothing but the sound of the wind and the crash and clatter of branches overhead. They turned to look at the house and their hearts sank. From attic and cellar not a light showed.

"But the Judge and his daughter are there," Colonel Snow muttered. He set off up the garden path.

The other car drew up. Its occupants sprang out. Finch paused to send the driver and Sampson on round the house in case anyone should attempt to break out by the side or back door. Then he and Slater hurried after the Chief Constable.

Superintendent Ennis, who was not without courage, went off to search for his two men.

Colonel Snow tried the front door, turning the handle gently. To his dismay the door opened—opened on silence and darkness. He stepped over the threshold, feeling for the electric light switch. Behind him Finch closed the door.

The colonel expelled his breath in a long sigh of relief. There was the hall just as he knew it. The warmth, the handsome Regency furniture, the cabinets full of china. Nothing was displaced. Nothing broken.

And then the silence caught at him again. The unnatural, all-pervading silence. A silence that was quite apart and unaffected by the noise of the wind.

Gradually another sound impinged on his hearing. That of the grandfather clock. Slowly, sedately, it ticked on in the silent house. A reminder of minutes lost. Of men who perhaps had delayed their arrival too late.

"Blast that clock!" Colonel Snow cried angrily. And then, "Horace! Kathie! Horace, old chap!" He heard his voice oddly thin and echoing, as if it called in a deserted house.

Finch said quietly, "You take that side of the hall, I'll take this." He threw open the door nearest to him, switching on the light. Drawing room, study—both empty and undisturbed.

Colonel Snow joined him. "There's no one here," he said. Sweat had broken out in great beads on his forehead.

Finch paused, his speculative gaze travelling up the wide shallow staircase to the darkness beyond. But what he said was, "Where is the side door your man mentioned?"

Colonel Snow's glance sharpened. "This way." He pushed open a door and switched on the light. He was conscious of an obscure feeling of comfort that the house was coming to life beneath his hands. He turned a corner and came to an abrupt halt. An involuntary cry was forced from his throat.

Mr. Justice Kelvin lay face upwards in the passage. His eyes stared sightlessly, his head lay at an unnatural angle. A sporting gun lay on the ground beside him.

Finch bent down to examine him. "Dead," he said briefly, straightening up. "Someone hit him hard on the jaw. His bones were brittle and the blow broke his neck." His eyes went past the body to where an open doorway gaped black. He switched on the light.

It was a storeroom of sorts. A room piled high with boxes and trunks and unwanted pieces of furniture. From these last the Judge had selected a small shabby armchair and an ornately carved Victorian table. On this stood an untouched thermos of coffee, a tobacco jar, and an unopened book.

"He'd prepared for a long wait," said Finch slowly, "but he didn't get it. He'd no sooner settled down when he heard his expected visitor arrive."

"But the gun? Horace Kelvin was a first-class shot."

"He was an old man. His reflexes were slow. He never had a chance to fire."

"And the intruder was already inside the house?"

"Yes. Miss Kelvin may have left the door open either inadvertently or for him to enter that way—but he came through this door"—Finch's finger jabbed in its direction—"and he left by the same way."

"She may not even have been expecting him," said the Chief Constable.

But Finch would have none of this. "She expected him all right. The Judge, as she thought, was playing chess at the vicarage. She herself got rid of the servants. She believed that she had at least an hour in which to find out exactly where she stood."

"Only the Judge was suspicious."

"Not as suspicious as our murderer," Finch retorted grimly. "He suspected that we might be guarding the house. And now content to have silenced one watcher, he must have circled the woods to make certain that that was the only one—"

Finch fell silent, his imagination caught by the picture his words had evoked. The daring of the scheme. The closeness with which they themselves must have followed on the killer's heels. A couple of minutes earlier— But what was the good of thinking of that?

He turned and made his way up what had once been the servants' staircase but which the Judge had transformed to make it a fit stairway for the woman who had been his son's beloved.

"But who—?" The Chief Constable's voice was almost a groan.

"A lover, of course. The man in her life. Remember I asked you?" It was a reminder, not a reproach.

The rooms at the head of the stairs had been arranged as a suite. Sitting room, bedroom, bathroom, compact and luxurious. Kathie lay half in, half out of the entrance to her bedroom.

She was wearing a green chiffon dinner frock. It had long transparent sleeves. A ruffle outlined the plunging neckline. It was a beautiful frock but all beauty had flown from its wearer. Her face was blackened, bruised. Her tongue was bitten through. Strong hands had strangled her. A clenched fist had struck her several times in the face. The bodice of her frock had been torn at the breast.

"A lover!" Colonel Snow's shocked voice cracked. "You said a lover!"

Across Kathie's dead body Finch looked at him. "D'you think that frock was put on for anyone but a lover? D'you think there was anything impersonal in those blows? No, the man who did that was cursing her in his heart. She'd made him put his head in a noose and he hated her for it."

Colonel Snow answered nothing. The soft lights and colours, the warmth, the flowers everywhere, all made the act of murder seem unreal to the point of lunacy. He watched in a sort of fascinated horror as Finch examined a pearl necklace around the bruised and swollen neck, and hated him sharply and illogically for the cool, surprised tone of his voice.

"That's odd," it said. "These pearls are real. The emerald ring too."

"I don't know about the emerald, but of course the pearls are real. The Judge gave them to—her—last Christmas."

Finch nodded. "So that's it. Miss Kelvin wanted money only that one particular time. Anything valuable she was given after that she kept."

"But what has that to do with the murder?" demanded the Chief Constable. "Kathie's dead. Horace Kelvin is dead. The murderer has escaped and you just stand here trying to prove yourself right about—" He broke off as he met the full force of the Scotland Yard man's gaze. A surprisingly cold, steely, and, yes, contemptuous gaze. He added lamely, "Well, I don't know what it is you are trying to prove."

"I'm trying to find a motive for murder. Two and a half years ago Miss Kelvin was in desperate need of money—and for some purpose of which the Judge would have disapproved. Otherwise she would have gone to him. I believe that that money was for her lover, not herself. For the man who was here tonight. The man who had the jewels she was supposed to have lost. He had them and the bulk of the insurance money."

"If you want to examine her jewellery, you'll find it in a safe somewhere in her bedroom. I remember the Judge telling me that's where she kept the stuff," said the colonel in muffled tones.

Slater looking brisk and alert came along the passage. "There's no one in the house but ourselves, sir," he reported. His eyes slid past Finch taking in the picture of the dead woman.

"They're both dead," Finch remarked, answering his look.

"The Judge downstairs. His adopted daughter up here. You'd better ring up the Lockbridge police station and tell them to send out the needful— Tell them to be sure of bringing a doctor with them. We shall probably need him. And I need the Templetons. They must be found and brought back. No, not the wife. I don't want any hysterics. Sampson may be able to tell you where they are likely to have gone. Then get in touch with the chap at the Hall. I want to know when the men of the household get back and whether there seems anything suspicious about their behaviour or appearance."

"Yes, sir." Slater hurried away to the telephone.

A few minutes later the front door banged open. Superintendent Ennis stumbled into the house. "I've found them," he said hoarsely.

"Are they all right? Alive?" The Chief Constable ran down the stairs. "Come on, man. Speak up."

"They've both been attacked and knocked out," Ennis replied. "The weapon might well have been the butt end of a pistol. Mason must have been taken completely by surprise. He was hit on the back of the head. He's *not* so bad. But Gunn must have heard something and turned. He'd caught it across his face. Broken his nose by the look of it. And that isn't all. I think some of his ribs have gone too."

The Chief Constable's dark eyes smouldered. "Someone kicked him when he was down?"

"Put in the boot. That's the expression of the modern hoodlum. But we'll catch him. See if we don't." For once Ennis and Colonel Snow were in complete accord.

"We'll have to," the Chief Constable retorted grimly. "Miss Kelvin and the Judge have both been murdered."

Ennis's already pale face turned a curious shade of green. "I was afraid of that. When I saw poor Gunn I thought—" He sank down heavily on a convenient chair. He covered his face with his hands. "I was afraid of that," he said again.

A party was formed hurriedly to bring in the two unconscious men. It consisted of Colonel Snow, Finch, the driver of the police car, and Sampson. Slater was still at the telephone. Ennis was in no condition to go although he gave clear enough directions as to where the two could be found.

Mason by the third pine, ten paces from the left-hand corner of the garden wall as they went out. Gunn had been hiding in the ragged copse close to the side gate. It had been the better choice since the murderer had had to cover an open space to get to him. Not that this fact had done the unfortunate man much good. The Chief Constable had sworn bitterly when, back in the hall, he had seen the extent of his injuries.

Finch's face too was grave. "Mason will do all right," he said after examining him, "but the sooner this other fellow is in hospital the better. We can clean up his face a bit but the rest will have to wait. If, as I suspect, he has internal injuries, other than the broken ribs, the less we mess him about the better."

"I'll see to him," said Colonel Snow harshly.

Finch nodded. He went back upstairs. Even when the man regained consciousness, he reflected, what would he be able to tell them? Not much obviously—or he wouldn't have been still alive. Finch went into Kathie's sitting room and began a search. A moment later he was joined by his sergeant.

Finch looked at him. "And what bad news do you bring, Archie?"

"I found these, sir, in the Judge's desk." Slater laid a small pile of receipted bills on the writing table in front of Finch. "It seems that he had the insurance money and that he bought the jewellery that replaced those pieces lost by Miss Kelvin."

Finch looked at the receipts one by one. Diamond ring. Single-stone emerald earrings. Emerald and diamond brooch— "At least she's not wearing any of this lot," he murmured. He sat silent, staring into the distance. "No, I can't be wrong about this. It fits together too well." He ran through the bills again. "All bought about the same time—during the last two weeks of March."

Again he fell silent. Then, "Jewellery supposed lost end of February. Insurance money paid in March. Jewels bought end of March—then in April Kathie borrows fifty pounds from Miss Chumleigh. Why?"

But now his thoughts seemed to go off on a tangent. A moment later he was telling Slater to ring up the man on guard at the Hall.

"Tell him to keep an eye on Louise Morton. Tell him it's important. If necessary he's to let everything else go."

Slater was startled. "You still think she's in danger?"

"More than ever. The beginning of the week there were three people who knew something to the murderer's detriment. Now there's only one left—Louise Morton. Pity is she doesn't realise what it is she knows—and certainly our murderer can't afford to wait for it to come to her."

A few minutes later the Lockbridge police arrived in force. They brought the manservant, Templeton, with them. The police surgeon followed in his own car.

Templeton was an elderly man. He bore a faint resemblance to the dead master whom he had served for so long. He seemed on the point of collapse.

"Oh, sir," he gasped, trembling and coming unsteadily forward to where Finch awaited him in the study. "I never should have left the house. I wouldn't have gone if the master hadn't said that it would be all right."

"He told you to go?"

"No, sir. Miss Kathie told me. My wife—Mrs. Templeton— she was in hysterics. Miss Kathie couldn't stand it. Take her in to her sister in Lockbridge, she said, before I start screaming myself. I didn't want to go but what with the two of them . . ." His distracted gaze was flitting about the room. His voice was thin and empty. "Then I thought that I would stop at the vicarage and ask the master—" He broke off, exhausted, trembling.

"Sit down, man," Finch urged. "Take your time."

Templeton's eyes filled with tears. "Yes, time doesn't matter now, does it?" He wiped his eyes openly.

"You saw the Judge?"

"Yes, sir. He was on the way back. I stopped the car and he said it would be quite all right for me to go as he'd called off his game with the vicar."

"Did he seem surprised to see you?"

"No, sir. Now you mention it, he didn't. He seemed more— grim, like. I thought at first he was angry with me but it wasn't that. He said I'd done quite right and then he—he wished my wife a comfortable night and he raised his hat to her—" Templeton's voice broke. After a moment he said, speaking with difficulty, "And that's the last I saw of him, sir. A real gentleman he was. Over thirty years it's been—"

Finch had to wait while the man recovered from his emotion. Then he asked him if he knew the combination of the safe in Miss Kelvin's bedroom.

This upset the old man all over again. He told Finch where it was and gave the combination. "You can see how it was, sir. The master trusted me. He trusted me."

Finch questioned him about Miss Kelvin's private life. Had she had any particular man friend? Had she kept up with any friends from her old life in London? Was there anyone who had written to her consistently, even if at long intervals, over the years? Had he or his wife ever suspected her of having a lover?

It became obvious that neither the old man nor his wife had liked Kathie but they knew nothing against her. She had had plenty of men friends. Occasionally the Templetons had hoped that she was going to marry one of them but always they had been disappointed.

Finch thanked the old man and told him that he would be taken back to his sister-in-law in the first returning police car.

Templeton refused the offer. "I should never have left here. I shouldn't have let my wife persuade me."

"You should be grateful to her. If you hadn't left you'd just have been another body by now."

The police surgeon, Dr. Hallam, was a youngish man, brisk and competent. When Finch went upstairs he found him repacking his medical bag, Sampson in attendance. "There's nothing new I can tell you," he remarked to Finch. "The Judge died of a single blow to the jaw which snapped his neck. This one," he glanced at the dead woman at his feet, "died of manual strangulation. Strong, large hands in gloves." He added grimly, "A right-handed killer." He indicated the torn chiffon. "Look, where he held her up with one hand whilst he struck her with the other."

Sampson turned an alarming shade of puce. "The bastard!" he gasped, deeply shocked. "The bastard!"

"The murderer pulled out a tuft of hair too," the doctor went on. "But that may have been accidental."

Leaving the doctor, Finch went into the dead woman's bedroom. The lovely room, decorated in white and differing shades of yellow, looked all ready to receive its mistress. The room was warm and had a faint feminine smell of scent and powder.

Finch located the safe behind a picture and opened it using the combination Templeton had given him. He did not expect to find any secrets stored away. A safe which could be opened by other members of the household was no place for such things.

He was right. It contained some dozen dark blue morocco jewel cases in varying shapes and sizes and nothing else. He emptied their contents on to the bed.. Slater brought in the murder bag, which contained a jeweller's magnifying glass. This Finch screwed into his eye, examining each trinket and identifying it from the list of receipts in his hand.

By the time he had finished, the Chief Constable had arrived and two pieces of jewellery had been separated from the others, a pearl brooch and a sapphire ring.

"They're genuine. The rest are fakes." Finch added thoughtfully, "So now we know why Miss Kelvin had to have that fifty pounds. It was to get this little lot made. It must have come as quite a shock to her to find that she wasn't getting the insurance money."

"Even so someone didn't do too badly," Slater commented. "Without the insurance money there were still two lots of jewellery, those Miss Kelvin said she lost and those the Judge bought and which she had copied."

"Whatever the reason for her actions they must have entailed a severe sacrifice on her part," said Colonel Snow rather sadly. "Kathie had a passion for jewellery. The Judge used to tease her about it."

Finch nodded. He had known other women with the same passion—and for the same reason. To insure against an insecure future. He said aloud, "And there we may have the motive for what happened this evening. Miss Kelvin wanted some return for her sacrifice. Love, perhaps even marriage. The fact that the Judge had promised to settle a sum of money on her may have made her feel that the time was approaching when, at last, she could afford to defy him."

Colonel Snow looked searchingly at the detective. "You're thinking of Jason Maule. Horace Kelvin certainly wouldn't have countenanced *that* match."

"Why not? As the Maules' heir I should have thought him a catch for anyone?"

"The Judge was prejudiced. There was this business of his hanging round Kathie when she was already engaged to Harry Kelvin. Then there was the manner and length of his disappearance."

"Wonder where he got to during those seven years?"

"The Maules have always gone into the army."

"The War Office says no—unless Jason enlisted under a false name."

Colonel Snow shook his head. "He'd never have done that. Not Jason Maule."

Finch nodded, his face thoughtful. "Perhaps we'll turn up some clue when we search these rooms."

But a search of the dead woman's suite—and indeed of the whole house—threw no light on that subject or any other. "Unless," said Finch, "you count the fact that Miss Kelvin kept nothing. No letters. No souvenirs. No diaries. Nothing."

"A woman without a past, eh?" said the Chief Constable.

"Perhaps," Finch corrected thoughtfully, "a woman who could not afford a past."

Chapter 15

The next day dawned grey, dreary, and still; for all that it was one of great and early activity. At Warley the search of the grounds and the adjacent wood was resumed as soon as it was light. The police car took Archie Slater into Lockbridge, where he roused the editor of the local newspaper and drove with him down to the office of the *Chronicle*. From there Slater went to the railway station, departing by train on a secret errand for his superior.

In London, where the death of Miss Chumleigh had passed almost unnoticed, the murder of Mr. Justice Kelvin and of his adopted daughter made the headlines in a big way. By train, road, and even by air reporters were out, converging on Tammerton.

At the Hall terrors born in the dark hours of the night were nurtured into the day. Added to the Maules' natural grief and horror was their unexpressed fears for Jason.

James Maule, when Finch called to see him, appeared to have aged ten years. His face was lined and grey, his eyes haunted. He asked the detective for details of the crime and then could hardly bear to hear them. He sat at his desk only to spring up again and pace the library with long scissorlike steps, shoulders bowed, hands locked convulsively behind his back.

"Horrible!" he said again and again. "Too horrible." And then in a complaining old man's voice, "I don't know what's come over this place. 'Pon my word I don't. Everything's gone wrong these past two years. First my brother Desmond's death. Then my niece's unfortunate marriage. Not that I've anything against the feller—more's the pity. I made enquiries at the time of the engagement. Strigent enquiries. I felt that that first meeting had been a bit too fortuitous." Mr. Maule seemed wound up. "But I was wrong. Roger Crane had been in the States for eighteen months. His ship had docked at Southampton only the day before. He was on his way back to Bideford in the next county and, since he had no cause to hurry, had decided to make a leisurely trip along the coast. That's how he came to find himself outside the gates of Miramar when his car broke down. Whole thing was an accident. Nothing more.''

"You found that he was a man of good character?"

"I did indeed. He had been a draughtsman in an engineering firm. They spoke highly of him. Said they'd be willing to give him back his old job. Then I looked up his old schoolmaster, feller called Braddock, and he spoke well of him. And I must admit that, since my niece's unfortunate illness, no one could have been more attentive than Roger. But the fact remains it was a poor match for a Maule. A damned poor match.''

Finch's next question brought him up short. "I understand that Mr. Jason Maule is your heir?"

"Yes. His father died when he was young. We—my wife and I—have come to look on him as a son.'' Mr. Maule spoke easily enough but his eyes had grown wary.

"You are fond of him no doubt—and he of you?"

"Yes, he's an affectionate lad. Devoted to us both and to Tammerton.'' Mr. Maule still felt himself to be on safe ground.

"And yet,'' said Finch and both voice and look were mild, "he could go away for seven years. Leave you and your wife in complete ignorance of his whereabouts. Not knowing even whether he was alive or dead.''

Mr. Maule halted in his restless pacing. "That's a damned offensive remark,'' he said angrily.

"It's also the truth, isn't it?"

Mr. Maule stared, realising for the first time that to this tall, sleepy looking man he was not James Maule, Esquire, J.P., Lord of the Manors of Tammerton and Triston Magna. He was simply an ordinary citizen, without any particular claim to privilege, faced with a police enquiry into murder.

"Oh, come, Inspector.'' He gave a good imitation of a light laugh. "It wasn't like that at all. The lad was on his own for the first time in his life. It was all new to him. He didn't feel the need to keep in touch with us old fogies. He was spreading his wings—and liking it.''

"You made him an allowance?"

"We offered to do so but he refused. Said he was quite able to support himself, which he was. Not surprising really. He was young, intelligent, able-bodied.'' Mr. Maule came back to his desk and sat down with sudden weariness. "You must realise, Inspector, that, at the time, he imagined himself to be deeply in

love. In the breaking of his engagement he had been desperately
hurt and he was at an age to do something drastic. Something on
the heroic scale. Break old ties. Throw himself into an entirely
different mode of life.''

''What kind of life?''

''The usual sort for a healthy young man—working his way
round the world.''

Finch's eyebrows climbed. ''Is that what he did?''

Mr. Maule smiled a wry acknowledgment of his own lack
of precision. ''An exaggeration, I fear. He did travel but mostly
in France and in what was then the French empire. We had
letters from Marseilles and from Algiers.'' Adding in explanation, ''Jason had a French nurse. He learnt young and kept it up.
Spoke French like a native.''

''France and North Africa, eh?'' Finch spoke slowly as if to
read something of significance into the words.

Said Mr. Maule hurriedly, ''He wrote to us from London
too.''

''You met, of course?''

Mr. Maule shook his head. ''Unfortunately it was only a
flying visit and made at a time when neither I nor my wife could
get away. She was down with a bad go of influenza and I
couldn't leave her. Apart from that there happened to be an
outbreak of fowl pest in the district. The home farm lost over
two hundred birds. A beastly business.''

''Where was your nephew staying in London?''

''Oh—I don't remember. It was several years ago.''

''He wrote asking for money?''

''Really, Inspector, I can't see where this is leading.''

''Nor do I. But in the spring of 1962 Miss Kelvin was
trying desperately to raise money. I wondered whether your
nephew was in the same predicament.''

''Are you suggesting that my nephew would have taken
money from Miss Kelvin?''

''I'm not suggesting anything. I'm merely asking questions.''

''Which I can see no point in answering.''

''I can get the information from your bank.''

''Indeed?'' Mr. Maule's voice was ironical. ''I should be
surprised if you did.''

''Then I am afraid you are going to be surprised. A court
order would do it.''

Mr. Maule's face turned slowly ashen. ''I think there is no
point in continuing this discussion. And in view of your attitude

I shall refuse to answer any further questions except in the presence of my solicitor." He added coldly, "I shall instruct the rest of my household to the same effect."

"Perhaps you are wise." Finch's voice was as cold as that of the man facing him across the desk but inwardly he was well satisfied with the result of his interview. He was certain now that his suspicions had been correct. Jason Maule had written home asking for money. Had come to London for just that purpose. And one other—to meet Kathie Kelvin.

As for the time when this had taken place, well, P.C. Sampson could furnish the answer. He had only to be asked when two events of local interest had coincided; Agnes Maule's influenza and fowl pest at the home farm.

Finch went next to the West Wing in search of Louise Morton, hoping to get there before the Squire's interdict had had time to penetrate. He knocked lightly on the sitting room door.

After a moment it was opened by Roger Crane. He looked worn and strained. "I should have kept my big mouth shut," he told Finch bitterly. "This business has pretty well killed my wife. You go and arrest Jason and it'll probably finish the job."

"Has the doctor been?"

"He's with her now."

"Then perhaps you can spare Miss Morton for a minute."

Roger stared. "Louise? I suppose so."

He withdrew, closing the door after him. After a short interval the girl appeared. She looked tired. Her green eyes were immense in her pale face but she was as trim and starched as usual.

"I can't stay long," she said coldly. "What did you want?"

"I asked you to write an account of what took place between Miss Chumleigh, Mrs. Crane, and yourself. Remember?"

Louise shook her sleek head. "You can't have it."

"You didn't write it?"

"Oh, yes. I wrote it."

"Well then?"

"I brought it down last night and burnt it, here in the drawing-room fire."

Finch looked at her sadly. "Now why on earth should you do a silly thing like that?"

Louise looked uncertain. "It didn't strike me as silly at the time. And, if it were silly, it's done now."

"You did it after hearing of the murders at Warley?"

Louise turned even paler. "I decided that I wanted to have

nothing to do with your investigations. Nothing at all. I'd neither defend anyone nor help to condemn them. It—it's all too beastly.'' Her groping hand felt behind her for the door handle. ''And now I must get back to my patient.''

Finch's eyes narrowed. His bland face seemed to harden in some curious way so that it became impressive, even alarming. ''Your patient? I've a bit of advice to give you there—if you don't find that silly too.''

The girl's slight figure stiffened defensively. ''What do you want me to do?''

''Not to leave Mrs. Crane alone. Stay with her. Just that.''

Louise stared at him in surprise. ''Is that all? In her present state of health I'd have done that anyway.''

She opened the door behind her and slipped through, quiet, composed, a nurse returning to her duty.

Finch went away. In spite of what Louise had said he went upstairs and searched her bedroom. There was a possibility that she had decided to burn the papers only when Finch had enquired after them and that they were still intact.

He was disappointed. They were not anywhere to be found in her room. Nor were there any hints as to their nature to be gleaned from the blotting paper nor from discarded sheets of paper in the waste-paper basket.

There were three people in the Great Hall as Finch came down the stairs. They were Mr. and Mrs. Maule and a small elderly and untidy looking man in baggy tweeds. He was introduced rather icily by Mr. Maule as Dr. Reed.

The doctor acknowledged the introduction, then returned to what he had been saying. ''There is no immediate cause for anxiety. Mrs. Crane has had a sedative, and that should keep her quiet for some hours. If necessary I can give her an injection to keep her under sedation for a further period. In any case I shall be out to see her again after lunch.''

To Finch, whom he followed from the house, he was not so reassuring. ''This is the devil of a position,'' he complained. ''Mrs. Crane's heart is in no condition to stand up to any further shocks. I was called out to her last night and, but for that nurse of hers, she'd have been gone before I got here. It was as near as damn it.''

Finch paused, frowning a little, recalling what Roger had said. ''You mean that an arrest in the family would kill her?''

''Not a doubt of it. And where that leaves us I can't say. Still you might perhaps keep me informed.''

Finch nodded. "I'll do that." As he drove away he was aware that Agnes Maule had come to the door. That she was standing there watching him, her pink face fixed in a stricken smile.

He drove first to Hill View, where he put in two long-distance telephone calls. The first was to Scotland Yard. The second was to his sergeant. Then he collected some papers from which he meant to work, and was driven to the police station at Lockbridge.

He was busy on his report when the Chief Constable came in. He looked pale and stern. His dark eyes were as hard as jet.

"P.C. Sampson's just come in with this. He found it not far from the path leading to the side entrance at Warley," he told Finch, presenting him with a cigarette end in a small box. "It had fallen on a stone overshadowed by another larger stone. That's how it came to be missed at first. It's a make smoked only by Jason Maule. As you can see for yourself it's damp but not sodden. There was no rain last night after that one sharp shower whilst we were in Sampson's cottage. Obviously this stub must have been thrown down after that."

Finch nodded his agreement. "After the shower and before the murders," he agreed, in his soft murmuring voice.

"It couldn't have been planted either," Colonel Snow went on a little regretfully. "As you know, I had a watch kept all night to prevent any such happening."

"Yes—Agnes Maule might have tried something."

"She did try," said Colonel Snow grimly. "Cool as you please. But when she saw the police she sheered off again."

A faint flicker of amusement passed over Finch's face. "Wonder what she had in mind?"

The Chief Constable's face darkened. "In view of this"— he rattled the cigarette end in its box—"what the devil does it matter?"

"What indeed," Finch murmured in agreement.

Colonel Snow snorted. "What time did Jason get back to the Hall last night?"

"Seems to be some doubt on that point," Finch was hunting through his papers. "Ah, here's Merridew's report. James Maule returned at exactly four minutes to eight. Roger Crane was the next to arrive—at two minutes past eight. The time of Jason Maule's return to the house is in doubt—if indeed he ever left it."

"How d'you mean 'if he ever left it'? We know he left it."

"So we do," Finch agreed. "Silly of me. Anyway Merridew states that the rest of the household had gone into dinner when Jason suddenly appeared coming down the stairs. It seems to have surprised him very much."

Colonel Snow glared at him. "Taken in conjunction with this cigarette end, I consider this no time for facetiousness."

Finch was pained. "I wasn't being facetious. It was only"—and a certain grimness sounded in his soft voice—"that I'd already worked out just what Mr. Jason Maule's part was in all this. It wasn't really difficult."

In the West Wing Roger Crane was preparing to leave for the office the late Desmond Maule had set up in Lockbridge, and from which Isobel's property business was managed.

"You're certain you wouldn't rather I stayed?"

"If I have a sleeping draught what difference will it make whether you are here or not?" Isobel retorted with uncharacteristic irritation.

Roger took it well. "O.K., Peaches. If that's how you want it." Adding with a rueful grin, "Some anniversary this is going to be."

Isobel's expression changed, softened. "I know—but we'll keep it just the same. The two of us quietly here. Louise can take the car and get the things we'll want from Miramar."

Louise, quietly clearing up after the doctor's visit, closed her lips in a firm line. She had not understood Finch's injunction not to leave her patient, but she meant to carry it out.

Roger too seemed to have his doubts. "I don't know that I like the idea of your being without a nurse—"

"Louise can go whilst I'm asleep. It shouldn't take her long. Maggie can sit in here whilst she's gone." Isobel closed her eyes. "Forgive me, Roger, but really I'm better left to myself."

But after he had gone Isobel seemed to regret it. She grew restless, tossing from side to side, and still the sedative remained untouched by her bedside. Louise pressed her to take it.

Isobel turned wild eyes on her. "I can't do it," she declared. "I'm afraid to sleep. The only time I slept last night I dreamt of Kathie—that she was coming for me with a knife. And, oh, Louise"—Isobel shuddered—"in my dream her face was all dark and bloated and most of her hair had been torn out, and her dead eyes were fixed in a stare of actual hatred. It was horrible."

"There's no need for you to take the sedative," said Lou-

ise. She spoke calmly, although inwardly she had been shaken
by the picture conjured up by Isobel's words. "Just lie quietly
there and try not to worry. As for the dream, I don't suppose for
a minute that it'll ever come back."

Isobel smiled rather bitterly. "I hope not." And then, "The
real trouble is that this house is bound up with memories of
Kathie, which is strange, for I'm not really here all that often.
But I *was* staying here when Harry Kelvin brought her down
here. I was here when he was killed. I was here when Kathie got
engaged to Jason, and here when it was broken off. And now
I'm here again when she . . ."

Isobel's voice trailed away. "As for bad dreams, I deserved
that one. God forgive me, but I believed that Kathie had killed
Edith Chumleigh. I told myself it was just the sort of reckless,
unthinking action I'd have expected from her. But she couldn't
have done it, because now she has been murdered herself."

Louise nodded. Better to talk than to lie there and think.
"But had Kathie any motive for wanting Miss Chumleigh dead?"

"That's the point. Edith knew far more about her than any
of us. And, thinking over the telephone conversation I had that
morning with Kathie, the impression grew—" Isobel broke off.
"But I was wrong. I can see now that I must have been wrong.
Poor, poor Kathie."

She lay silent for a time. Gradually the lines smoothed from
her face. She seemed to have found a less painful subject for her
thoughts. "About going into Lockbridge. I made out a list of
what I wanted several days ago—"

"Then someone else can have it. Young Mr. Maule perhaps," said Louise sedately, "for I certainly can't leave you."

Isobel opened her eyes, turning her head a little to look at
the girl. Louise was surprised to see a faint twinkle in their
depths.

"I wasn't going to suggest that you should. I've got a much
better idea than that. It came to me quite suddenly. I thought I'd
get up and go with you."

Louise stared. "Go with me?" she echoed slowly. She was
startled but, thinking it over, it seemed to her to be an excellent
idea.

"To Miramar. Why not? I'll be much better away from
here, and if Roger telephones I shall tell Maggie to say I'm
asleep. He *is* such an old fusspot. We can get out without going
through the hall, and no one need even know we've gone."

"Dr. Reed must know."

"All right. Telephone him, then. But I warn you it'll make no difference if he says no. I shall go just the same—even if I have to go alone and drive myself."

But Dr. Reed was all in favour of the idea. "Once she gets into her own house she may decide to stay there. I hope so. I'll be round about two to see how she has stood the journey. If you should want me before then ring up the surgery. My receptionist will know where to find me. Oh—and Nurse, better give the police a ring when you get to Miramar."

When Louise went back to the bedroom to report the success of her mission she found her patient already dressing. She had a faint colour and her expression was animated. She greeted the girl almost gaily. "We'll leave the house through this wing. Maggie shall push me down the back drive and you can pick me up with the car out of sight of the house. With any luck no one will know that either of us have gone until it's too late to object."

Once dressed she told Louise to look out into the passage to make certain that the way was clear. Then, reassured and delighted with her scheme, Isobel was pushed through long winding corridors to emerge into a part of the garden Louise had not seen before. Tall trees hid them from the house and walks of pleached limes ran in all directions.

"We part here," said Isobel. "Louise, you'll find a path to your right which will bring you out by the garage. Here is the key. You can't mistake my car. It's a white Jaguar. Turn left as you drive out. I'll be waiting for you."

Chapter 16

The Jaguar was the latest model, sleek, shining, and powerful looking. It seemed to Louise unlikely that anyone would catch them up once they got under way. She slid in behind the steering wheel, adjusting a cushion behind her back. She felt a thrill of pleasure as the great car throbbed into life, and slid smoothly into the open.

"Louise!" Jason came striding round the corner, smiling and waving.

Louise's heart seemed to displace itself in the oddest manner. "What d'you want?"

"To talk to you."

"But I don't want to talk to you." Louise did not look at Jason but she was conscious that his smile had gone and that he was favouring her with one of his long thoughtful stares.

"Meaning that you think Kathie and I were still lovers? Well, we weren't. She just implied that to bedevil the situation."

Louise wished her heart would stop thumping. "That's easy to say now she's dead," she remarked scornfully.

"I wanted to say it yesterday, but you didn't give me the chance."

"Are you surprised?" And then, "I *know* you were lovers—however unwillingly on your part."

Jason's face hardened. "What did you say?" There was a quiet grimness in his voice she had not heard before.

Louise forced herself to turn her head and look up at him. "Oh, don't pretend. I heard you in the yellow drawing room. The room was in darkness. I didn't mean to eavesdrop. I just didn't know anyone was there."

A startled look stole over the hard reckless face. "What exactly did you hear?"

"I heard Kathie say that she'd never give you up. And that it was no good your thinking that she would."

"And you told the police this?" The voice was politely curious. He was smiling again, a deadly chilling smile.

"No, I didn't." Louise's voice choked. "I don't know why—but I didn't."

"I see." He was not looking at her now but away across the yard. His face wore the strange blankness she had seen once before—on that first night when she had fancied that he had recalled where it was he had seen Miss Chumleigh—and Miss Chumleigh was dead. Come to that Kathie was dead too and could no longer hold him to anything. She—

Jason's voice broke in on her thoughts. "So you haven't told the police. Not very wise of you, was it?" His voice was soft, reflective and, to the girl infinitely menacing.

In sudden panic she started the car. It shot forward. She heard Jason shout her name but she did not stop.

"Louise, how white you look," Isobel greeted her. "D'you think the car is going to be too much for you?"

"No, the car is wonderful to drive," Louise answered, truthfully. "It's just—well, I was overcome suddenly with a longing to get away."

"That makes two of us," Isobel assured her. She climbed, with the little maid's help, into the front seat beside Louise. "Goodbye, Maggie. Remember I'm depending on you to hold the fort until I get back."

"I'll see to it, ma'am." Maggie smiled and waved. The great car sped on, down the winding drive and out on to the road.

"The bliss of getting away," Isobel murmured, "and no one knowing we've gone."

But Jason knows. Suppose he came after us? Louise thought. Indeed she could not see what else he could do. She had not told the inspector what she had overheard and Jason could not afford for her to do so. And Isobel was in no condition to be embroiled in an argument.

Louise repressed a shudder as she tried to close her mind to what might be called the ultimate in argument.

She found herself glancing again and again into the driving glass, scanning the road behind them for some sign of pursuit. But there was none. There were the trees and then the flat fields and the road stringing out behind them, empty of traffic.

Not very wise of you. Not very wise of you. The words became a mocking accompaniment to their flight.

They stopped on the outskirts of the town whilst Louise got

out and did some shopping from a list Isobel gave her. It seemed a lot of food for two women and one meal. The shops were busy and it took her eighteen minutes by her watch. When she got back to the car she found that her companion had managed to move into the back seat.

"We have to pass Roger's office," Isobel explained. "If he sees the car I don't want him to see me as well. I may even duck down at the crucial moment."

They went on through the centre of the town, Louise following Isobel's directions. They passed several policemen but Louise dared not stop to speak to them in front of her passenger.

She consoled herself with the thought that as soon as they reached their destination she would ring up Inspector Finch and tell him all the things she had so far kept to herself.

The car was climbing steeply now. The sea lay in front of them and the town behind. There was only a vast expanse of sky, empty downland—and a single white house.

Designed by a famous architect Miramar had been built round three sides of a paved fountain court. There was a charming small white pavilion not far from the house, the whole standing in three acres of formal garden.

Inside it was expensively luxurious. There was the most modern of lighting and central heating. The furniture was in the pale woods of Scandinavia. Carpets were so thick that they deadened every sound. Lined curtains in the richest, heaviest of silks were drawn over the windows.

"And how warm it is," Louise cried in surprise.

"The heating is still on. One of the gardeners comes in every evening and regulates it according to the weather," Isobel answered, looking about her and smiling with the pleasure of being at home. "Don't bother to draw back the curtains here. Only in the sitting room." Adding contentedly, "This is really a very comfortable house."

She walked across the hall, determinedly if haltingly. Louise, following her, paused to pick up a small lump of wet mud, left by the gardener, she supposed, and dropped it into a neighbouring pot of trailing ivy.

She drew back the curtains in the sitting room and caught her breath in amazement at the view.

Almost the entire wall was of glass. Beyond was a flagged terrace, a strip of green lawn and then nothing but sea and sky.

Behind her Isobel laughed. "It is breath-taking, isn't it?" She leaned forward and opened one of the long windows. "I love this view, even on a dull day like this. Even when it's raining.''

"Is there a beach down there?"

"Yes, my father had a stairway made through the cliffs. The entrance is concealed in the little pavilion."

"M'h'm! Marvellous!" Louise turned away reluctantly. "I suppose I'd better take the things we bought along to the kitchen, if you'd tell me how I get there."

She was relieved to have reached the shelter of the house. Pleased too with her patient, who not only had stood the journey well but who looked much better for the change.

"And there's the telephone," she remarked thankfully. "I suppose there's an extension. I mean"—she smiled radiantly— "if I should want to ring up the doctor."

"There're plenty of extensions," Isobel answered carelessly, "but you can't use them. I always have the telephone cut off when I'm away. It's one of my things. I can't bear the thought of anyone taking advantage of my being absent and making calls in my name."

Louise halted, staring at her in dismay. "But how about the doctor?" And the police—particularly the police.

"Blow the doctor," said Isobel gaily. "I don't want him."

Louise went on staring. "I wish I'd known before we came here," she said slowly. At the back of her mind she felt a fluttering of fear, remote, intangible as one of the clouds passing outside. She had been so delighted to get Isobel away from the Hall, from her memories of Kathie, from those unspecified dangers of the inspector's. And now here they were, alone, isolated, completely cut off. Their presence known—and this was the final irony—only to the murderer.

Isobel began to laugh. "It's not the end of the world so stop worrying and go and make us some tea." She gave Louise directions to get to the kitchen. Then, still laughing, gave her a little push in the direction of the door.

In the hall Louise paused to examine the fastenings on the front door. She was relieved to find that, although there was neither bolt nor chain, it was fitted with a burglar-proof mortice lock and could not be opened by any other means than by the rightful key. The windows too were fitted with a burglar-proof device.

Looking through the glass, she could see beyond the gardens the empty sky, the wide sweep of the downs. In the distance some sheep were feeding on the coarse grass. There was no other living creature in sight.

You could call and no one would hear you. Cry out and no one would come. Who had said that? She remembered that it had been Mrs. Maule at that dinner party. In spite of the warmth in the hall Louise shivered involuntarily. She turned dispiritedly away.

The kitchen was a large square room, very bright and wonderfully equipped with everything one could possibly want for cooking, for hygiene, and for comfort.

There was a hatch set in one wall. Louise pushed it open and found herself looking into a smallish dining room intended for use when the family were alone.

Here too the curtains were drawn, making it dim and shadowy. Tall chairs, graceful and pallid, were pulled up to an oval table of the same pale wood. One wall was composed wholly of sheets of looking glass so arranged that they gave back, over and over, confusing reflections of the same objects.

Rather odd, Louise decided. Like a do-it-yourself Picasso.

She plugged in the electric kettle. She found glass and crockery behind sliding doors in cupboards large as small rooms. She laid the tea things on a tray and put out some biscuits.

Louise stood still, feeling apprehensive. What's wrong here? she thought. What is it? The kettle boiled. The chill moment passed. Louise made the tea and took it along to the sitting room.

Isobel sat in a low armchair before the fire, looking relaxed and peaceful. Louise felt a sudden surge of protective affection for her. She wished Inspector Finch had been more definite about the danger in which Isobel stood. She reflected unhappily that he could never have visualised the particular danger by which her patient was now threatened.

A large sheet of paper hung from the mantelpiece, held in place by a green onyx cigarette box shaped like a large egg on small golden legs. It read in Isobel's rather sprawling handwriting:

> *This is to certify that Louise Morton cannot be held responsible for my being in this house. Nor for anything that may happen whilst we are here.*
> *Isobel Crane.*

For a moment Louise stared in the utmost dismay. If only it were true, she thought. Or better still, if it were only the joke Isobel seemed to think. She managed to laugh quite creditably.

Isobel's answering laugh was far more genuine. "So now sit down and have a cup of tea." She frowned slightly. "You've only brought one cup."

"Yes, the tea is for you. Whilst you're drinking it, I'll get on with the lunch."

Isobel looked up at her. "And then whisk me back to civilisation? Well, we shall see. Meanwhile, if anything untoward happens, I'll ring the bell—madly."

Louise smiled. "I suppose it's silly of me to be so anxious, but I don't like being cut off. After all, you are my responsibility."

Isobel shook her head. "I absolved you. Remember?" She poured herself a cup of tea, sighing luxuriously. "If only Roger were here it would be perfect."

Yes, and how could we get in touch with him? Louise wondered. Or with anyone else, for that matter.

Again she paused in the hall, looking about her. At the wide shallow staircase. At the strange green plants standing about. At the few modern paintings hanging on the walls. How expensive it all was—and how quiet!

Outside leaves had rustled in the wind and a lark had sung high in the sky. Here, in the well built house, not a board creaked. Not a window shook. There was only a silence that seemed to emphasise their isolation.

A silence too complete for the strong feeling that had come to her. The feeling that someone else was in the house with them. Jason! Could he have overtaken them after all? Taken a short cut perhaps and now be hiding somewhere waiting to catch her alone?

Upstairs maybe?

Her eyes were drawn to the staircase, curving gracefully to the floor above. Her unquiet mind followed his imaginary trail. Up the stairs. Into some room she had never seen.

She pictured him there, lean, tall, hard-faced, standing just inside the closed door, listening even as she was listening. Hurriedly she turned on all the lights and stared upwards. The doors on the landing remained obstinately shut. The silence was unbroken.

Louise switched off the lights. She hurried back to the kitchen. We must finish up here and get out, she told herself. We must finish up here and—

She found a tray which, she discovered, opened very cleverly to form a tabletop. She washed the salad. She put out the food she had bought. She added cutlery, glasses, a water jug, working neatly and fast. And as she worked she found herself thinking of the lump of mud she had picked up in the hall. Something about it had been strange. But what? And then suddenly, she knew. It had been wet and not dry as it would have been if it had been in the warmth of the house all night.

So it had not been dropped from a shoe on the previous evening.

It had not been dropped by the gardener.

It must have been brought into the house that morning.

It had been there when she and Isobel had arrived.

So the murderer had got here first.

Louise felt her veins turn to ice. Terror took the strength from her limbs. The murderer was no longer Jason. He was faceless, formless, the cowled figure of Death itself. No longer upstairs but all about her. Outside the door. Beyond the hatch—

"Is anyone here?" Her voice sounded abnormally loud in the empty room. There came not a sound in reply. No door opened. No steps echoed. No one called out in answer. There was only the background silence and against it, her own anxious breathing.

Shuddering she tried to regain some measure of calm. The hatch caught and held her gaze. How suggestive it was of a spy hole. A darkened window through which someone might stare unnoticed. Slowly, reluctantly, Louise crept across the floor and peered into the room beyond.

Although the heavy curtains were drawn the room was not really dark. Mentally she took an inventory. Chairs, table, sideboard, those queerly arranged mirrors—to her fevered fancy it seemed that in their gleaming depths the furniture had developed a life of its own. It took her a minute to sort reality from illusion. To satisfy herself that no one was there.

Louise went back to work.

She found a coffee percolator and put it on the tray. Milk, sugar, what else was needed? Salt and pepper. She wondered where she would find them. In that long wall fitting, perhaps.

She hurried across the kitchen passing the hatch with a casual glance. Her impetuous speed carried her past the opening. Then she halted, staring straight in front of her, touched by such a degree of fear as she would not have thought possible.

The chair at the head of the dining room table had been occupied.

She turned stiffly, forcing herself to retrace her steps. She came to the hatch and looked through. She closed her eyes and drew a deep breath of relief. It had been a mistake. No one was there. The chairs were all empty.

She opened her eyes and a small scream ripped from her throat. A man's head and shoulders filled the hatchway, blocking out the room beyond.

At police headquarters time passed slowly. There was good news of the two constables who had been attacked on the previous evening. One was to be allowed home that day. The other was making excellent progress. Neither could identify the assailant, although Gunn had seen that he wore a black stocking drawn over his head.

For some time there had been no news from the Hall. Then Harris, the plain-clothes man who had relieved Merridew, reported that Roger Crane had left for his office in Lockbridge. Three quarters of an hour later he rang up to say that Mrs. Maule and Mr. Jason Maule had left the Hall in the Rolls, driving furiously by way of the back drive.

Richardson (this was the man sent to reinforce Harris) had managed to get to the garage in time to ask them where they were going but had had no answer unless you could count Mr. Jason Maule's invitation to take a running jump at himself.

"Mr. Maule is endeavouring to escape," Ennis cried, striking an attitude of despair.

"Taking his aunt with him?" snarled the Chief Constable. "Talk sense, man."

Fifteen minutes later Harris telephoned again. The Hall was being besieged by reporters and James Maule had gone for a shotgun.

"Intolerable!" cried Colonel Snow, springing up. "This can't be allowed."

Finch squinted at him through his cigarette smoke. "The reporters or the shotgun?"

"The reporters, of course."

Finch looked amused. "You could offer them a statement. That should draw them off."

"That's what I will do. I'll speak to Harris . . ." The Colonel was interrupted by the telephone ringing again. He snatched off the receiver. "Yes, put him through." He turned to Finch. "It's for you, Inspector. It's your sergeant, speaking from Bideford."

Finch nodded. "Thanks." And then, "Hullo, Archie, what's

the news?'' His bland face registered no change of expression, yet suddenly everyone was still, acutely attentive.

Finch replaced the receiver.

"Well, man?" snapped the Chief Constable.

"Slater tells me that the Bideford police have no record of any woman, whose son had been in trouble, hanging herself."

"Oh?" Colonel Snow looked as if he were expecting some further elucidation of the subject, but Finch had gone on to speak of something else.

"I told Slater to cover the same ground as Mr. Maule covered when enquiring into the character of Roger Crane. Slater visited the engineering firm for which Crane worked before going to Alaska. He visited the man's old schoolmaster. They all extolled his character. Only"—and here Finch's voice became even softer and more drawling—"the man we know as Roger Crane is not the man they knew."

The Chief Constable stared, speechless for once.

"Did your sergeant prove this to his complete satisfaction?" The superintendent's tone of voice suggested that he at least would not have been so easily satisfied.

"He had with him a photograph of the bridegroom taken for the Lockbridge *Chronicle* at the time of Miss Isobel Maule's marriage."

"And he's not the same man," Colonel Snow repeated in a stupefied voice. And then, on a higher note, "D'you mean to tell me that Isobel isn't Mrs. Crane? That there never was a Roger Crane?" And again, "But the cigarette end found at Warley. Didn't that prove that Jason Maule was the murderer?"

"Only," said Finch gently, "if you can tell me when he smoked it. It wasn't before the attack on the two constables. They would have seen the lighted end glowing in the darkness. It wasn't during the attack. The attacker was wearing a stocking over his face. It wasn't after the attack. There wasn't time."

"Then you think it was planted there? A false clue left by—by— Damn it, man, we must go on calling him Roger Crane."

Before Finch could make any answer there was a knock on the door. The man who had told Finch of the loss of Kathie's jewellery came in.

"I thought you ought to know, sir," he told Finch, "one of our men has just come off point duty. He says that, about fifteen minutes ago, he saw Mrs. Crane's white Jaguar driving fast in the direction of Miramar."

Finch sprang to his feet. "Who was in it?"

"A young lady driving and he thought there was someone in the back. May have been Mrs. Crane."

"I thought that expedition was off," commented Finch slowly. And his face expressed the uneasiness he felt. "The doctor said he'd left Mrs. Crane under sedation."

"But if Miss Morton does go to Miramar does it matter so much?" the Chief Constable asked anxiously.

"We keep getting back to the fact that of the three people who could have recognised Roger Crane for the imposter he is, two are dead," Finch answered. "If Crane knew or even suspected that Miss Morton was going to Miramar he would be there waiting for her."

"But he's at his office," the superintendent objected. "There are men watching the back and front. He can't get out unnoticed."

"Of course he can get out unnoticed. He's got to." Finch added thoughtfully, "Come to think of it he must always have been able to get out unnoticed. How else did he meet Kathie Kelvin?"

The Chief Constable had been silent, visualising the building in which Roger Crane—for so they continued to think of him—had his office. Now he said, "It's a street of narrow three storied houses. Crane has his office on the top floor. Mrs. Crane has obtained planning permission for the area and isn't renewing any of the leases. Consequently most of the buildings are empty, including one at the corner which faces on to another street. If Crane could get to this via the roof, he could leave and our men would be no wiser."

Finch looked at him. "Then that's what he has done," he said slowly.

A new thought struck the Chief Constable. "But if we arrest Crane, the shock will kill his wife," he cried in dismay.

Finch nodded. "That," he said grimly, "is our problem. How do we rescue Miss Morton without killing Isobel Crane? Anyone got any ideas?"

A dismayed silence fell—and grew. The problem appeared insoluble.

Chapter 17

Louise went on staring through the hatch. "I never heard you come in."

"Why should you? I'm not the Mayor of Lockbridge to be announced. I live here. Remember?"

Louise nodded, held by shock and the sheer amazement of recognition. Miramar was his home. Yet she had last seen this man on Dartmoor on the day on which her father had been killed. Roger Crane was an ex-convict—if his name were Roger Crane. And at once a ghostly voice echoed in her ear. *"Convicts? The newspapers said nothing of convicts."* Louise seemed to be living on two planes.

An anticipatory shudder shook her. "Who are you?" she asked.

The man laughed, white teeth gleaming sharp and white against the darkness of his beard. "Appropriately enough my name is Death. Martin Charles D'Eath." The head made a little ducking bow, mocking her. "I think you've heard it before."

Louise stared dumbly. Two voices rang in her ears. The one carried her back down the years. A man's rough voice ordering, as she now realised, one of his charges back to the working party. The other, her own voice, echo of a child's mistake. *"Someone else shouted that someone was dead. . . . I didn't hear what was said very distinctly."*

And then suddenly something else about that happening of long ago became clear to Louise. She knew just why Kathie had driven so blindly onto the main road. Why Harry Kelvin had looked so furious. Kathie had recognised in one of the convicts the man she loved. Harry's case had not been so simple. He too had recognised the convict. Recognised him as the man whom he had defended unsuccessfully at the Old Bailey. Recognised, too, in that moment of approaching disaster, that Kathie had deceived him. That whilst he, Harry Kelvin, had made her the centre of his world, this man would only have had to crook a careless finger and she would have turned and followed him without a regret or a backward glance.

Poor Harry! And poor Kathie.

"I knew you'd recognise me in time," the voice said suddenly from the other side of the hatch. If it held the slightest touch of menace it passed her by.

"It was seeing you like that," said Louise simply, giving him only a part of her attention. "It was the open car window all over again."

"But you were on the verge of recognising me, girly." There was a grisly facetiousness in his voice. "You recognised Kathie and I saw how you stared at me that night I got back from London. And all those questions to my wife. You didn't think she'd repeat them, did you?" He raised his voice in a high falsetto. "Is he away now? Doesn't he find it quiet after Alaska?" His voice dropped to its natural tone. "Oh yes. You were suspicious all right."

Louise shook her head. "I wasn't, you know. It was just that Isobel liked talking about you." But the head was gone. The hatch showed vacant, an empty square of sad grey light.

With a quick stab of fear the reason for which was still not clear to her, she turned and looked towards the doorway leading from the small dining room.

He was standing there—the man whom she still thought of as Roger Crane. The same—and yet not the same. She puzzled over the difference.

It was difficult now to think of him as Isobel's husband. Not so difficult to see him as Kathie's lover. But if he had been Kathie's lover, it followed that he must have been the man with her in the darkened drawing room. The man to whom Kathie had said, *"Don't think I'll ever give you up. For I won't. Not ever."* She, Louise, had thought that it had been Jason with Kathie. But it had been Roger.

She might have derived some pleasure from the line of thought if another, shattering one, had not followed it. "You," she said unsteadily, "you are the murderer. You killed Kathie—and the Judge."

"That's right." He grinned cheerfully. It might have been a plumbing job he discussed. "Kathie had it coming to her. She actually thought I was going to leave Isobel and go off with her. Always on at me she was. Then, when that doting old fool promised to settle some money on her, she tried to force my hand. Wanted me to meet her in the woods. Threatened to tell my wife just how well we knew each other. That was the payoff. So . . .'' He opened his hands in a mock rueful gesture. ''As for the Judge—I didn't aim to kill him. He just happened to be too nosey for his own good. Not that I minded killing him. He was the spitting image of the old geyzer who sent me down for life—and that counted against him.''

''Had you—'' Louise gulped. ''Had you killed anyone before?'' She was progressing slowly and painfully from one awful moment to another, like a barefoot paddler stepping on sharp rocks, driven by an incoming tide.

He nodded. ''My Aunt Bess, the silly bitch. Always saying to me, 'Don't ask for money now. When I'm dead it'll all be yours.' But it wasn't. After I'd done her in I found she'd left it to some charity, the old . . .'' A stream of obscenity poured from his lips.

It reminded Louise suddenly that Isobel was in the house. Isobel who, all unwittingly, had married this monster. It was her voice that echoed now in Louise's ear, raising the most immediate, the most urgent problem of them all.

One of these days perhaps a moment of crisis will arise and then Roger will emerge in his full stature for all to see.

Isobel had said that about her husband. Now the crisis had arisen and Roger could be seen for what he was—but not by Isobel. She must not see him like this.

''Stop it!'' Louise cried urgently. ''Stop it! Your wife will hear you. She's here—in the drawing room.''

Roger grinned unpleasantly. He wagged his head in mock admiration. ''Smart, aren't you? But you're not smart enough to fool me. I 'phoned the Hall before I came here. Maggie told me Isobel was there, asleep in bed.''

''I know.'' Louise almost wrung her hands. ''I was in the room when Isobel told Maggie what to say if you rang up. You must believe me. Your wife is here—in this house.''

He raised his heavy eyebrows in cold disbelief. ''An actress too! Pity it won't do you any good—but there it is.''

''How d'you mean—won't do me any good?'' Louise whispered, whispered because the answer was already an icy coldness in her blood.

''Well,'' again that deprecating smirk, ''there isn't room in the world for both of us—not as things are. So I decided you'd better go over the cliffs—and go over alive. An accident, see? You went too near the edge and that was that. And anyway the police won't be interested in me. They'll be after Jason Maule. I tipped them off myself. Walked into the police station bold as brass.'' He began to move towards her silently, smoothly. If she had had any doubts about his being a killer they would have gone now. His eyes were bright, pitiless. His arms—she had noticed they were long arms—now seemed to hang to his knees.

''You'll never get away with it.'' Terror thickened her voice so that she scarcely recognised it for her own.

The grin widened. ''I shan't do anything else to you. I'm depriving myself there. But, like I said, an accident.''

Louise fell back a step. ''Keep away,'' she whispered frantically. ''Keep away or I shall scream. I shan't be able to help it.''

His eyes narrowed, thin slits of cruel amusement. ''Why not?'' he asked. ''Why not?'' And then raising his voice, ''Go on! Scream! Why don't you—?''

As if in answer to his question a door opened off the hall. Footsteps sounded coming towards the kitchen, hesitant, limping. ''Louise, what is it? Who's there?''

Roger stiffened into a dreadful immobility. A fearful anguish showed on his face. Sweat gathered in great beads on his forehead to trickle sluggishly down into his beard.

Isobel stood in the doorway, supporting herself against the doorpost. ''Roger''—her voice was a mixture of delight and astonishment—''what are you doing here?''

He swung round, head lowered. He broke into words, rough accusing words, overwhelmed by what, obviously, he thought of as undeserved disaster. ''That's a question I ought to be asking you, isn't it? I 'phoned the Hall and was told that you were in bed and asleep.''

''And all the time I was up and about.'' Isobel laughed. ''Poor Maggie! She was only doing what she was told.'' She gave him a fond wifely smile. ''I knew you'd make a fuss if you heard that I'd gone out in the car.''

He laughed harshly. ''You're too right. I am making a fuss. When I'm told you're at home and in bed I expect you to be at home . . .'' He broke off, seeing the look of dawning astonishment on his wife's face. He made a great effort to regain control of his temper. ''I'm sorry,'' he said gruffly. ''I guess I shouldn't have bawled Louise out like I did.''

He mopped his face with his handkerchief. For a moment one eye peered over its edge at the girl. In its suffused depth Louise saw reflected his perplexity, his desperation, and the hint of some dreadful knowledge that had been revealed to him.

As if there had been between them sympathy and not antagonism she realised the full force of his dilemma. If he himself were to live then Louise might not be the only one who would have to die. Unless some unforeseen solution presented itself the goose that laid the golden eggs would have to be sacrificed. The dear doting goose whom he had fought to keep alive all these months.

And if he did kill her and get away with it what was left? At best he would become a pensioner of the Maules. At worst a penniless man. Mentally Louise shook her head. Something of her desperate anxiety was assuaged. Roger himself, she felt, would find some way out short of murder. He had too much at stake for it to be otherwise.

Isobel's voice broke in on her thoughts, a gay happy voice. "Why, Roger, you silly boy! You really are upset. And there isn't any need. Coming here hasn't done me any harm and I was so longing to get away from the Hall." And then, as they stared dumbly, she added, "So if Louise will forgive you for being such a bear you can stay and we'll all have a nice cosy picnic by the drawing room fire."

A nice cosy picnic with a murderer and his next two intended victims! Louise could have screamed with laughter. Only, if she once began to laugh she felt that she would be unable to stop. She wondered suddenly what Jason was doing. Jason who, she now realised, must have known the identity of the murderer for some time. So—where was he? Why didn't the police come? Even as she asked the questions the answer came to her.

If anyone attempted to arrest Roger the shock would kill Isobel. By Louise's own idiot folly in bringing her patient here she had made of her a kind of hostage. It was Isobel's life against Roger's. It was a sobering thought.

"You two go back to the drawing room," Louise said. "I'll finish putting the things on the tray. Then I'll bring it along." The smile felt stiff and her voice sounded thin and empty in her ears but Isobel seemed to notice nothing wrong.

Roger's brow darkened. "Oh no you don't. I'm staying here."

"I can manage."

"I don't doubt it." He caught his wife's eye and added hurriedly, "The tray's too heavy for you. Isobel, you go back to the drawing room, love, and I'll give a hand here."

Isobel nodded. "Then don't be long." But still she hesitated uncertainly. Roger saw that something more was expected of him.

"You're walking!" he cried. "What a dolt I am!" He struck his temple with a clenched fist. "Here was I so angry with Louise for risking your health that I never noticed a thing like that." He forced a wide grin. "What d'you know? You're walking!"

Louise thought suddenly, of course he knew that Isobel could walk. Kathie would have told him everything that went on at the Hall. She had been perfectly placed to spy on everyone and everything.

Isobel's colour came and went with pleasure and pride. "Only with a stick," she said. Her voice came a little breathlessly. "But it is a beginning. And Dr. Reed says I'll soon be able to live an ordinary life."

"An *ordinary* life?" To Louise's ear Roger's tone was sickeningly ingratiating. "Why, Peaches, and you the most extraordinary woman I've ever met."

Isobel smiled and blushed. She looked at her husband with love and confidence. "Roger, you absurd creature." She left them standing one each side of the kitchen table, listening to her halting footsteps as they grew fainter and fainter.

"And now what do we do?" Louise hissed furiously.

"I shall think of something." Roger looked at her, all his intentions for her mirrored in his sharp furtive gaze. "The way you two left the Hall no one knows where you are."

"Dr. Reed knows." And Jason. Her heart rose a little at the thought. "He's supposed to be coming round about two." Louise wondered if this were the answer. If the doctor knew of their predicament? If he came prepared? Only—prepared to do what?

Roger scowled at the clock. "It's not twelve yet." And then mistrustfully, "Why d'you tell me about the doc?"

Louise sighed impatiently. "Because, for widely different reasons, we have the same objective in view—to keep Isobel alive. Since the doctor is going to call you've got to know."

"Don't want me to do anything hasty, eh?" Roger's face darkened ominously. "A right pickle we've got ourselves into and no mistake." He added with vicious suddenness, "But don't you go getting any fancy ideas in your head. I don't go to the gallows for anyone! Not for you. Not for Isobel. I'll strangle you both first with my bare hands. And don't you forget it, baby."

Louise looked at him with loathing. "I wish you'd stop those phoney Americanisms."

"They're not phoney. I was born and brought up in Canada. My parents came back to England when war broke out."

"In Canada? Isobel said Bideford."

Roger grinned, sharp and cruel. He had seen a way to break her spirit. "That was the other chap. The one who died in the plane crash. Poor fellow! He died on the very morning the rescue team arrived." He laughed, adding carelessly, "But then I couldn't afford for him to do anything else. He was just about my height and age. He had all his papers with him and he'd talked a lot. There wasn't anything else for him to do but talk. He couldn't move."

Louise felt that she had reached the ultimate in horror. She heard Roger's hateful voice coming as if from a long way away.

"What's in a name," it said. "I've heard my wife say that. There was something daft about a rose as well but that first bit was the one that always tickled me . . ."

His voice faded from her hearing. She saw the crashed plane lying on the windswept hillside. Saw the snow-covered bodies of those already dead. She saw the two badly injured men. Realised something of the helpless terror that must have come to one of them at the last. Recognised, too, the iron determination that had driven the survivor as he struggled to change clothes with a body not yet cold—*and all because a new identity had been wanted by a man whose sour jest it was that his name was Death.*

Roger picked up the tray. "That frightens you, doesn't it? You won't be so quick to try anything foolish, will you?" He went out of the kitchen, chuckling.

Louise leaned for a moment against the table, trying to control the sudden shaking of her slim body. She no longer had any confidence that the nightmare would end, that Roger would find a way out other than that of murder. Sooner or later he would decide that Isobel's money must be sacrificed in exchange for his freedom. And then—?

"Hey, Louise!" Roger's voice, amused, derisive, came floating down the corridor. "Come and get it!"

He saw the piece of paper hanging from the mantelpiece. He went over and read it. "That's rich," he said, roaring with laughter. "That really is rich. So Louise isn't to be held responsible, eh?"

Isobel gave a happy crow of laughter. "Louise was so horrified to find the telephone wasn't working. Really, to hear her one would have supposed that, without Dr. Reed, I was liable to drop dead.''

Roger left the room still chuckling. He came back carrying a bottle of red wine. The macabre meal began. Roger, Louise noticed incredulously, ate with a good appetite. His preoccupied silence was met with no more than an amused raising of an eyebrow from his wife.

"You never told me, Roger, what brought you here," she said. He appeared not to hear her. "Roger!"

He looked up. "Eh? Oh—me?" Louise wondered whether under the stress of circumstances he had gone back to being Martin Charles D'Eath. "What did you say?"

Isobel gave a sigh of mock despair. "I don't believe you've been listening to a word. What is the matter?"

Roger looked at her. His gaze was deep and brooding. "I've got a bit of a problem on my mind," he answered truthfully. "Something to do with the police. I thought at the time I was doing the right thing. Now I'm not so sure."

Isobel's face sobered. "Something about Jason? I seem to remember not so long ago your telling me to take comfort from the knowledge that none of us three was a murderer."

Roger looked at her briefly. "You go on doing just that, Peaches," he told her.

The meal continued. The silences between the three grew more frequent and longer. Roger seemed preoccupied and Isobel content to gaze lazily at the view. Louise had been pursuing her own thoughts, her mind searching for some plan of escape. But whichever way she turned she found herself faced with the same problem—the precarious state of Isobel's health.

And yet their stay in isolation could not be prolonged indefinitely. Isobel's doctor would call to see her. The gardener might come round to regulate the heating. Jason or the police might decide on desperate measures. And from Roger's uneasy glances at the small gilt clock on the mantelpiece she fancied that his absence from somewhere else was already giving him cause for anxiety.

Her strung nerves ticked the seconds into minutes. And there were sixty minutes in an hour. How was she going to bear the slow crawling of time?

And then suddenly the silence was broken by the sound of a car coming up the drive. Across the table Roger looked up with sudden uneasiness. To Louise came the exultant realisation that he was vulnerable, that it was now his turn to be frightened.

"Who can that be?" Isobel asked, looking round.

"One of those darned reporters maybe." Sweat had broken out on Roger's skin and at the roots of his dark hair. "They were nosing round the office when I left it."

The car stopped. The next moment the front door bell rang, loud, insistent. Roger sprang to his feet, staring at the closed sitting-room door. His head was sunk low between his broad shoulders. "It's too early for the doc," he muttered. And then, "Has anyone a key beside us two?"

"Why—Andrews has one to the back door." This was the gardener in charge of the heating.

"Who else?"

"Miss Chumleigh had one. She used to fetch papers for me from here."

Roger laughed harshly. "It's not likely to be Miss Chumleigh. That's for sure."

"Roger!" There was bewilderment as well as pain in Isobel's voice. "What a horrible thing to say."

"Sorry, Peaches." He smiled at her awkwardly. Striving to think himself back into the part of Roger Crane. It was as useless as for an insect to try to re-enter the chrysalis it had outgrown. This was the convict, the killer. The man who had lived by the rules of the jungle. He had emerged from the wastelands for a while and now had returned. It was as simple as that.

His forced smile still lingered. He went to sit down again so as to reassure his wife. It was at that moment that the door opened and Jason Maule walked in.

Chapter 18

For Louise, and perhaps for Jason too, there was one terrible tense moment when he came through the door. If Roger had moved then— But he didn't. Jason walked past him unchallenged and, at that moment, Roger lost the initiative.

"Jason!" Isobel had sprung to her feet. "How lovely to see you. But how did you get in?"

He stood looking down at her, tall, elegant, composed. "I rang the bell. No one answered so I tried the door. It opened so I came in."

"That must have been Roger. How careless. But never mind. How did you know that I was here?"

"I didn't know. I came to see Louise."

"Louise?" The sudden mischievousness of her gaze showed that she was not as surprised as she sounded.

Jason nodded. "I've been trying to court that gal ever since I first saw her, but she's persistently eluded me. So when I heard she was going to be here I thought now's my chance."

Louise smiled in his direction. Clever Jason to think of the one explanation that might be acceptable to Roger. "You were at the front door—oh, for ages." She spoke slowly so that all the anguish of waiting could be heard in her voice.

"I went to the kitchen first," Jason smiled across at her, a smile so reassuring, so sweet, so intimate that Louise with astonishment realised that he did indeed love her.

Her whole being was irradiated by happiness. It was not the time nor the place for happiness but she could not help it. She did not know if it were love she felt for him but she was happy. She looked back at him steadily. Even if we don't get out of this alive, her heart was saying, Thank you for loving me, Jason. Thank you very much.

"But Jason, is it safe for you to be here?" Plainly Isobel had just remembered what she thought of as the precariousness of her cousin's position. If anything could be done to thwart the law, her expression said, she was ready to do it.

Jason remained standing—perhaps because it gave him the ascendancy over Roger who, however reluctantly, was still seated. "Don't worry, Isobel. The police don't suspect me any more." Adding deliberately, "They're on the track of some fellow from Kathie's past. A stranger. Someone you've never even heard of."

Again there was a moment of extreme tension. How would Roger react to this statement, plain enough to the murderer that his true identity was known or, at least, suspected.

Roger said nothing—only the sweat broke out again glistening on his skin. He picked up a table napkin and wiped his face with it.

The happy colour had flown into Isobel's cheeks. "Roger, did you hear that?"

Her husband nodded, his face expressionless. "Yes, I heard."

"Have they actually arrested this man?" Isobel asked.

"Not yet. I suppose the fellow could still escape. For instance he might get hold of a boat and get away across the channel."

"But surely the police will have thought of that and be watching the coast," Isobel protested.

"Not the whole coast," Jason answered carelessly. "There're still one or two quite seaworthy boats hidden away in private bays."

"Like mine? What an immoral suggestion," Isobel laughed. Her colour was high. Too high for health. Her breathing was a little uneven.

"I suppose anyone with imagination might amuse themselves speculating how a man on the run could best escape," said Jason. His voice was casual. "Money? He'd want to meet up with some solid citizen who'd just been to the bank—like myself for instance. Passport?" And now there was a kind of angry grimness in Jason's voice. "I imagine a man capable of doing what this fellow has done, will know how to get along without one."

"But who exactly is this man," Isobel persisted. "Had you ever heard of him, Jason?"

"I knew that there was someone with whom Kathie was in love. I used to think that if only she'd give her mind to it she could snap out of it. That's how we came to be engaged. And that's why, three days before the wedding, she came and told me she couldn't go through with it.''

A great light seemed to dawn on Isobel. "So all the time it was she who jilted you—and Miss Chumleigh knew it."

Jason nodded. "Kathie was terrified the Judge would cut up rough and change his will if he knew. So I offered to jilt her."

It was a most extraordinary position, Louise reflected. This discussing of Roger's guilt with only his wife ignorant of the fact that he was the murderer. She could feel her heart pounding.

"Kathie," said Isobel sadly, "always hankered after security."

"I think," said Jason dryly, "she hankered after being a wealthy woman. It seems this fellow wouldn't marry her otherwise."

Isobel's face clouded. "Poor, poor Kathie."

"What about the man?" Roger demanded sourly. "Maybe he didn't want to marry her anyway. Maybe he was tired of her long ago. Some women are like burrs. You just can't brush 'em off."

"From what the police say," and now anger was making Jason's voice colourless, "it seems that this man didn't refuse to be helped by Kathie—and that more than once."

"Maybe he didn't refuse because each time it seemed to give him a chance to get away from her," Roger growled. "And anyway she probably liked doing it. You know what women are."

"Oh hush," said Isobel with a troubled look. "It's Kathie we're speaking about. Kathie whom we all knew and were fond of." She added with a sigh. "Still, I can't help wondering how she kept her secret and who this man could have been."

Jason smiled rather stiffly. "I imagine that the police will find that out. I imagine too that the further away this fellow gets the better for the state of his health." His voice grew warmer, faintly cajoling. "Isobel, why doesn't Roger go off and do any business he has to do, whilst you wait here for Dr. Reed."

Louise could see that they were approaching another crisis. She stood up with an abruptness that, at any other moment, might have brought disaster with it. "You'd better have your heart medicine, Isobel. I've got it here in my bag."

Roger was shaking his head from side to side as if it pained him. "I got to think," he muttered.

Isobel smiled at him. "Now, Roger, what is there for you to think about? Dr. Reed will arrive. He'll suggest I stay the night here. Then he'll go away, leaving me another sedative."

Roger looked at her from under his heavy brows. "You're

pretty certain to be right about the sedative,'' he said with a certain grim humour. It had been, Louise thought, a completely impersonal look. It made her think that Roger had decided to fall in with Jason's plan. And why shouldn't he? It offered him a chance, money, and boat.

Frowning thoughtfully, Roger produced a cigarette case from his pocket.

"So you got your case back,'' Isobel remarked, taking her medicine from Louise's hand.

"Oh, this?'' Roger looked at it carelessly. It was as if, in his heart, he had already abandoned the life epitomised by such expensive symbols. "Yes, it came by this morning's post.''

"And the one I lent you?''

"It's somewhere in my pockets.'' Roger hunted through them. He found the case and, still with that air of discarding something of no value, tossed it carelessly on the table among the plates and dishes.

It lay there, beautiful, ornate. The gold glowed dully. The jewelled initials winked and sparkled—but sparkled no more brightly than the wisp of something caught up in them. Twined innocently about them.

Gold, emeralds, diamonds and a curling strand of ginger coloured hair.

Roger rapped out an oath. He would have grabbed up the case but it was too late. Isobel had seen it.

"Kathie's hair,'' she whispered. And then again in agonised tones, "Kathie's hair.'' She put up a hand to shut out the sight. It was a curiously childlike gesture. Yet when she lowered her hand and looked across at her husband there was nothing remotely youthful in her face. It was ravaged, bleached, majestic in its acceptance of knowledge. It was as if she gazed from a great distance at a stranger—and that another stranger stood in her place and was herself. Then, suddenly, her hand went gropingly to her throat. She made an odd choking sound and crumpled to the floor.

Louise gave an exclamation of dismay. She dropped down beside her, but there was nothing she could do. She had seen enough of death to be certain of that.

"Shall I get some brandy?'' Jason asked urgently.

Louise rose to her feet. "It's no good,'' she said simply. "Isobel's dead.'' For a moment they stood together, their hearts full of regret and sorrow, forgetful of the evil man who had brought this fresh disaster on them.

Jason was the first to remember him. His face darkened. He looked round, eyes narrowed, and dangerous.

The newly made widower was moving swiftly and silently across the room. He had nearly reached the open window. Jason snatched up the egg shaped onyx cigarette box from the mantelpiece and sent it hurtling, like a hand grenade, through the air.

It struck Roger squarely on the back of his head. He fell to the floor and lay sprawling, unconscious.

The square of paper, written on so recently by the woman who now lay dead, and released by the removal of the cigarette box, fluttered to Louise's feet, the little joke coming to her like an echo from some lost and distant past. *This is to certify that Louise Morton cannot be held responsible—*

The words faded unintelligibly. For the first and last time in her life Louise fainted. There seemed a great noise going on in her head and in the room. Through it she heard Jason's voice from very far away, "I know it's not what we decided, Aunt Agnes" it said.

And another voice that was Inspector Finch's, from still further away, "No but it does very well," before fading into the general darkness that enveloped her.

It seemed to the Maules that a vast indignity had been done them. The man whom they had known as Roger Crane would stand his trial. The story of Isobel's marriage would become public property. To their grief for her death had been added all sorts of other emotions. The only good thing that had emerged was that Jason had fallen in love with Louise. The spell that Kathie had laid on him had been broken at last. Louise herself was not conscious of any definite feeling towards Jason. She had liked him. She had even been strongly attracted to him. But that all seemed long ago. Now she felt empty, drained of all emotion.

"I blame myself," Mr. Maule declared, tramping the floor. "I blame myself very much. And you, sir," he came to a halt before his elegant nephew, fixing him with an unaccustomedly fiery eye. "Disappearing as you did. Is that going to help matters, d'you think?"

"No, sir," said Jason meekly. "I'm sorry."

Mr. Maule snorted. He resumed his pacing.

"James, do stop tearing yourself to pieces," his wife besought him. "How could you have known that the Roger Crane you were enquiring about wasn't the man whom Isobel wanted to marry?"

"I can't help feeling that it'd have been far worse if Isobel had lived to see her husband hanged," the Chief Constable urged. "Far worse if Miss Morton had never held that conversation with Jason outside the garage. Or if he hadn't followed her to Lockbridge. Left it to Inspector Finch to think up some way of rescuing her. Eh, Miss Morton?"

Louise smiled faintly, shuddering inwardly.

"I nearly went out of my mind," said Agnes Maule in her hoarse voice. And her face changed with remembered terror. "From the first moment that Jason told me that Roger Crane was the murderer I kept right on trying to warn you, Louise. Willing you to be on your guard—although what you could do, poor child, I could not think."

"It seemed a lifetime to me," said Jason slowly. "That fantastic drive—with Colonel Snow and the Inspector crouched on the floor of the car in the back. And Aunt Agnes under my feet in front." He laughed a little unsteadily. "I must admit that if I hadn't wanted Miss Chumleigh's key to Miramar I should have bypassed the police station altogether. In which case I should certainly not only have got there quicker, but I should have stood a better chance of spiriting Roger away."

The Chief Constable smiled rather grimly. "I believe Judge Kelvin once warned you against underestimating the inspector. He had that place sewed up so tightly that I doubt if even a fly could have left."

Jason looked up, his narrow face amused. "Including the seaward side?"

Colonel Snow nodded. "Including the seaward side."

Jason's grin widened. "Too bad. Still, I doubt if I'd have sounded as convincing if I'd known that Roger hadn't a chance."

Shortly after this Finch arrived. He paused on the threshold of the room and was greeted with somewhat old-fashioned courtesy. There followed an interval for congratulations, for small talk, and for hospitality. And then, suddenly a silence fell. The room was full of ghosts. Isobel with her plain clever face. The Judge, thin and urbane. (My oldest friend, James Maule thought desolately. Known him all my life.) Kathie, with her hollow cheeks and flaming ginger hair. Edith Chumleigh, in her neat twin set and sensible low heeled shoes.

Said Agnes Maule dismally, "I really don't see how we are going to get through these next few months. I really don't."

James Maule asked the colonel, "That feller? The one Jason knocked out. What's happened to him?" He could not ring himself to call the man by either his false or his true name. Ie was to remain "that feller" from then on.

The colonel cleared his throat slightly. "He has recovered consciousness and been charged with murder."

"The murder of Edith Chumleigh?" asked Mr. Maule.

Colonel Snow shook his head. "He was charged with the murder of Miss Kelvin and the Judge."

Mr. Maule stared. "Then who the devil killed poor Edith? I mean—I know the feller was supposed to be in London but he could have nipped down, couldn't he?"

"He could but he didn't," said Colonel Snow briefly. "It was Kathie who nipped. She went through the woods when she was supposed to be having a bath. She was still in the cottage when Oswald Philby called with the Judge's note. Fortunately for him he didn't see anything suspicious."

"Kathie! Good God!" said Mr. Maule feelingly. And then, "What was this feller? A kind of Svengali?"

"I suppose he could be called that," Colonel Snow answered reflectively. "The inspector here has learnt quite a bit about him—from one source or another. Trouble is the information arrived a bit late."

"Roger Crane's real name," said Finch, taking up the story, "was Martin Charles D'Eath. Kathie was barely seventeen when she first met him. They had much in common, both being unprincipled, reckless, extravagant, and fond of luxury. They fell in love and with Kathie it was for keeps. She had no life apart from him—was his doormat, his slave. Quarrelled with him only to make up. Left him only to go crawling back.

"At that time he was part owner of a garage. His partner was sent down for five years for dealing in stolen cars. D'Eath would have gone with him if he hadn't already been serving a life sentence, for the murder of his aunt, rather unsavoury old party.

"She was the widow of a prosperous publican and alternated between long bouts of drinking and even longer bouts of hymn-singing repentance. It was during one of the former periods that he killed her. He had planned it to look like an accident but, unfortunately for him, one of his aunt's old cronies, coming to visit her, saw him leaving the house.

"He heard old Mrs. Parmenter give a piercing scream," Finch went on. "When this was followed by the approach of running footsteps he took the precaution of hiding in an adjoining doorway. Later D'Eath was arrested and charged with mur-

der. And since, at that time, he had plenty of cash in hand, h
approached the well known firm of Spooner & Silk to undertak
his defence. They in turn briefed Harry Kelvin, then a risin
young barrister and the first seeds were sown of the tragedy tha
was to affect so many people.

"The defence was that D'Eath was drunk and could remem
ber nothing of what had happened. The prosecution could no
prove that he had expected to gain from his aunt's death. Indee
there was the evidence of the will to suggest the contrary. If the
could have proved it D'Eath would have hanged. As it was h
got a life sentence which, in practice, usually works out at te
years.''

"I find it a bit puzzling that nothing came out about Kathi
at the trial," Mr. Maule, who had been listening intently
remarked.

"That too was a bit of luck for the defence. Kathie hap
pened to have quarrelled with her lover shortly before the murde
and had moved out of his flat. At the time of the actual killin
she was on the continent on business for the textile firm fo
which she worked. No doubt it was on the defence's suggestio
that she kept in the background during the trial. The appearanc
of a young, expensively dressed mistress could scarcely hav
helped the man on trial for his life. Furthermore because th
murder was a very ordinary one it didn't attract much publicity.

"I'll touch briefly on Kathie's life during the next ten years
As you know she became engaged to marry Harry Kelvin. Tw
years later he was killed in the motor smash of which we have al
heard. After his death the Judge kept in touch with her an
finally persuaded her to make her home with him. Knowing he
nature I don't think she schemed to become his heiress but I d
think that, after her engagement to Mr. Jason Maule was broke
off, she must have realised that it was futile for her to try an
break from her lover. From then onwards I think we must see he
as waiting for two things. Her lover's release and the death o
Mr. Justice Kelvin.

"In February of 1962 Martin D'Eath was released fro
prison. He decided to take up the offer of a free tract of land i
Alaska and so begin a new life. I suspect by now he had lon
fallen out of love with Kathie. He found her useful and, o
course, there was always the possibility that Mr. Kelvin woul
die and make her a rich woman in which case she would becom
even more useful.

"It was Kathie who determined that D'Eath should make a

good start. How she raised the money we know. She gave him her jewellery and then reported it lost. She could not, as she had hoped, give him the insurance money but she did give him her quarterly dress allowance. She borrowed from Miss Chumleigh. She had the jewels the Judge bought replaced by fakes and, I suspect, she borrowed from Mr. Jason Maule.''

Jason nodded. ''Yes, Kathie wrote to me through my bank. Said she was in a jam and desperately in need of money. I came over to London to meet her. I gave her what money I had and I borrowed more from my uncle here.''

''To give to Kathie?'' Mr. Maule sounded astounded. ''Why didn't you tell me that at the time?''

Jason smiled rather bleakly. ''I knew you wouldn't approve. That was why I insisted on paying it back.''

''You lent it without knowing what Kathie Kelvin proposed doing with the money?'' Finch asked.

Jason's face hardened. He spoke with distaste. ''Why not? I am no money lender.'' He added more temperately and with a slightly apologetic glance at Louise. ''It may seem strange but I was always sorry for Kathie, even when I was most furious with her.''

''I'm sorry for her too,'' said Louise slowly. ''It's not often that someone loves only once in a lifetime. It was sheer bad luck for Kathie that it was with someone as loathsome as Roger Crane.''

Jason said nothing to this, but he bent on Louise a look of such loving attention that her heart seemed to come alive again and stir in an unaccountable manner.

James Maule was still staring at his nephew. ''But could you have done nothing to persuade Kathie of the possible consequences of her continuing to love this man?''

It was Finch who answered. ''Nobody could have changed her. Nobody could have stopped her doing what she did do. There's really something rather frightening about such an obsession. Kathie was right in thinking herself doomed.'' He took up his story again. ''Martin D'Eath sailed for the States in the late April of 1962. In May of the following year he was involved in a plane crash. By then he must have been in low waters financially, otherwise he would not have seized upon the opportunity to change his identity, to hide behind a false name and a beard.''

Poor fellow! He died—but then I couldn't afford for him to do anything else. Louise shivered, hearing again the hateful jovial voice of the man called D'Eath.

"Martin Charles D'Eath was buried and the new Roger Crane lay in hospital broken and penniless and the fact that he had been able to shed his convict background must have seemed to him an ironical jest on the part of fate. Meanwhile Kathie must have been frantic at her lover's plight. At the distance separating them and still her Justice Kelvin lived on. Then Desmond Maule died and his daughter, Isobel, was left both rich and lonely."

The atmosphere altered and grew taut, and Finch's audience stirred and stiffened. A little like dogs, he thought, hearing the far away footsteps of an intruder.

"We can picture the idea growing in Kathie's mind. Why shouldn't her lover return to England and marry Isobel? Judge Kelvin was not immortal. Sooner or later he must die and leave her a rich woman. Why should not Isobel fill the gap until then? If a meeting could be arranged—"

A groan burst from Mr. Maule. "A pretty pair! And Isobel their dupe. It—it's nauseating."

"Yes, but although Kathie did not know it, she was about to encompass her own ruin. In all her dark plotting it never occurred to her that her lover might come to prefer Isobel to herself. To enjoy being accepted as a man of substance and a respectable citizen. Even, perhaps, to be proud of having married a Maule."

"As well he might," Mr. Maule muttered. "As well he might."

"But slowly the true picture must have become apparent to Kathie. She became jealous of Isobel. To hate her with a deep and consuming hatred. A hatred that found expression in the telegram sent in an endeavour to prevent Miss Morton's arrival on the scene. The two conspirators must have been thrown into a state of panic. Since Miss Morton had recognised Kathie, they must have argued it would not be long before she recognised in Isobel Crane's husband the convict she had seen on that fatal day when her father had been killed.

"But it didn't work out like that. It was Edith Chumleigh who recognised his presence on Dartmoor. She had known that Martin D'Eath had been sent to Princetown Prison. And, hearing Miss Morton's account of the accident, she realised that, as a child, Louise had heard, not the announcement of her father's death but the warder's voice calling to Martin D'Eath to come away from the car and rejoin the working party to which he belonged."

James Maule held up a bony expostulatory hand. "One minute please. If Miss Chumleigh knew Martin D'Eath why didn't she recognise him in Roger Crane?"

"She had never actually seen him. She knew him in the sense that her firm had acted for him. She knew his story. She knew that Kathie had been his mistress. She knew that Harry Kelvin had fallen violently in love with Kathie. And here I think we come to the real reason for Miss Chumleigh's final disenchantment.

"Kathie must have persuaded her that her love for D'Eath was dead. That she did love, and mourn for, the man whom the older woman had looked on as a son. It was only when listening to Louise Morton's account of the accident that Miss Chumleigh realised, not only that Kathie had never ceased to love D'Eath, but that at the last Harry Kelvin had realised this truth."

"Of course," said Louise. "That was why he looked so furious and so surprised." She seemed to hear an echo of her own voice. *"I know his face must have expressed other emotions but these are the two I remember."*

Finch nodded. "Miss Chumleigh felt that she was no longer bound by her promise to Harry Kelvin, and so Kathie understood when she telephoned to Isobel Crane. Her position now was desperate. Miss Chumleigh would tell the Judge about her past. Worse still, it would not be long before one or other of those two acute minds would begin to speculate as to the present whereabouts of Martin Charles D'Eath. Everything was at stake. Kathie, who had done so much for her lover, now became a killer for his sake. And perhaps, in her tormented mind was the thought that, through this terrible deed, he might come to be tied to her even as she was tied to him."

"So," said Finch, "we now have Roger's return to the Hall, after Miss Chumleigh's death, anxious to know what was going on. We also have Kathie's returning to her former hopeless subjugation."

"And I suppose," said Mrs. Maule, "that Roger had an appointment to meet Kathie in the yellow drawing room that night?"

Finch shook his head. "If he'd been in the habit of being as rash as that their secret would have come out long ago."

"I suppose," Jason said reflectively, "that Kathie wanted to tell Roger that the Judge was going to settle some money on her. That they would soon be able to go away together."

"A thing which Roger Crane had no intention of doing. But

he was a smooth worker. I don't know what he told Kathie but, whatever it was, she must have experienced a second moment of truth—and one no less painful than the first. She must have realised that he no longer loved her. Perhaps even that he had not done so for years—and the realisation made her dangerous, or so he thought. At any moment she might betray him to Isobel. He could not meet her in the woods next day because he had some business to do for his wife in Lockbridge but he arranged to drop in at Warley on his way back to the Hall.''

"But if it's true that Kathie saw through him, why on earth did she agree to empty the house so that they could meet there?'' demanded Mr. Maule.

"When I came on Kathie in the woods that afternoon, she gave me the impression of being beyond feeling, beyond hope. She could still react to protect Crane but for herself—?'' Finch shrugged. "I don't think she cared any longer. She may even have suspected his intentions and acquiesced in them.''

"Suspected that he intended to murder her?'' The inspector was going too far. James Maule was scandalised. "Nonsense, man.''

"I'm not insisting on it,'' Finch answered mildly. "But there have been authenticated cases where a woman, usually a wife, has realised that her husband intends or is actually engaged in killing her and has made no protest.''

"Kathie *might* have realised,'' said Mrs. Maule in her matter of fact voice. "That would have accounted for the new frock. She would have wanted to look her best.''

"Never,'' said Jason. His voice was low and he had turned very pale. "Kathie loved life. She would never have decided to give it up.''

"Perhaps,'' said Colonel Snow dryly, "she found the idea preferable to that of hanging.'' This, not unnaturally, brought the argument to an abrupt close. After a moment the colonel continued, changing the subject. "By the way, Agnes, there's one thing you can explain. What were you doing when you shut yourself up in the sitting room at Glebe Cottage?''

Mrs. Maule was not at all put out by the question. "I could see that the room had been rearranged and I wanted to make certain that nothing had been put there to incriminate any of my family.''

"I'd like to ask the inspector how he managed to get so much information about this feller?'' James Maule asked. "Has he been talking?''

"No, but he will at the trial," Colonel Snow rejoined grimly. "You'll have to be prepared for that. He'll talk—and he'll enjoy it."

"I got my information from Scotland Yard," Finch answered, watching the smoke curl from his cigarette. "It was there all the time for the asking. Just as soon as I realised what Kathie might have wanted that money for I asked C.R.O. for information about any prisoners released from Dartmoor in February, 1962. They sent it down on the next train. There had been two men. One of them was Martin Charles D'Eath. When I saw his photograph I recognised him. He hadn't got a beard then but I couldn't mistake those expressionless, deep-set eyes."

Louise shivered. "It's odd that I've only just realised it. His smile never went further than his lips."

"He smiled a lot," said Agnes Maule. "Particularly at Isobel. It biased one in his favour."

"There is one mystery still unsolved," said Finch looking at Jason. "Just where was it Miss Chumleigh and you first saw each other?"

Jason looked embarrassed—at least as far as such a self-possessed and hardy young man could look embarrassed. "That was when I was away."

Colonel Snow grinned widely at him. "You may just as well own up. Inspector Finch has already worked out where you went and what you did."

Jason looked startled. "How the devil did he do that?"

"It wasn't difficult," Finch assured him. "I'd noticed the family predilection for the army. I'd tried the War Office with no result. And then Mr. James Maule gave me the information I wanted."

"Me?" It was Mr. Maule's turn to look startled. "But I didn't know where Mason was myself."

"You did—if you'd thought about it. A young man with his heredity. Writing to you from Marseilles, Algiers—"

For the first time that evening James Maule's face really relaxed. "What a dunderhead I've been. Star-crossed and romantic!" He caught his nephew's arm in an affectionate grip.

"I was a young fool," said Jason briefly.

"When you have all finished your cross talk," said Agnes Maule, "perhaps one of you will tell me where Jason spent all those years."

James Maule was chuckling again. "I'll tell you, Agnes. The boy had joined the Foreign Legion."

Louise was conscious of a feeling of shock. It had been such childish thing to do. Her eyes examined Jason's face closely. There was nothing childish about its harsh lines. Nor in the grave enquiring gaze that now met hers.

She was conscious of a sudden feeling of excitement. It was almost as if she were about to find the answer to some great secret.

"And Miss Chumleigh?" Finch asked. "Where did you see her?"

"That was four years ago." Reluctantly Jason left off looking at Louise. "I was in Corsica at the time, helping to train recruits. It was one of those blood feuds with a touch of the Mafia thrown in. A young man was shot in the back. We heard the sound of firing but Miss Chumleigh, who was holidaying in Corsica, actually saw it happen. She burst out of the trees, shouting abuse and shaking her sunshade at the bandit leader. Fortunately for her, he didn't understand what she called him. The whole lot of them vanished into the trees and when we got there, there was only Miss Chumleigh, the dead body of the young man and the hot sun beating down—" Jason's voice died away. Then he said abruptly, "She had plenty of pluck. It's odd to think it was Kathie—"

A silence fell on the room. It was broken by James Maule.

"We're all strangers," he declared darkly. "Whom do we really know?"

"It's enough if you know one person," Mrs. Maule leaned forward. Her bright little pig's eyes beamed affectionately into his.

Her husband nodded. "It's enough," he agreed, smiling back at her. "It's enough."

The little incident set off a whole string of reactions. Jason and Louise looked again at each other and now they smiled.

Septimus Finch was reminded of his parents who next day would have been married for fifty years.

The Chief Constable's reaction was purely practical. "Well, Inspector, if I'm going to run you into Lockbridge to catch that train—?"

James Maule, rising, took Finch's hand and shook it with solemn care.

ABOUT THE AUTHOR

MARGARET ERSKINE has written over a dozen mystery novels in the classical tradition—carefully shaped and plotted and highly literate. The Erskines are a Lowland Scots family connected with the Stuarts by many inter-marriages and, from Bannockburn to Culloden, they fought on every battlefield of Scotland. Miss Erskine was educated by governesses and the vast resources of her father's library in South Devon. She now lives in London.

Inside Boston Doctor's Hospital, patients are dying.
No one knows why,
No one but . . .

THE SISTERHOOD

Nurses bound together in mercy. Pledged to end human suffering. Sworn to absolute secrecy. But, within the Sisterhood, evil blooms. Under the white glare of the operating room, patients survive the surgeon's knife. Then, in the dark hollow silence of the nighttime hospital, they die. Suddenly, inexplicably, horribly. No one knows why. No one but the Sisterhood.

One man, a tough, bright doctor, risks his career, his very life, to unmask the terrifying mystery. One woman, a beautiful and dedicated young nurse, unknowingly holds the answer. Together they will discover that no one is safe from . . .

THE SISTERHOOD

A Novel by
MICHAEL PALMER

"Compassion turns to terror . . . Riveting reading, I couldn't put it down."

—V. C. Andrews, author of *Flowers in the Attic*